Destiny Falls

Aspire to Inspire

ANGELA ENGNELL

Destiny Falls

ISBN 978-1-63844-437-4 (paperback)
ISBN 978-1-63844-438-1 (digital)

Christian Faith Publishing, Inc.
832 Park Avenue
Meadville, PA 16335
www.christianfaithpublishing.com

Printed in the United States of America

Acknowledgement

This book was so much fun for me to write. However, I would not have enjoyed the process as much, nor would I have been able to get it published without the help of those around me.

I would first like to thank the numerous coffee shops that allowed me to sit and write for hours: *Ambrose Coffee, Bogart's Coffee House, Cafe 86, Cafe de Leche, Civil Coffee, Coffee Gallery, Dinosaur Coffee, Go Get Em Tiger, Hey Hey, Jones Coffee Vroman's Bookstore Cafe, Jameson Brown Coffee Roasters, Lavender and Honey, Mantra Coffee, Rosebud Coffee, Starbucks,* and *Verve Coffee Roasters.*

Thank you, Jessie Early, for your EP, *Wild Honey.* I played it on repeat while writing this book to get the creative and emotional energy I needed!

Thank you to my mother, Cheryl Engnell, for supporting me in the process, reading through the rough drafts, and offering help and encouragement in any way. Thank you for introducing me to *Christian Faith Publishing*!

Thank you, Beth Schmeisl and my brother, Anders Engnell, for the advice and insight I needed to write this book well.

Thank you to my illustrator, Melissa Van Der Veen, for taking the time to read through some of the roughest drafts of this book and still manage to create magic on your first attempts. Melissa, I have loved working with you and experiencing how you have brought this book to life with your awe-inspiring skills!

Finally, thank you to the many wonderful people of *Christian Faith Publishing* for helping me make a dream become a reality!

1

*H*e wandered along the uneven, jagged path like a toddler through a messy room. His head drooped low, as if to try and bring a center of balance to his wobbly footing, and his eyes sank even lower. It was late afternoon, and the hot sun was not helping the situation as it seemed to suck more energy from him.

Despite feeling and looking quite exhausted, he was a horse built strong and beautiful, unbeknownst to him. Although he was creamy white in color with a long mane to match, he had some darker spots here and there on his body that bugged him to no end. They were imperfections he couldn't fix. Majestics don't have those—imperfections.

At this moment in time, however, he wasn't feeling sorry about his imperfections; he was feeling bad about his own exhaustion. In reality, it wasn't his fault that the new Stars he met last night kept him up almost all night. He reminded himself that strong creatures—like the strong, magnificent Majestics—can push through exhaustion like it's nothing.

Though he wondered what the Stars think, about his reason to keep going.

Aspire brought himself back to reality by looking at his surroundings. The sky was a clear, vivid blue, and the sun was bright and hot overhead. It was a different environment for Aspire. He was familiar with wet climates perfect for growing plants. This place, however, was dusty and dry. There was no green plant or fresh grass in sight. The dirt on the path felt packed hard, and the rocks, boulders, and ground seemed to share variations of the same reddish-brown color.

Aspire decided that he liked this new place. Even though he felt as if his mouth was becoming drier with every step, he felt proud that he was embarking on this journey on his own. He liked the change of environment.

He went back to thinking about the Stars. They left him alone about a quarter to dawn processing everything they spoke to him. One of the Stars he met last night, Perchance, managed to leave a couple of sentences that still bounced around in his mind. One, in particular, couldn't quite settle down. "Aspire, where exactly are you going?"

Then she dared to ask, "Why?" right after without a pause. It wasn't that those questions were difficult. The answers seemed to be quite obvious to Aspire. But the way that Perchance asked them sunk a lot deeper in Aspire's soul. She was asking for more than simple answers. Now the questions seemed to almost bounce out of his head, off the rocks jutting out from the ground beside him, and back into his heavy noggin again.

He thought over Perchance's questions. Where was he going?

"Well, Destiny Falls!" Aspire couldn't help but express his frustration, and the answer, which was so obvious to him, out loud.

He thought, *Isn't that anybody's planned destination on this trail?* The Stars should know. They told him themselves that they see countless creatures embark on this journey to get their dreams at the falls.

He thought about the other question. Why was he going to Destiny Falls? Well, that was obvious to him too. He questioned to himself with sass, hadn't the Stars seen him? Didn't they catch what he was missing? What he looked like? He was not perfect and was seeking that very thing.

He stumbled on a sharp rock and let out an unmentionable. Immediately, he felt worse about what came out of his mouth than what the rock did to him. He realized that the Stars were beginning to leave quite an impression on him. He wondered why he was feeling bad for things he hadn't thought about before.

Why did the Stars' opinions matter so much to him now? He questioned. He felt a fire burn in him. Who gave them the power to dictate whether or not certain uttered words would define the success of a creature's mission anyway?

"Who are these Stars?" Aspire blurted out his question as if to ask the rocks around him if the Stars were legitimate.

To preface, along his journey to Destiny Falls, Aspire met these unexpected creatures. They were rather strange and unorthodox Stars. During his first evening on the trail, he already met a few families and a rambunctious group of young friends shimmering above him. To him, they looked like tiny bright, white beings with arms and legs that seemed almost to move and sway like a dance in their place in the sky.

Despite their size, Aspire felt surprised that he could hear their voices quite well. He had never known before that right above him lived an entire town of Stars. He was also surprised that they cared to notice him and what was happening in his life.

He had never seen them from his town. But he heard stories about the Stars and how sometimes they would interact with creatures who stepped out onto the Adventure Trails. However, he never entirely believed the stories, let alone that the Stars were so close to him.

As he embarked along the trails the previous evenings, he talked with the Stars. Aspire enjoyed them a great deal. He also noticed how they would whisper corrections to his wrong turns or steps. Sometimes they would even whisper to him before he made a decision. The Stars would even lull him to sleep when he laid down to rest for the night. Except for last night.

Last night was different. Some new Stars showed up. They were Stars that were a little different from the rest. He didn't hear about them at first. These Stars made him question himself and his motives; they spoke differently than the other Stars Aspire had met. They also dug deeper into Aspire. They made it uncomfortable and almost unfamiliar for him to answer what seemed like obvious questions. They even had him second-guessing who he was.

He had tried his very best not to let the Stars know that their questions and opinions shook him up like a snow globe. They unsettled his little world, but there was no escaping the confused and hard-thinking looks that would creep on his face like a moving shadow. He found himself hoping that they chose to rest when the sun began to wake so he could be alone with his swirling thoughts. He was confused about why this snowstorm in his head would not settle down.

He felt concerned that the Stars were watching him as he bumbled along the path in the heat with a weighty mind and funny looks on his face. He thought about resting to calm his mind and reenergize his body. Yet none of the large rocks and boulders littering the path seemed to invite him to stay a while. So he kept going. He had wished a couple of times already that he could see over this rocky mess and get a drink of water. But none of these stone-cold masses before him wanted to budge, let alone acknowledge him.

Aspire had already expressed his frustrated tiredness through a sigh enough times. So he decided to resort back to mulling over his conversation with the new Stars he met last night. He tried to remember their names. He thought, *There was Perchance, Wistful, Deferring, and…what was the other one? Oh, yes, Believe.* They were an interesting crew. They immediately caught his attention when night fell, and he began to look around the sky for the Stars he had met the nights previous.

These four specific Stars—Perchance, Wistful, Deferring, and Believe—shone a shade different from the others. They seemed to like hanging out in the darker parts of the sky together on their own from the other congregating clusters. When Aspire caught sight of the four, they almost immediately began to talk to him like they already knew him.

He realized that they must have been watching him on his journey from the beginning. They asked questions, made statements, and offered advice like they knew who he was and what he was about. Another odd thing about them was that sometimes, their words did not affirm what a previous Star had said. Each had her own opinion different from the other, but each one also agreed with each view presented. It made them quite confusing to Aspire and even flat-out strange.

As his mind carried him off to other places, he hadn't even noticed that he had walked into a large canyon. He realized where he was after the boulders and rocks around him had grown to make walls on either side of the path. The path was wide enough for about five creatures of Aspire's size to walk side by side, and the walls were high and mighty. Aspire stopped to stare at the magnificence of it all in awe that the earth could form such a thing.

Aspire didn't stay in that place long, as he remembered his mission. He knew that he could never settle as a simple horse in a simple field lounging kind of life. He wanted to be what everyone looked up to, the fierce, magnificent, strong, creature, the unicorn.

His mind shifted, and he remembered another thing that struck him as unusual about the four Stars. They cared very little, if at all, about unicorns. They didn't rave, exchange fan stories, or wish they could interact with one, let alone be one. Maybe that is what made their questions and comments throw him for a loop, he thought.

For the first time, Aspire met beings who did not think that unicorns were a big deal, and that felt like uncharted territory for him.

Soon other tidbits of advice began floating to the surface of his brain. A couple, in particular, floated high and almost turned into neon lights before him. The Stars told him to stick to the trail. They strongly warned him that venturing off or taking any shortcuts would be dangerous for him. They made it clear that he did not want to get lost off the Trails. He wouldn't do that, he assured himself.

Then, his mind trailed off to his little mistake earlier, when he said the unmentionable. He had hoped that the Stars were sleeping and didn't hear what slipped out of his mouth from the agony that rock caused him earlier. He affirmed his action by choosing to believe it was justified. It had to be. The rock was cruel enough to make him stumble. The least he could do was make it known that the rock had hurt him.

He thought again about Deferring's opinion. She made it known her distaste for the dirty mouths of certain creatures. She had mentioned a couple of times how those creatures' mouths made them "so simple" and "not at all worth" what they were seeking. It didn't matter if it was a horn, fire breathing, the ability to fly, a tantalizing appearance, or whatever a creature desired.

Aspire got distracted and thought about how cool it would be to have a horn and wings. He thought that even fire breathing would be great. He shook his head in awe of the sight of himself with those things. He saw himself flying through the sky, and his horn sparkled as he breathed fire to move a cloud out of his way. *Wow*, he thought, *that would be so cool.*

Aspire thought about Deferring's words again. They were still making him question his actions. He hoped his little mess-up didn't make him "so simple" and "not at all worth" the horn of his desires, let alone what he imagined himself as before.

That would be plain awful if it were true, he thought. His mind began buzzing with the options he had left if that were the case. Going back home is an option. He wasn't that far. He could forget what he wanted and pretend that he only imagined seeing a unicorn in the Ever After Mountains.

Hah, but how could that be? he thought.

How could he forget the eye contact of acknowledgment, the hair flip of recognition, and the glorious neigh of invitation?

He remembered that day like yesterday. He remembered looking out his window after a long day and seeing a unicorn for the first time. He was so excited that he dropped everything, ran out of his room, out of his house, and straight to the mountains.

The unicorn looked at him from above. It nodded his head in acknowledgment to Aspire. The unicorn proceeded to shake his mane and gave a bold "neigh" to the world around him, as Aspire watched in gaping awe.

It was an inspirational moment for Aspire. He could feel a stir in his soul, and it was almost as if bells were ringing everywhere. Aspire felt right then and there that it was meant to be. He couldn't deny this dream that began to grow inside him.

He wanted to be a unicorn.

Aspire decided to keep moving forward, no matter if he was simple or not. He couldn't let go of his divine inspiration moment and risk embarrassment before everyone at home who thought he would never make it anyway. He had to keep going. He also decided to prove to the Stars that he was not simple, but he was worth the journey. He was worth his horn.

Aspire stopped. He wondered, had he seen that rock already? The one that looked like it had a face and a tongue sticking out at him? He realized he did. He must have fallen so lost in his thoughts that he turned in the wrong direction somehow. But how? He felt confused.

He paused. He saw yet another rock resembling a face with its tongue sticking out. That one looked a little different. He started to question, did he not get turned around after all?

Suddenly, it seemed like every rock ahead of him had a face with its tongue sticking out. Not too soon after, Aspire began to hear a rumbling noise that was growing louder. Then rocks started tumbling down the walls that stood tall to keep him from seeing beyond them.

Some smaller rocks jutted quickly beneath and past his feet. One skimmed his hoof and left a jagged scratch. The noise grew louder and louder as rocks started falling closer and closer to him. The falling rocks also seemed to be getting bigger in the process! Aspire started to pick up his pace to get out of the situation as quickly as he could.

He started to feel a great deal of anxiety and looked behind him to see what the situation was. He remembered he was not going back, so he decided to run forward faster and faster until he could hear his heart beating. He had to get out. A fear flooded over him that, at any moment, a huge rock could fall and badly hurt him or, worse, flatten him like chewing gum on pavement.

He glanced at each side of the path before him, and it seemed that the rockslide didn't have an end. Why the walls were not getting lower because of this was beyond him. *Where were the rocks coming from?* he wondered.

Anxiety was adding more to his sweat that kept increasing from his brisk running. A few questions and thoughts in his brain started to run the stressed pace with him. Why was he doing this? Was he going to die?

Without time for him to process what was happening, a rock hit the joint of his front leg and instantly took him down. A couple of small rocks pelted him on the side, and it stung.

But at that moment, his attention was immediately drawn to blood dripping from his left front leg. He tried to get up. He decided that he'll have to take care of that later. He started running again.

"Does this have an end?" Aspire yelled out only to hear his question muffled by the sound of the rocks.

He wanted out. This was scary, but most of all, it was getting in the way of his mission. He started to feel mad about the situation as rocks poured in the path before him. He felt so mad now that he stopped and looked at the rocks falling before him, beside him, and behind him and yelled, "*Stop!*" swishing his tail as if it would help him force as much sound out as possible.

The rocks didn't stop falling. Aspire whimpered a bit not because his leg hurt, but because the rocks paid no attention to him. He slumped forward and quickened his pace again as rocks kept barely missing him.

He shook his head in frustration as he had to hop over a pile of rocks that had stopped in his path. He wanted to get to a place where he was not fearing for his life, but he kept going. The only way was forward.

He heard a loud crack behind him and nervously glanced back. He saw that a rather large boulder fell and broke over a sharp rock jutting up from the ground about six feet behind him.

"Stop!" Aspire whined a little more quietly this time. By now he was in so much of a swirl of fear, anxious energy, frustration, and anger that he was feeling drained from the whole ordeal. He kept pushing forward nonetheless. He reminded himself that he had no choice.

He tried to think about good things to distract himself from the situation. He looked up at the sky before him and considered how pretty the soft blue was as it was beginning to change its color to dusk, a yellowy pink. As he began to think about other things, the noise of the rocks started to quiet, and the pelting around him began to slow. Now about as suddenly as it started, it all stopped.

Everything was quiet again. The walls were just as high as before, but Aspire felt oddly safe now as night was getting closer. The walls seemed to be promising to keep away predators. Aspire stopped to catch his breath. *Whoo, that was a doozy*, he thought. He noticed that the walls around him looked different at this point in the journey; they were more flat than jagged.

As he moved forward, there were a lot less ragged and sharp rocks on the path too. He looked at his leg. Most of the blood had dried, so it must not have been that bad of a wound.

It was official—he had survived. He was not prepared for the rockslide, but despite that fact, he overcame that difficulty. Now, he realized his thirst again. He was hungry too.

This presented another issue now, because all he had seen for quite a long time were rocks, dirt, dried-up brush, and more rocks. Also, at this point, the sun was setting, and the daylight was dimming.

Aspire began to walk faster as if it would help him keep the daylight longer in his search for water and food. But around every rock and every corner were more rocks and more corners. Now it was starting to get quite dark and hard to see. Then something caught his eye.

It looked green and leafy, and he became interested. He moved closer, and lo and behold, he found himself staring at a small but abundant cluster of bushes off the path protruding from a low crevice of the rock wall. Aspire felt relieved. He also felt surprised that it was there; everything around was dried up and dead. But his hunger took over, and he forgot his surprise.

He settled down by the meatiest-looking bush, mindlessly ate to his fill, and then rolled over to look at the sky to digest his dinner. This also seemed like a good place to stay the night as the ground around the area was smooth and free from uncomfortable rocks. There were a few small ones that he only had to nudge away.

He chose an excellent spot to rest, for now; the Stars were beginning to show up one by one with their dancing arms and legs as lights on a front porch at dark. He began to search for his favorite family but immediately caught sight of the four again. In a chorus of different tones, he heard, "Hello, Aspire!"

Perchance, Wistful, Deferring, and Believe were all there shining their different lights. Aspire had wholly forgotten his shame from earlier and was happy to have something familiar back with him before he went to sleep.

"Hello!" he responded. He shifted in a more comfortable position feeling ready for a good conversation.

Deferring was the first to talk and straight to the point. She said, "It's good to see you're still taking on the trail. Made it past the rockslides I see."

Aspire felt her gaze on his leg and remembered the bump in the trail he had hit earlier. "Oh, yeah, it's a scratch I guess. I made it just fine."

"You were brave!" Wistful smiled. "I'm happy you didn't turn back, especially after what you probably heard."

"What I heard? What did I hear?" Aspire felt confused and curious.

"Well, as always, talk of those who take on Adventure Trails spreads fast in the sky, so all the Stars know about you. Have you talked to any others yet?" Perchance came to the next words a little slower, "Few Stars think you have it in you. Some don't think you're the type for this journey."

"Oh." Aspire felt his face getting hot. He felt embarrassed, by himself. "I've talked to some, but they didn't say anything about that." He wondered if any of the previous Stars he had met didn't think he would make it. He couldn't help feeling betrayed. He needed hope. "What do you think?"

Aspire had to wait on the answer for a moment as the Stars began to whisper amongst themselves. He heard one whisper from Perchance, "Well, what should we tell him?"

The whispering ended when Believe said in a very audible whisper with frustration at the other Stars, "Well, Artist said he could do it. I think Artist might help him too. Artist already has."

This made Aspire think. Who is Artist? And why did he need Artist's help? Believe brought Aspire's attention back to the Stars.

"I think you can!" Believe tried her best to comfort Aspire. All the Stars agreed.

"Only time will tell though," Deferring said thoughtfully. They all agreed again.

"You never know what could happen! Some creatures have gone as far as the forest and have turned back. I have even heard one creature got lost in the mountains almost right by the falls!" Perchance said this with such positivity that Aspire didn't know what to think.

"That's true!" All the Stars chimed in once more with agreement pulling Aspire's attention back on their opinions.

"But maybe you'll be the one," Wistful offered nicely. The Stars all danced in agreement this time giving no verbal response. He wondered, was it because they couldn't verbally agree, or did they move so because they all felt the agreement so strongly? Aspire couldn't tell. He secretly wanted to know.

Yet Aspire went back to the idea of being "the one." He loosened up and settled back after getting a little tense from the Stars' opinions. He liked the idea that he could be the one. His mind wandered to a picture of him in all the unicorn glory, as a Majestic.

He could see himself on a precipice in the Ever After Mountains. His mane was flowing powerfully in the wind, a beautiful, perfect coat, and the magnificent horn glinting in the sunlight. He thought about what he would look like flying too.

Perchance interrupted, "So why exactly did you leave your hometown for the falls?"

Aspire came back to reality and immediately responded with a laugh. "Well, have you seen my town?"

"No!" The chippy chorus was going strong at this moment.

"Why haven't you? I mean, why did I have to leave my town to meet you anyway?" If curiosity and frustration could blend together, Aspire was feeling that emotion. Aspire had to give the Stars a question now.

"Well, we don't like to shine over boring creatures," said Deferring quite frankly.

Before Aspire could feel offended, Perchance chimed in. "It's not that we don't like boring creatures. Mundane shines its own lights so constant and bright all the time that we're not needed over there.

But it's true. No one has anything interesting to say anyway. Many in Mundane couldn't even care less to notice us in the first place."

Aspire thought for a moment. The town always had bright lights. It seemed that the same kind of light shone all the time, a placid, warm light that never shifts tones from daylight to the street-lights at night. He thought about how the Stars considered the creatures of Mundane boring.

"We also like to shine over creatures who notice us and talk to us too," Wistful chimed in.

Aspire understood that statement.

"So what got you out here? What made you different from the rest?" Believe questioned with intent and interest.

Aspire knew this question could bring on a story and dig up some metaphorical photographs from the past. "It's kind of a long story."

"It's early in our day!" Wistful pressed cheerfully.

Aspire started from the beginning. He told the Stars that he was born to a small family of gardeners. Growing vegetables and fruit to sell at markets was his family's trade. That's all they have ever known living in a town of creatures doing all they had ever known. Everyone stuck with their specific family trade, and no one ever changed.

So Aspire had learned everything he knew through the eyes of his forefathers, the gardeners. Because of that, he had heard enough gardening illustrations and puns to spout at least one a day. Although, he tried to avoid them as best as he could. The puns made him cringe with annoyance. His family was great but corny.

Oh no, he thought and kicked himself for saying a garden pun.

Though Aspire's family was so content with their gardening way of life, he always felt a fire inside him for more, for something differ-ent. His bedroom window faced the Ever After Mountains, and he would stare out at the mountains daily wondering what life was like beyond them. He could remember the first time he heard about a sighting of a unicorn in the mountains.

He was young and learning how to plant and foster the growth of seeds. He was practicing the best technique with a watermelon seed when he heard commotion beyond his family's picket fence.

A group of creatures around his age was running down the street toward the mountains. He heard many questioning a creature that was leading the group, "Did you really see a unicorn? What did he look like?"

The word *unicorn* started to run through Aspire's mind after that, and he remembered asking his family. He laughed now as their description wasn't so accurate. He had proof because he saw one. His family tried to make the unicorn very small compared to what it was.

He described to the Stars his small interaction with the unicorn a couple of years ago. Since then he had been trying to figure out how to become a unicorn, get to Ever After, and become a part of the Majestics, that glorious tribe of unicorns.

Aspire also went on to explain that when he wasn't forced to garden with his family, he was spending his time trying to learn about the unicorns in Ever After. Mostly, he wanted to learn how to become one of the Majestics. That's when he learned about Destiny Falls.

He remembered the day he was in Mundane's library because he was stuck on the fact that he needed a horn to be a unicorn, but he didn't know how to get one. He thought a book could help. That's when he found a piece of gold. It was a magazine with an interview from an actual unicorn who didn't begin his life with a horn in Ever After, and he was from Mundane!

The unicorn's name was Complete. In the interview, Complete talked on his trip to Destiny Falls on the Adventure Trails; he told of a few pretty sights as well as some roadblocks. He spoke of some difficulties, but he said they were so worth the journey. This unicorn also explained that Destiny Falls gave him his horn; the waters were magical or something.

Complete described that after he made it to the waters, he slept for a couple of days, dreamed weird dreams. He then woke up, drank a lot of water from the pool, and then discovered the gorgeous horn he now has! He said all one had to do was find the entrance to the Adventure Trails south of the town of Mundane and it would lead right to Destiny Falls.

Aspire explained how elated he felt because his dream seemed so attainable! He had an invitation from a unicorn and the knowledge to get what he wanted. He was ready to go. He was so done with the gardening days—they were over. He was going to be a unicorn.

But his family had a different idea. They didn't want him embarking on the journey until he could prove he knew how to garden. They wanted him to carry on the family's trade in case he couldn't complete the journey. Aspire explained that it was a miserable time for him. But he made it through, and when his family said he could go, he left as soon as he was able to say goodbye.

He told the Stars how his first time stepping out of Mundane was weird for him. It became quite bittersweet to him as he realized he was leaving all familiarity behind and was crossing over on foreign ground. He admitted to questioning his decision to leave his town with each step out at that point. But it turned out to be quite fun because he discovered the beach and ocean for the first time. It was close by the entrance to the Adventure Trails.

Aspire expressed how beautiful he thought the beach was. He had seen pictures, but it was nothing like what he saw. The sky was a different blue than he had seen before. The ocean seemed to roll up to him in a friendly greeting making him so excited and hopeful for his upcoming journey. He thought he could stay there forever in that sweet moment, but he remembered he had a mission to complete. Thus to the Adventure Trails entrance he marched.

When he passed under the entrance, it marked a special moment for him, so much so that he felt a rush of excitement that made him run on the trail for a good mile. He realized that he'd better walk before he fainted.

Following that experience, when night came, he met all his Star friends. He first met the families. He met a crazy group of friends. Then, he met the four. Now, here he was wandering through Trap Canyon after passing through a big difficulty of the trip.

Aspire thought out loud. Many creatures, especially his family, warned him it could be hard. He figured it most likely would be, as on all Adventure Trail experiences there were difficulties for the travelers. He had heard a couple of stories. But he was fine with that. No issue. He especially felt good after making it past the rockslide with little difficulty. Kind of, he remembered his injury.

Aspire took a deep breath after finishing his story. He felt he hadn't taken a good breath in a while. He realized that after he was telling his story. His own story. That was a first for him. He had a story. Now, he was noticing his eyes feeling droopy, and a big yawn followed.

"And now you're here," echoed Wistful.

"And it's only just the beginning!" Perchance exclaimed.

"Yeah." Aspire yawned. "You know, I think I might turn in for the night. I'm sleepy."

"One last thing," Deferring butted in. "We should warn you to be prepared for tomorrow. If you thought today was hard, you might change your mind after tomorrow, just so you know."

This news perked Aspire's ear up and might have made his eyes wider than he wished. Before he could ask any questions about what was ahead of him, the four Stars bid him a good night's rest in hopes that he would gain energy for the next day. They proceeded to pull away and converse with each other.

But Aspire, with the unknown of tomorrow's battles ahead of him, found it hard to fall asleep all of a sudden. Questions ran through his mind. Would there be an even scarier rockslide? Or something else? What would make what he went through pale in comparison? And why would the Stars tell him that in the first place? His worries seemed to keep him awake longer than he wished. But before he could catch himself, he drifted off into a hazy sleep.

2

B oom. Crash. Aspire burst out of sleep to find himself in a growing puddle. As he was being pelted by heavy drops of rain, a bright flash of light caused him to realize that he was caught in a rather large thunderstorm. He also realized that he was sopping wet to the bone and now quite miserable.

It wasn't morning yet, and he still wanted to sleep. Aspire stood still for a moment trying to figure out what to do as he pulled out of his sleepy stupor with every flash of light and a loud boom. He decided there was no point in lying there getting pelted with rain, so he forced himself up and took to the path again.

It was hard for him to see straight ahead because it felt like his eyeballs were magnets attracting each raindrop to them. He kept his head low glancing up now and then to see where he was going. He was glad the walls were there to let him know if he was going straight or not.

A flash lit up the path like daylight, and a boom followed not too long after shaking the rocks around Aspire. He could hear some rocks tumbling in the distance. Aspire thought that he should find some kind of shelter. He started to walk closer to the rock wall on the left to get some relief from the pounding rain and to feel semi-protected.

Suddenly, a big streak of light came slicing down and touched a tall rock jutting from the ground about ten feet in front of him. A quick boom followed that was almost deafening. That was enough to get Aspire to stop in his tracks and almost hug the wall beside him. He had never experienced anything like this before, and he was beginning to wonder if he was going to make it. He hoped that this would pass really soon. Otherwise, he didn't know what to do.

As he leaned against the wall in a bit of shock, he tried to figure out his next move. He started to walk forward a little slower and in more of a crouched position, very cautious of his surroundings. He tried to be very attentive to the flashes of light. He saw a lightning bolt cut through the sky in the distance, but the thunder was not that loud this time, so he loosened up a bit.

To urge himself forward, Aspire started reminding himself of why he was on the journey. He wanted that horn—he needed that horn. His life was for more than gardening for a living, and he desperately wanted to make the journey to the falls. He started picturing himself as one of the Majestics on the Ever After mountain. His horn stood tall while his mane blew in the wind, and he was all that he wanted to be in life. Creatures in the town of Mundane would see him and know that he was valuable and magnificent. A true Majestic.

A streak of light and a rather large boom following it brought Aspire back to reality. This was not where he planned on being, but it was a struggle on the journey, and he would get through it. At least he was not in the town of Mundane anymore, and he was doing something to get his horn. He was making the trek. That thought gave him a little more energy to push a little harder and walk a bit faster. He was not going to let the silly thunderstorm keep him from getting to his dream destination, so he pressed on.

He trudged through the trail that was now turning into mud and puddles. Sometimes, he would shrink back from more aggressive streaks of light. Eventually, the storm quieted down until it became a plain rainfall. By now, dawn was arriving on the horizon, and the sun was preparing to rise. The rain slowed to a drizzle at this point, and colors in the sky began to reveal themselves in a beautiful coral, peach, and violet. As they appeared and grew more vivid, Aspire could feel his spirits lifting.

As Aspire pressed on, face toward the sky, the colors shifted to become a puffy white, peach, and popsicle orange. The backdrop was a vivid blue as the cheery yellow sun began showing up to the scene. It was breathtaking. At this point in the show, the sun looked like it had a halo of golden rays and bleached white clouds as it began to rise in the sky. If that wasn't enough, Aspire looked to the far right of the sky and saw it, a brilliant rainbow in a complete arch.

The rain was still falling ever so slightly making Aspire blink his eyes a couple times in amazement at the magic of the scene. Aspire vowed to remember that day. He saw that out of an ugly, scary mess, true beauty shone through, and he would want to remind himself of that scene for the rest of his journey and life.

As the sun took to its place in the sky, Aspire continued on the path carefully avoiding some streams of water still flowing from the rain. He also had to dodge some rather large puddles with murky clouds. He was feeling good though. He completed another difficulty with a wonderful treat at the end.

He carried on through the canyon and enjoyed the coolness and brightness of the morning. It was a refreshing walk, and his mind was so clear that his imagination carried him far. His head was up deep in the clouds imagining life as a unicorn, so much so that he didn't notice the time passing.

It was now close to noon, and the sun was beginning to heat up everything. It also drank up all the leftover water from the rain; it must have been thirsty from its morning performance and was now beating fairly strong on Aspire's back. It didn't bother Aspire too much until a little later when the air began to absorb the sun's heat as well, and everything felt hot: the rocks, the ground—everything. Aspire couldn't find shade anywhere either, so there wasn't much of a point to look for rest from the heat of the sun.

As time went on, Aspire began to feel like a melting popsicle, and it wasn't so fun trying to walk over the hot ground either. He started to feel miserable again forgetting the glorious views from before. The sun was hot, he was dripping sweat everywhere as he walked, and he could not get relief.

He told himself he had no choice but to keep going. But every time he took a step and accidentally knocked a rock or two off the path in overheated clumsiness, the noise seemed to laugh at him and his decision to keep going. As he inched his way through the hot canyon, salty sweat started to drip into his eyes and in his mouth. He could almost see his sweat leaving a little trail on the ground behind him.

This is the worst! he thought in frustration.

He felt so hot that he imagined his body would be soft enough to mold and shape into something entirely new. As he was thinking about that image, he saw some rocks in the distance that looked like they were moving.

He squinted his eyes, and as he came up closer, he saw small creatures, like lizards, sitting on the rocks sunning themselves. As he approached them, they didn't seem to notice him. They appeared distracted by basking in sun-filled paradise. He was in awe of how the lizards enjoyed the heat so. Then he made eye contact with an orange-and-red speckled one.

"Who are you?" the lizard questioned Aspire without even moving. He didn't seem that excited to have a visitor in his area, but he also didn't seem to care to do anything about it.

"Um, I'm Aspire," Aspire said through his sweat.

A couple of lizards opened their eyes and watched the conversation.

"What are you doing here? You shouldn't be here. This is our space." The lizard was straight-faced, and Aspire could read no emotion whatsoever.

"I'm going to, um, the Destiny Falls. I'll just be walking by," Aspire assured, hoping to soften the lizard's tone.

"Oh, well, good luck on that!" laughed the lizard, still not showing any emotion on his face. "You already look like you're having a hard time. You don't know this sun, do you?"

"Uh, thanks…" Aspire didn't feel encouraged by the lizard very much but felt okay with at least a laugh from the lizard. "Yeah, it's pretty hot out here."

"It's perfect." The lizard stretched more into the sun.

"How can you handle the heat like that?" Aspire wondered, but more so under his breath, but the lizard heard nonetheless.

"We like this sun. The hotter, the better," the lizard said this proudly with his eyes closed now as he continued to enjoy the heat of the sun as if to claim ownership over what was torturing Aspire.

"If you really need out of the sun, there is some shade over there." He pointed further down the trail. "Don't interrupt me again. I can't help you."

"Oh, good." Aspire felt some relief already. "Thanks."

Aspire took that as his cue to leave the little spa session and go find the shade. He quickly hopped around the other lizards sunning themselves avoiding their glares and moved on. The lizard was right. Aspire did not know a sun like this one, and he couldn't handle it, so he searched hard for that shady spot.

Aspire had to push through the heat and deal with his sweat a little longer. Until, a distance ahead, he discovered a small rocky cavern where glorious shade lived welcoming him. Aspire trotted faster to it, as well as he could in his exhaustion, and practically threw himself in the shade. What a relief. He lay there for a while basking in the shade just like the lizards were basking in the sun.

After about five minutes, he realized how thirsty he was, but he was too tired to think about it at that moment. So he lay there for a while resting his body, thoroughly enjoying the coolness the little rocky cave provided. His brain was too tired from the sun to think, and before he knew it, he had fallen asleep.

Aspire woke to something tickling his face. It startled him, and he jumped back practically smashing into a rocky wall in the tiny cave. Aspire warmed his eyes up to the daylight and saw what looked to be an orange fox standing not too far from him settling on top of a big rock. Despite its good appearance with a shiny copper coat and luscious tail, it had a funny look on its face. It was a stare that suggested Aspire was weird to the creature and that he shouldn't be there.

After keeping eye contact above Aspire a couple seconds, the fox promptly hopped off the rock. Still holding the same stare, now at Aspire's level, the fox walked up to Aspire. It stopped in front of him, now seeming to judge Aspire's tired, sweaty appearance. Then suddenly, without a hint, he broke the tension with an assured smile.

"I'm Confident." The fox held out his paw.

Aspire, in shock, took a second then jutted out his hoof. "I'm Aspire."

They shook a friendly greeting.

In a relaxed tone, Confident stated, "You look thirsty."

"Oh. Yeah. I am." Aspire, who was still making it back to reality, tried to return the same coolness, but it turned out a little awkward.

"Follow me then." Confident began to walk off to a nearby path, a smaller one found around the large rock that deviated from the main one. Aspire slowly got up still in shock from Confident's greeting and started to follow Confident.

The hope of fresh water and the curiosity of a new potential friend gave him interest and a livened step now. He began to feel a little excited and curious to see what was next.

Confident led Aspire through a smaller crevice in the rocks that was a bit of a squeeze for Aspire to get through. In one part on the way, Aspire's hips got stuck, and he had to do a quick shimmy to get through without being too obvious. He didn't want to draw much attention as he felt silly for not fitting well through the crevice that Confident so easily led him through.

Aspire was starting to lag farther behind Confident. Confident's quick feet and perfect balance had him jumping from here and there on the rocks and on top of the crevice in a smooth and agile fashion. Aspire couldn't imagine himself being able to do that well. He was built more for speed and strength, he thought.

During the detour for water, to boost his confidence, Aspire imagined himself in all the unicorn glory. He added fire breathing for good measure but could have been overcompensating for how he felt. Even so, there he was again this time lounging around the falls refreshed and hydrated, cool as a cucumber, he might add. He was climbing up on the rocks by the falls, his mane flowing nicely and horn shiny and sparkly.

Once he got to the top, as a way to celebrate the victory of being in his stature, he let out a majestic neigh. He breathed fire like a beacon high in the air to let the world know of his existence. He got so lost in his mind that he didn't notice Confident had stopped, and Aspire was now walking past him.

Aspire stepped down to reality again realizing Confident was no longer in front of him. He turned around to see that the space had widened a bit. Confident was sitting at a water spring dribbling from the rocks into a small, clear pool. Some lush green plants sprinkled around the water.

Confident was giving Aspire another one of his stares suggesting that Aspire was ridiculous in his way. But Aspire had no time to think about that as his attention was directed to the fresh water now. He quickly skipped over, threw his face in the pool, and lapped up as much fresh water as his body would allow. He hugged the pool out of pure appreciation to the best of his ability.

"Geez, save some for the rest of us," Aspire heard from behind him.

He got up and turned to Confident. At the same time, he wiped his mouth of the cool water that was now clinging to his eyelashes, soaking his chin, and dripping down his neck. Confident stared at Aspire this time with more of a curious look. He seemed to be trying to figure out what kind of creature he had discovered.

Aspire and Confident stared at each other for a fair amount of time as Aspire began to look sillier with his wet, dripping face and growing quizzical look. Then, out of nowhere, Confident let out a howl and started to laugh and hard.

Aspire's quizzical look turned to a smile and then full-out laughter after he realized the hilarity of the moment. Soon they were both rolling on the ground in side-splitting laughter with tears falling from their eyes to top it off. After another minute, they both had to catch a breath, and Confident got up to get his fair share of the cold water from the pool.

When Confident finished, Aspire grabbed another couple of sips. Both creatures decided it was time to relax and stay by the water in case if they wanted more in a few minutes as it was a hot day. Aspire snacked on some of the green plants for a couple minutes too. They were silent for a while until Confident broke the silence with a question.

"Aspire, where are you from?" He didn't get up from his relaxed position and only turned his head slightly to ask the question, but his face showed a curious interest.

"I used to live in Mundane," Aspire said, lifting his head.

"Used to?" Confident turned to face Aspire more head-on.

"Yeah, well, I don't want to live there anymore. That is not where I feel I belong," Aspire explained.

"What's it like over there?" Confident was now sitting up slightly. His whole body faced Aspire curious about Mundane, which caused Aspire to give a little more detail about the town.

"Well, it's a nice town. Everyone's nice there. Everyone has nice homes, and the land is nice. Not like this place at all. It's not bad, but everyone grows up to be a gardener, fence maker, furniture or house builder, and other stuff like that. My family is a bunch of gardeners, but I don't really enjoy doing that. I want to do something else."

"What do you want to do?" questioned Confident further.

"Well." Aspire paused. "Don't laugh, but I want to be a unicorn and live in Ever After with the Majestics. My town is right by the Ever After Mountains, and I saw one with my own eyes once." Aspire thought about that interaction with the unicorn for a second. He replayed the scene in his head, stopping at the part where the unicorn acknowledged him.

"Oh, yeah, I've heard of the Majestics. Haven't seen any though. But I have seen some creatures like you take the trail to become a unicorn." Confident shifted his position, relaxing a little more again.

"Oh really? Did they make it?" Aspire perked up and for some reason wanted to know of the possibility of the journey. He was still trying to figure out why so many creatures, even his family, did not fully believe in what he thought was very possible.

"No." Confident laughed. It did not make Aspire feel so good. "I mean, there was one or two that I didn't see come back, but I'm not going to bet on them making it to the falls. Just the same, few creatures come out this way anyway in the first place. Few can make it past here."

"Oh," Aspire said it a little more quietly. "Do you think I'll make it? Just wondering." Aspire was fishing for hope.

Confident shrugged his shoulders. "I don't know."

"Oh." Aspire put his head down a little. That wasn't the answer he wanted, but at least it wasn't a straight up "no."

"I guess you seem a little different from the others, less spoiled, so you might make it. I mean I did show you to my pool, which I don't really do. So that kind of says something." Confident seemed to be trying to assure Aspire.

Aspire appreciated it. He liked this fox.

"Okay. Cool." Aspire nodded and let that sink in and give him the hope he wanted.

"So what is it about Destiny Falls? Can it actually give you your horn?" Confident asked.

"Yeah, I guess. You're supposed to drink the water or something, and it transforms you from what I read. That's what I learned from a unicorn who used to be a regular horse. I've also heard from the Stars that you can get other things from the water too. Some creatures go to breath fire, some to fly, and other stuff." Aspire was now curious if Confident wanted to upgrade himself too. "Do you want to be anything…different?"

Confident turned and stared off in the distance. "Maybe."

Aspire went on, "I bet you can think of anything you want, and the water will give it to you." Aspire thought for a second that he might be exaggerating, but he was trying to sell his point.

Aspire knew Confident was thinking as he could almost see Confident's mind mulling over what to say. "I've always wanted to be a king. You know of a tribe of creatures or something."

"I bet the water will give that to you!" Aspire began to think of how fun it would be to take on the trail with this new friend, Confident. He really did like Confident, and Confident seemed to be liking him too. He could also introduce Confident to the Stars; Confident would probably like them!

"Yeah, sure." Confident didn't seem as interested in going to the falls as Aspire had hoped. So Aspire had to press the idea a little further.

"You should go to the falls too." He hoped that Confident would agree with him.

"Maybe…nah." Confident remained quiet. He didn't seem 100 percent sure that the water could actually give him what he wanted.

"Okay." Aspire tried to say it with Confident's kind of coolness. Inside he was hoping that Confident would agree to join him on the journey. He wouldn't beg. At least not yet.

They sat in silence for a little longer. By now, the sky was shifting color, and the sun was an orange gumdrop melting into the horizon. It was a colorful view. Aspire and Confident watched together in silence until the sun fully dissolved and evaporated out of sight. Now the air was fresh and cool, but it was getting dark.

"Are you going to continue on your journey now that it's cooled down?" Confident questioned after the silence.

Aspire thought about traveling through the small cavern and trudging on the trail alone in the dark. "Mm, I think I'll start tomorrow," Aspire said, internally cowering back.

"Okay." Confident seemed all right with Aspire's decision to stay there the night. It probably gave him more time to think about joining Aspire on the journey to the falls. "Here, I'll show you the best place to chill for the night."

Confident got up and started walking a little farther in the cavern, and Aspire followed his lead. Soon enough they got to a bit of a divot in the cavern where a bed of brush stood, and overhead covering was plentiful. Confident moved some brush over for a bed for Aspire.

He then promptly took to his spot circling around it, smoothing it down to his liking, and then laid down. Aspire wondered if he should do the same for his little bed. He attempted to circle it and smooth it like Confident did but got a little dizzy and, more so, fell into his bed than anything else. Confident gave a chuckle and then tucked his face in his tail.

Aspire tried to get more comfortable but found it difficult. In the process, he remembered the Stars.

"Oh, Confident!" He jutted his head up. "Do you know the Stars?"

Confident pulled his face out from his tail slowly. "Kind of. We don't talk though. I keep to my business, they keep to theirs."

"They're actually pretty cool," Aspire offered. "I talk to them a lot, and they're really interesting. They make me think."

"That's great." Confident returned and laid his head back.

"Do you want to go out and talk to them with me?" Aspire leaned into the question.

"Mmmaybe… I don't know." Confident seemed to lean more to the option of sleeping. He also seemed wary of the Stars, and it made Aspire curious about why.

"They're interesting to talk to! They make me think. A lot. But it's good," Aspire assured. "But you don't have to talk to them with me. I probably won't talk to them for long." Aspire sat for a second then got up and went out to the path. He sat down and looked up at the night sky.

He started searching for his four Star friends. He certainly had some stories to tell them. It was kind of a cloudy night, and he began to wonder if he would be able to find his friends. He searched and searched and then saw them. The four, Perchance, Deferring, Wistful, and Believe.

"Hellooo!" Aspire chirped.

"Good evening, Aspire!" the four chimed together.

"Glad to see you here!" said Believe.

"You're still making it!" said Wistful.

Aspire felt encouraged by their words and enthusiasm.

"How was the day for you? We had seen that storm coming in." Perchance sounded curious even though the Stars seemed well aware of the obstacles Aspire had to get past that day.

"Crazy. First, there was a thunderstorm, and then it got sooo hot. But I saw a rainbow and made a friend!" Aspire said, quite proud of his adventurous day.

"Yes, the fox," said Deferring, with less approval than Aspire had hoped. "You two get along?"

"Well, yeah." Aspire felt a little defensive. He looked over at Confident who was watching the scene with a less-than-pleased look. Was there bad blood between the Stars and Confident? Aspire looked back at the Stars. "Why do you ask?"

"We never interact. He keeps to himself. Plus, we don't know why he chooses to stay in Trap Canyon," Perchance clarified for Deferring.

Meanwhile, Confident, who was clearly listening and seemed to have had enough of the Stars' words about him, hopped out of his bed and sat by Aspire. He huffed at the statement. He obviously didn't like what they said about him as he looked frustrated at the Stars.

"Hey, this place is nice with all the caves and the pool and stuff. I like it. Plus," Confident added with a dignified tone, "I'm going to Destiny Falls with Aspire." He said it so matter-of-factly that it threw Aspire off guard but then made him happy and excited because he was sure that Confident meant it.

"Yes!" Aspire couldn't contain his excitement over it either.

"I see." Perchance put her gaze on Confident. "What do you want to get there?"

"I want to be a king, of a tribe." Confident puffed up his chest before the Stars.

"Well, well. Ambitious," said Deferring.

"That's great!" Believe smiled at Confident. It was a smile that seemed to soften his face.

"Thanks," Confident said in his cool way.

"Going on the journey together could be a good idea." Perchance said to Aspire and Confident. "We wish the best to you."

"Yeah, you could really make it," said Wistful.

Aspire beamed. He was happy about this. He was also glad that the Stars were taking well to Confident, his new travel companion. Aspire looked at Confident and smiled. Confident nodded and took this as his leave to get out of the situation and went back to his bed.

Aspire watched, sad that Confident seemed done with the Stars for the night, but he moved on and turned to talk to the Stars more about how his day went. He and the Stars laughed together about the weirdness of the lizards and chatted about the cool spring in the rocks.

Soon enough though, Aspire found himself tiring out for the night. So he said goodnight to the Stars and retreated to his bed feeling a fresh excitement for the journey to come.

"The Stars might be okay," Confident said as Aspire laid down in his bed. "Believe is kind of cool anyway."

"Yeah, they're my favorite." Aspire yawned as he began to fall asleep. "You should meet some of the other ones too."

"I might." Despite his words, Confident had a new tone in his voice. He sounded like he may be hopeful and excited about this potential new change to his life. "See you in the morning."

"Yeah, see ya." Aspire and Confident both fell to a sound sleep almost instantly. Little did they know of the journey ahead of them and how much they would need each other along the way.

*A*spire's eyes fluttered open. Immediately, he could hear birds chirping suggesting to him that it was a good time to get up. He yawned with rebellion, slowly rose up, and looked around while trying to remember what happened the previous day. When the memory hit him, he recalled his new friendship with Confident. Aspire quickly looked to the bed beside him and discovered that Confident was nowhere in sight.

He instantaneously felt nervous worrying that Confident had ditched him. He hopped to his feet and started searching around every corner and crevice to see if he could find Confident. When he got to the little spring and pool of water in the rocks, he still couldn't find Confident.

He suddenly got distracted by his thirst and decided that a good drink and morning snack were necessary before anything else. Just as he was taking in his fill of the fresh, crisp water, he heard a voice behind him.

"Morning, Aspire."

He turned to see Confident with a meal of his own. Aspire felt immediate relief knowing that he wasn't ditched and returned with a happy "Good morning!" and a mouth full of food.

"Are you excited for the journey?" Aspire asked after finishing his food, hoping Confident was still on board.

Confident didn't respond right away. He made half a noise as he had sat down and started to eat his meal. For some reason now, he didn't seem as interested in the journey.

"You're coming, right? 'Cause you told the Stars—" Aspire began to sound worried but got suddenly interrupted by Confident.

"I might still," Confident said it quickly but coolly paying more attention to his food, not acknowledging his sudden change of mind.

"Oh. I thought you said you would..." Aspire was now feeling deflated. He liked the idea of having a friend to travel with along the trail. Now, it looked as if he was going by himself again. He didn't realize how much he had wanted a companion until now.

Confident looked up from his food. "I mean, it sounds nice and all, but Adventure Trails is long and really hard to finish. I still need to think about it. I know of some stories and experiences, and, well, let's say they don't sound very fun." Confident went back to finish his breakfast.

"But don't you want to be the king of a tribe? Don't you at least want that chance?" Aspire worked harder to convince Confident. "The journey has to be worth it for what you want! I promise! Plus, the creatures that failed were probably by themselves. I bet we'll make it just fine since we won't be alone!"

"Maybe." Confident sat silently now staring ahead in the distance over his finished meal.

"Well, I'm going no matter what. You can join me if you want to or not." Aspire was hoping that this last statement would be the final convincing argument. He then realized, after it came out of his mouth, that it probably was going to be of no help to him.

Yet Aspire could see Confident rethinking over his decision to go to the falls with him. Confident was definitely not as sure about taking on the trip as he was the night before. Aspire had to acknowledge the fact that Confident had a whole night to think over such a rash decision. But Aspire thought that Confident was still interested in becoming a king of a tribe.

He could see it in his face. He could see the longing. But he could tell that Confident was content and might feel safe with his life somehow in Trap Canyon. Though Aspire wondered why. There clearly wasn't much to do in Trap Canyon; there was barely any room to begin with. It seemed that Confident's only enjoyment and entertainment was watching and interacting with other creatures that passed through the canyon.

Aspire started to believe that Confident could be something. Confident's life could have more, and Destiny Falls might be the answer to that. Something in particular, however, seemed to stop Confident. Aspire had no idea what it was but was curious about what held Confident back. They just had to follow the Adventure Trails to the falls, right? He thought so.

After some time, Confident broke his stare and looked at Aspire with a plain face. "I'm going, don't worry." He stated it so matter-of-factly that Aspire felt surprised for a second.

"Okay! All right!" Aspire laughed a little to himself. Watching Confident in his thought process with his intense stare was oddly entertaining for him at that moment. Aspire was very interested in this fox and his character. Aspire also felt a great sense of relief that Confident was going to keep his word from the night before. He knew that he wouldn't want to embark on this journey alone, and he was not about to, even if it took all of him to convince Confident to come.

"Well, let's go, I guess." Confident sounded less thrilled than Aspire would have hoped.

"Yes, let's!" Aspire began to feel excited. He felt refreshed and ready for the journey too.

Aspire got up followed by Confident. They each grabbed a quick drink of water, and Confident led the way on the little path back to the main trail. When they made it to the main road, Confident suddenly slowed his pace down with Aspire almost tripping over him. He let Aspire go ahead of him. Though he kept trudging on, Confident gradually started to fall behind.

Aspire's step was light, however, because he once again felt excited for the journey like when he first started. He now had a new friend to take on the trails with him.

Though Aspire walked with a smile, Confident, on the other hand, let a mix of emotions play over his face. It looked as if brackish waters were swarming in his soul.

Aspire would glance back occasionally to see if Confident was still there. He would notice Confident exude boldness when they made eye contact, but then he would suddenly show fear as he looked ahead of him further down the path. Aspire thought that Confident seemed to know something about what lay ahead as he appeared to move toward it cautiously.

It looked like it was going to be another hot day. The sun was high and already projecting heat. Both Aspire and Confident were aware they would have to face another hot one, but they pressed on ignoring the fact. They walked in silence, each beginning to entertain themselves with their own thoughts.

Aspire was daydreaming about unicorn glory hastily moving forward to his goal. Confident still lagged behind slowly. They were steadily heading to the end of Trap Canyon; Aspire could see it in the distance. Confident could see it too, and he seemed to begin to take more of his time walking on the path as they got closer.

They still pressed on and soon began to pass by another group of lizards sunning themselves. Aspire tiptoed so as not to interrupt them this time. But for some reason, Confident stopped in the middle of it all and seemed to have another idea. Maybe Confident wanted to stall time and get his mind off the torment obviously playing inside his head. Or perhaps he just saw a fun opportunity and wanted to take advantage; that didn't matter.

Just the same, when, to his relief, Aspire made it past the lizards enjoying the glorious heat of the sun, he turned in time to see Confident let out a loud howl. Then Confident began to jump around and over the lizards with a playful bouncing while Aspire watched in growing horror. His jaw dropped as one by one all of the lizards woke up with a glare as hot as the sun above them. He tried his best to avoid eye contact.

However, he wasn't the one the lizards' attentions were on because their hating glares were entirely toward Confident. He was still hopping around them occasionally stopping to poke, nudge, and put his face right in the personal space of some. One reasonably sized lizard went after Confident with his mouth but was too slow. He missed the quick, agile creature who would not stop his troublemaking for anything.

Aspire tried to speak up softly, "Uhh, Confident, I would stop. They really don't like to be bothered." Aspire was feeling nervous and wanted the whole thing to end.

"But it's so fun! Look at me!" Confident proceeded to run through a row of lizards. He treated them like an obstacle course dodging and swooping around them with ease, very much at the frustration of the lizards and even Aspire.

The lizards were now starting to yell things at Confident and Aspire too. Many of the words don't need to be mentioned here, but a couple of them went along the lines of "Who do you think you are, numbskull?" and "You idiot, you'll regret doing that!"

One line caught Aspire's attention, "Hey, let's get Emperor. He'll get rid of them. He owes us." Aspire immediately trotted over in earnest trying to catch Confident.

"Confident, you need to stop, or we're going to get hurt. Didn't you just hear? They want to get Emperor after us!"

"Who's Emperor?" Confident seemed not to care as he started running figure eights around some lizards.

"I don't know, but it doesn't sound good!" Aspire was starting to lose his breath from trying to stop Confident. He was also feeling bad for almost stepping on a couple of lizards in his attempt. He wasn't even listening to all the names he was being called now as he wanted to get him and Confident out of there. But Confident would not stop with his rambunctious attempt at having fun.

Suddenly, the sound of a loud rattling grew and made everyone stop in their tracks. Confident found himself face-to-face with a big, intimidating rattlesnake. It had to be Emperor. Many growls and hissings were passed back to each other while Aspire slowly backed away as far as he could, sweating even more than ever.

The lizards stared with contentment almost easing back into their original places in the sun. The troublesome fox was about to be silenced by Emperor.

"Confident! Please, please leave him alone," Aspire was whispering but also practically begging this time. He felt scared, and his heart seemed to sound louder than his words now.

Confident and the rattlesnake were having quite a stare down until in a quick flash, the snake went for Confident. There was a yelping sound, and Aspire felt an orange rush zoom past him. He decided he should flee the situation too, and he quickly followed, escaping the scene of the crime, very relieved to get away.

Confident ran out quite fast but had slowed down. Aspire closely followed Confident as best as he could until Confident found a spot of shade and slumped into it assessing his front paw. Aspire couldn't see any damage from his distance, so he ran up to check out the results of the tiff. Once he caught up, Aspire didn't see blood, but Confident was licking his right paw just the same.

"Are you okay?" Aspire asked with worry.

"I'm fine. It's just a scratch. I've had worse." Confident proceeded to spit off to the side after licking his paw and went back to licking it. Despite no evidence of blood, it did look a little limp and possibly a little larger than before.

"Wait, you've been bitten before?" Aspire questioned in shock.

"Yeah, it's no problem. This really wasn't a bite. But uhh, I do need you to do something for me." Confident seemed quite calm for the situation but slow to the question.

"Sure, how can I help?" Aspire was hoping that his new friend was going to be fine and was ready to do anything that would help make the situation better.

"I'm going to need water, and there is another small spring, like mine, ahead near the end of the canyon. Can you help me get there?" Confident's seemingly strong presence was now a little diminished as he was currently looking slightly helpless.

"Uhh, sure."

Aspire began to wonder how he would help Confident get to the water. Yet almost as soon as the thought came, Confident stood up, keeping his injured paw lifted, and jumped right onto Aspire's back. It would have been fine if Confident had the use of all four legs, but since he was out one, his balance wasn't the best. To steady himself, he used his claws, except those were now in Aspire's back.

Aspire, who was surprised by Confident's choice, was even more surprised when he felt the sharp pains from Confident's grip near his rump. This caused him to shriek and set off running to find the water. This, in turn, took Confident by surprise, causing him to slip off Aspire's back grabbing Aspire's tail with his teeth.

Aspire began to shriek even louder creating quite a sight as he ran through the canyon. (This moment, though quite an uncomfortable experience for both of them at the time, would soon be a laughing subject later.) Aspire ran and ran dodging rocks and pebbles, not even noticing his breath getting short and his body getting tired.

Aspire thought he saw something out of the ordinary in the rocks, and Confident was clearly trying to say something. But Aspire ran on, feeling flustered, and his tail was still in Confident's mouth, so it was hard to make out what he was saying.

"What?" Aspire sounded confused and quite out of breath.

"I shed, shtawwwp!" Confident was now attempting to tug on Aspire to stop, and Aspire could feel it.

Aspire turned and saw that he had passed another little spring with a pool in the rocks as he had seen before. He realized that was the water Confident was talking about. In reaction to his observation, Aspire, without thinking, quickly turned. He ran up to the water halting so fast at the edge that he accidentally threw Confident right into the little pool.

Aspire stood in shock and suspense as he waited for Confident to emerge. Suddenly Confident's head popped up from the water choking and spitting with quite a few of Aspire's hairs still in his teeth. Aspire began to feel the soreness of those missing hairs on his rump as he recognized the strands in Confident's teeth.

"Geez, why'd you do that?" Confident finally said through his choking.

"Well, you were the one hurting me!" Aspire defended, wondering what his backside looked like at that moment.

Confident coughed a few more times and then settled in the pool to let his paw soak while Aspire stared at Confident wondering what to do at that moment. After a few moments of silence, Aspire went back to his first question at the beginning of the incident.

"Are you okay?"

Confident took a good breath, leaned back, and closed his eyes. "Yeah, I should be fine. I was quick. He barely got me. It's just a little scratch."

"Okay," Aspire said warily.

After a good ten minutes of silence as Confident rested and soaked his body in the refreshing pool, Aspire sat nearby in a bit of angst. He watched to see when Confident felt better and if he was actually all right.

Finally, Confident opened his eyes and said, "Okay, I'm good now."

Confident hopped out of the pool landing very lightly on his hurt paw. It looked all right, maybe a little swollen, but nothing terrible. He continued on the path dripping water as he went walking only slightly awkwardly. Aspire watched stunned by his quick recovery. He hopped up to follow, keeping an eye on Confident and then staring straight ahead through the canyon.

With all the chaos going on before, he didn't even notice how close they were to the end of Trap Canyon. They walked a few more minutes, and as they rounded a slight corner, he could see the end with so much green in sight! Aspire took it all in with growing excitement. But once they got to the very end of the canyon with a beautiful stretch of green land ahead, Confident stopped, and he wouldn't budge. He only stared off into the distance. Aspire noticed and sat down by Confident.

"Are you okay?" Aspire worried that Confident's paw was bothering him.

Confident stared off in silence for a minute then came to reality. "Uhh, yeah," he said slowly. "I guess I haven't left this place in a long time..." His sentence trailed off as he was still staring at all the land ahead looking quite unsure.

"Oh." Aspire was hoping again that Confident wouldn't back out on him. However, he had no choice but to wait on Confident, so he too sat there and took a long look at the land before him.

It made him so happy to see green everywhere. It also gave him hope for the journey even though this was only the beginning. After a moment of silence, Aspire questioned Confident with excitement in his voice, "So are you ready to keep going?"

"You don't know what's ahead of you, do you?" Confident said, turning to look at Aspire, and there was uncertainty written on his face. "When the trail starts to turn, it goes through a marsh, and it is swarming with gnats and other bugs. They say things. Bad things. Like really bad. The gnats also make it so hard to see, so you don't even know where you're going. They call it Liar's Loop." Confident was now staring ahead at the land before him again. He seemed pretty content to be staying right there, not moving forward.

"Oh, come on, how bad can it be? There's two of us." Aspire didn't know the difficulty ahead, but he didn't want Confident to give up on the journey. They both sat there for a bit until Aspire got up and said cheerfully, "Okay, let's go!" and he began to take to the trail again.

"You really don't know what is ahead of you!"

Confident didn't budge as Aspire started to walk forward. Aspire kept going and gave no evidence of turning around, until Confident let out an obvious heavy breath. So Aspire stopped and turned to face Confident. He saw Confident's paw. It looked a little stiff and swollen, but it seemed manageable as he started to hobble toward Aspire.

"Will you be okay?" Aspire wasn't so sure it was good for Confident to walk on his paw.

"Yeah, it's just a bit of a scratch from the snake's tooth. Maybe a little venom got in there, but I've had worse before. I think I'm past the worst of it. I got most of the poison out in time."

Confident seemed sure that he would recover all right from the wound but still not so sure to move forward as he sat down when he reached Aspire. He was slowly inching his way out of the canyon though. But Aspire was ready and excited to move forward on the journey, so he continued walking as soon as Confident reached him. He hoped that Confident would continue to follow.

"Hey, slow down! Injured fox over here!" Confident shouted from behind.

"Oh, sorry!" Aspire slowed and turned to see Confident picking up his pace and hopping over. Aspire moved to meet up with

Confident and began to walk at his pace. He was glad that Confident decided to leave Trap Canyon entirely. He had officially stepped out to the other side. The land around the trail was lush and beautiful. Fresh green grass was everywhere littered with clusters of clovers and white flowers. The sky was a vivid blue speckled with some fluffy clouds that looked like puffy white pillows waiting for a creature to rest on one. There was also a glorious view of the vast ocean in the distance to their left.

Aspire and Confident spent a fair amount of time in silence taking in all the beauty, a sight for sore eyes after being in Trap Canyon for so long. Despite the two water springs, the canyon was dry and brown and unwelcoming.

It was now past afternoon, and both Aspire and Confident realized how hungry they were, so they decided another break was in order.

Both of them left the path to fetch their respective lunch preferences and met again to rest and stare at the sky after. As they waited for their food to digest, they proceeded to watch the clouds and equally wish they could sleep on them. But Aspire found himself anxious to go, so they moved on and continued the journey again.

They enjoyed the view even still. But as they walked at Confident's pace, Aspire could see a bit of a dark fog in the distance. It began to grow and grow the closer they got until, finally, it slowly showed up when one single gnat got into Aspire's eye taking him out for a second. When Aspire recovered, he and Confident found themselves surrounded by thousands of gnats and other gross flying things. They swarmed in clouds all around them making it difficult to see where they were going. The swarm was now quite dense, and the gnats were very attracted to Aspire's and Confident's eyes.

"Get ready," Confident said with remorse.

Aspire and Confident pressed on shaking the irritating gnats from their heads quite often. The sound of continual buzzing remained steady by their ears.

"This isn't so bad," Aspire said this mostly to himself as they continued on.

But then, something changed. Aspire couldn't tell at first what it was. But he began to notice how the irritating buzzing was starting to sound more and more like a constant whispering of voices. Then, he began to hear his name as if it was being passed around like a ball from gnat to gnat until, rather unexpectedly, Aspire overheard a new thing from a gnat. A bad thing.

"You really think that you're going to make it to Destiny Falls? You can't be strong enough."

Then another thing came out of left field. "What makes you think you'd ever be able to become a unicorn? Have you seen what you look like?"

How did they know what he was doing, what he was so sensitive about?

Another gnat chimed in on the discouragement as well. "You can't be a Majestic. It's impossible."

And another, "The Majestics wouldn't even like you anyway."

And another, "Adventure Trails is too long and hard for you. You should give up now."

Aspire was starting to feel sick, really sick, and not physically but mentally. These comments stabbed him in the gut like a knife, and he was starting to believe them.

He looked over to Confident and saw that he seemed to be feeling the same way. The whispers from the gnats continued to come from all directions. Aspire could feel himself slumping lower and lower as he walked slower and slower.

"I told you so." Aspire looked over to see Confident looking at him. His eyes were watery, and his limp was looking worse. Aspire turned away and kept his head down. His eyes were watery too, but he didn't want to acknowledge it. He felt emotionally beat up, and he was beginning to second-guess taking on the trails.

Aspire and Confident tried their best to trudge through the bug fog, but the whispers were getting to be too much. The whispers were also starting to hit Aspire and Confident harder and harder like many sucker punches to the gut. One whisper shot into Aspire's ear and was like pulling the final Jenga block to topple the whole structure over.

"You're not supposed to be anything more than a gardener. You were only meant for that."

Aspire couldn't take it anymore, so he sat down and cried like a baby. Confident sat down by him too but was silent, clearly not knowing what to do. The gnats were still swarming around them proceeding to whisper their string of thoughts that seemed to have no end.

Finally, Aspire's tears slowed to a halt, after feeling like he ran out of tears, and he stopped to catch a breath.

"You want to just go back?" He turned to see Confident looking at him again with quite a discouraged look on his face. Confident seemed ready to give in.

Aspire thought for a moment then felt a rush of strong emotions. "No! This is ridiculous. I'm not going to let these dumb gnats control me! I'm going to keep going." With that, he got up and pressed on to his goal.

Confident was the one to show surprise this time. No matter how much he seemed defeated by the whispers or how much disgust he showed for the annoying gnats, he responded well to Aspire's courage and strength to press on. So he too made the conscious decision to believe that it was worth it to continue as well. He got up and walked alongside Aspire.

Both Aspire and Confident continued to slowly push through the thick cloud of disgusting, flying bugs. They tried their best to ignore what the bugs kept whispering in their ears, and they each kept an eye on the direction of the path. It was a lot to handle at once. Aspire wondered if he would break under pressure.

Suddenly, Aspire heard a different noise outside of the buzzing. It was the sound of humming. It caught his attention, and he began to search for what it was and immediately caught sight of an emerald green hummingbird. It flew quickly before him, behind him, and finally settled between him and Confident. What came next was like music to Aspire's ears amidst the cacophony of the buzzing gnats. Though it was quiet and took Aspire and Confident a couple tries, they heard the bird whisper something to them. "Speak truth, hear truth. Speak truth, hear truth."

It sparked something in Aspire's mind, but Confident was the first to blurt out.

"You know, this place must be called Liar's Loop for a reason. I bet everything these gnats are saying are just flat out lies!" This realization caused Confident to show some strength. He seemed to feel a breakthrough in his fears of the place. He turned to look at Aspire with a flicker in his eyes.

"You're right!" Aspire agreed and was grateful to come to that conclusion as well. "We shouldn't believe a thing they say."

Just then a gnat whispered into Aspire's ear, "Confident doesn't like you. He is just using you." Aspire turned to look at Confident. Confident must have heard a similar thing about Aspire. They both made a face at each other that suggested they equally felt rejected by one another.

"Ugh, these lies! Enough is enough!" Aspire shouted. "Confident, don't believe what they say!"

"You don't either!" Confident shouted in return.

Aspire tried to look for the hummingbird hoping to hear more of what it had to say, but it was gone. He proceeded to remind himself of what it said earlier, "Speak truth, hear truth. Speak truth, hear truth."

"I think you're really cool, Confident!" Aspire tried to shout loudly over the lies as they pressed on, heads low.

"Really? I kinda think you are too!" Confident continued the effort by shouting over the lies.

"Kinda?"

"No, I do!"

"Thanks!" Aspire was feeling energized again. Yeah, he can do this!

Aspire and Confident both walked forward with their heads a little higher. They both continued to yell out compliments to each other to keep each other going. The gnats were still annoying as ever, but both Aspire and Confident took that energy and used it to push each other forward and help each other out.

"Thanks for helping me out after the snake today!" Confident continued loudly over the gnats. "I'm sorry I hurt you."

"You're welcome, and it's all right. I'm glad you're okay now!" Aspire returned.

"I like that we're taking this journey together!" Confident looked at Aspire with one of the most appreciative looks Aspire had ever seen.

"Me too! I don't think I could be doing this by myself." Aspire returned the look back to Confident.

They continued a conversation that was only weird because they had to keep yelling over the noise of the gnats. They tried to avoid any silence that would let the gnats' lies come through. Slowly though, they were running out of things to say. Plus, their throats were getting tired. Then, to their dismay, a dreaded silence came. They were both blindsided with a nasty whisper from a couple of gnats hitting right at Aspire's and Confident's being. It led them to question why they were worth anything at all.

"Agh, we can do this!" Aspire forced himself to say through a whimper. "Remember, 'speak truth, hear truth.'"

Aspire and Confident decided to give their voices a break and try a new technique of tuning the whispers out with their own thoughts. When that got tiring, they both decided it was best to keep reminding themselves it was all lies. So they instead filled their minds with their own words of truth.

They were still taking hits from the lies, but they worked hard to fight it with what they knew was true. By this time, the sun was beginning to set. With every inch of the sun that disappeared into the horizon, the gnats started to decrease until all that remained was fresh air and a dark sky. The gnats were actually and finally gone.

Both Aspire and Confident breathed a huge sigh of relief together. They looked at each other in wonder and shook their heads. Confident chuckled, and then they began to laugh and laugh. The laughter bubbled from being so happy to have made it past Liar's Loop but also at the hilarity of the whole day they had finished. Now, after all that they went through, they felt like they could do anything. They were suddenly on a high as they were standing in the victory of completing yet another obstacle.

After the sun had fully disappeared, the sky remained littered with thick, dark puffs of cloud. It was hard to make out the Stars even after Aspire and Confident found a place to sleep. Aspire realized that he was most likely not going to see the Stars that night. He felt bummed because he wanted to tell them about his crazy day. But quickly, he and Confident got distracted by reviewing the events of the day together.

The two were really beginning to bond and become good friends even after knowing each other only a couple of days. After quite a time of event recounting and side-splitting laughter, they both fell into a heavy sleep. They were thoroughly exhausted from the tumultuous day. But they were sleeping with smiles on their faces, because they were officially conquerors.

A spire woke to the sound of a faint whimpering. It was early, and the sun hadn't risen yet, though the sky was already beginning to brighten for the day to come. He raised his head sleepily and looked around. As he turned, he found Confident trying to soothe his still slightly puffy paw with his tongue.

It seemed to be quite achy from the altercation with the snake followed by the rest of the activity from the day before. Even though Confident said it was only a scratch, that snake venom was strong. Aspire looked at his surroundings to see if water was in sight or if anything, for that matter, was nearby to help soothe Confident's paw.

It was still hard for him to see as the light of dawn was still making its way through. But he could make out a long stretch of grass spanning out far speckled here and there with what must have been rocks. It looked like there was an extensive mountain range in the distance, but that was of no help. He turned to Confident to see if he wanted anything and if Confident knew how to get it as Aspire gave up on trying to do it himself. He stood up, stretched, and walked over to Confident.

"Hey. Morning! Do you want water or something?" Aspire got close to Confident's face to see him well. But he got so close that it startled Confident, distracting him from his paw. This jutted a morning dose of caffeine-like energy into his system causing him to spring straight on his back, paws covering his face in surprise. "Uhh, sorry." Aspire was trying to keep from laughing.

When Confident realized it was only Aspire and that Aspire was clearly not going to harm him, he pulled his good paw and his puffy paw from his face. He looked at Aspire with a little embarrassment and frustration. He followed by turning over and going back to licking his paw again. "I'm fine," he said it coolly as if nothing ever happened.

"Okay." Aspire was hoping he didn't offend Confident enough to make him upset. "I was just wondering if you wanted something for your paw."

"I'm fine."

They both sat in silence for a while as Confident continued to tend to his paw. By now, the sky was beginning to become a beautiful periwinkle blue. The sun was peeking over the horizon in a way to make sure everything was ready for his entrance to another adventurous day on the trails.

There were no clouds to shield the sun's excited light as it began rising over the mountain range in the distance. It seemed to be looking forward to the day. Aspire tried to welcome the sun, but it was too bright, so he ended up looking up at it with a squinty, semicheesy smile.

Aspire turned to view his surroundings, which were clear now and actually not very different from what he saw before. Aspire and Confident lay at the entrance of a rather expansive grassy valley. Small boulders and patches of cornflower and buttercream flowers spotted the valley. There was also a vast mountain range on the right side and a distant rocky drop off to the coast on the other side.

The valley appeared as a bowl holding nothing but grass, large rocks, and flowers, so Aspire and Confident could see for miles. Much of the trail lay plain before them, and it looked endless as it cut through the bowl-shaped valley.

It was a beautiful sight to Aspire, something he had never seen before except in a few pictures in some catalogs in Mundane's library. He was never able to see that much land all at once before. He could see some greenery and another mountain beyond the first mountain range. The mountain behind looked massive even from that far of a distance. That specific mountain caught Aspire's eye, and he began to focus intently on it until Confident broke the silence.

"That's called Mount Impossible. I think that's what they call it anyway." Aspire turned to see Confident staring at the mountain too. "It's on the Adventure Trails, you know." Confident turned to look at Aspire with a face that suggested to Aspire he didn't know very much about the trails, which was definitely true. Confident went back to soothing his paw.

"Oh." Aspire turned to look back at the mountain. "It's far… and big."

Aspire's mind began to open more to the reality of the journey. If the mountain was on the trail and far away as it looked, it was going to be a long journey. He began to wonder if the mountain was as big as it seemed, and if so, how they would be getting around it. Would they have to climb over it? Go through it? Or under it? Would it be easy?

He didn't like the idea of climbing over it. Also, he questioned how many obstacles they would have to go through before they got to the mountain. He had seen that Adventures Trails already was not a straight line to the falls. Aspire's mind went back to Mount Impossible. Did Confident really say it was on the trail? Not by the path? The idea started to bother him until he had to make sure what the situation was.

"So the mountain is on the trail? Like, will we have to climb it or something?"

Confident shrugged his shoulders. "I don't know." He was beginning to leave his paw alone now and was taking in the size of the mountain as well. Either he was tired of licking his paw or it stopped hurting as much, Aspire couldn't tell. He was starting to feel overwhelmed about the journey, so much so that he could not stay still anymore. He had to get going.

"Okay, let's go then." Aspire quickly got up without thinking anymore and started taking to the trails. They had spent too much time staring at what was ahead. He needed to make progress on the trails. But he did look back to see if Confident was following.

Confident didn't look ready to get up and take to the journey again. He did not seem too excited about what was ahead either, even after getting past the gnats. His poor injured paw had set him at a disadvantage. He took a second to get up and a bit longer to catch up to Aspire. He still had a noticeable limp and took a few quick breaks here and there holding his paw up from the ground.

Aspire could tell that Confident was not a fan of this temporary disability to his usual quick and stealth self. He seemed to work hard to push through and ignore the discomfort. They continued to walk together, however; Aspire tried to push the pace to get to through the valley faster.

"Hey, stop for a second. My paw is throbbing. I think it has a heartbeat." Confident was a little out of breath, but he said it loud enough for Aspire to hear quite well even though Aspire didn't want to listen. He wanted to keep going. Confident paused and immediately sat to tend to his paw.

It took Aspire a bit to stop pretending that he didn't hear Confident at first. He did not want to halt the journey anymore because they had to stay on track for the finish line. They had to make progress and figure out how to make it past Mount Impossible now.

But he slowed, remembering that he wanted Confident on the journey with him. He turned and sat down by Confident, feeling anxious about what was ahead. It was clearly written all over his face, and Confident noticed.

"It's just a mountain. Creatures make it over all the time," Confident assured.

"Really? A lot of creatures?" Aspire perked up to the idea of the journey being easier than he thought.

"Yeah...I've heard of a couple, I think." Confident ended the last two words of his sentence quietly. Maybe he didn't actually have very much evidence to support his first statement.

"Oh. We could make it, right?" Aspire wanted hope for the journey and was searching for it in Confident.

"I hope." Confident turned and looked at the mountain again. He didn't look very hopeful at the giant mass of rock that would be in their way on the journey to the falls. This did not make Aspire feel any better, and he started to feel nervous about the journey all over again.

"You ready? I think we should get going." With that said, Aspire got up and looked to Confident. He didn't give Confident much of a choice as he started moving. The two had a great deal of travel ahead of them.

When Confident stood up, the pressure he placed on his paw made him wince. But he got no sympathy from Aspire who was now heading off on the trail again and definitely faster this time. Confident was going to have to catch up. He injured himself in the first place.

Aspire started to feel bad for not giving sympathy and stopped to let Confident catch up. Confident slowly began to pick up the pace Aspire had set; he was obviously limping but trying to make light of it. After meeting up with Aspire, he stopped.

"Why did you stop? We have a destination to get to." He looked plainly at Aspire while he held up his paw, resting it as well as he could.

Aspire laughed. "Okay, let's go!"

Both Confident and Aspire continued a quick pace together for quite some time. Aspire was hoping to make up for what he thought seemed like lost time, believing that his speed would shorten the journey more than it actually could. Confident seemed to take on the challenge and to begin to forget about his paw as he looked ahead with determination.

They continued on in silence for a while focusing on the trail. Occasionally, they admired the beauty of the valley. The clear skies, the flowers that sparkled in the grass, and the birds that would fly overhead singing a happy tune were soothing.

This went on for a while. The valley seemed to stretch out for miles. Slowly, both Aspire and Confident got tired from their speed and slowed down to a more comfortable walk.

After a few hours, Aspire began to notice how strange the valley was becoming to him. Nothing looked different from where they started to where they were now, and it didn't look different ahead either.

Flowers and small boulders seemed strategically placed. The sky was an even blue, and the grass synchronized from a light breeze flowing in from the coast. Aspire also began to pay attention to the amount of time between when a couple singing birds would fly by. He noticed that each time there was little variance.

As the day continued, Aspire found himself not caring as much about the beauty of his surroundings. It was repetitive, and there was nothing new to see for miles, which caused him to keep his eyes on Mount Impossible continually.

He was sizing it up and partially studying it trying to figure out how he could overcome it. A significant thought ran through his mind: how would he overcome it?

He imagined himself in a daydream getting to the mountain and meeting beautiful, kind unicorns who knew the secret of how to get past it. They would lead him and Confident through a secret cave full of sparkling geodes that led to the other side right where the Destiny Falls flowed.

Aspire's thoughts were moving faster than his walking pace as he began to think of his limping friend. The idea came to him suddenly that Confident must have tried to get to the falls before. How else would he know so much about what was ahead? Confident had dropped a few hints here and there, especially when it came to his knowledge of the trails. Aspire's curiosity peaked, and he had to ask Confident about his attempt.

"Confident, have you tried to get to the falls before?"

"Uhh…yeah…" Confident seemed hesitant to open up about the fact.

"So did you get close?" Aspire was hoping to learn more. He realized he should have read more about the trails when he visited the library. The interview from that unicorn was proving to not be very helpful now.

"I…I didn't make it past the gnats." Confident awkwardly laughed. He was obviously not comfortable with this vulnerability. He didn't say anything more until Aspire pressed for further information.

"Really?" Aspire suddenly felt bad. His question may have sounded loud and demeaning, so he tried to soften the seaming blow of his question. "I guess that would have been really hard to do alone."

"Yeah. I'm honestly so surprised we made it. Tons of creatures don't. So many come crying back."

"So you didn't think we would make it? Why did you go with me then?" Aspire was at first confused and then upset that Confident didn't have faith that they would make the journey. Nonetheless, the fact that he and Confident had made it farther than a lot of creatures before them gave him comfort.

"Well, I don't know. Maybe I got excited about being a king again. I hadn't thought about it in a while." Confident seemed to unintentionally and unknowingly open up a bit to Aspire on his own accord. But he caught himself in the process and made a disgusted face at his vulnerability. He clearly did not want to open up about his weaknesses and shortfalls.

"How long have you had that dream?" Aspire saw the crack in the door to Confident's life and peered in with his question.

"Uhh, my whole life, I guess." Confident started to let Aspire in by opening the door, but only a little. Aspire began to wonder if Confident had ever talked about this to any other creature. He seemed to have a hard shell and to keep a lot to himself.

"Have you always lived in Trap Canyon?" Aspire tried to peer in farther.

"No, actually. I used to live outside Aimless. It was so boring there. I didn't like it at all. I tried for a second to start a tribe when I lived there, but no one cared. Some of my friends came to join, but they didn't want to do anything, just hang out. They eventually left. It's okay. They were boring anyway." Confident stared straight ahead, avoiding eye contact.

Aspire felt interested to learn about Confident's past life. "When did you leave?"

"I kind of ventured out of Aimless one night and somehow got on the Adventure Trails. I saw some creatures stopped along the path. They were talking to the Stars about Destiny Falls and how it gives you what you want. I had figured that's probably what I needed to do, so I left Aimless and never came back." Confident looked down at the ground as they walked. He had opened the door for Aspire to see into his world, and he seemed not to know how to react.

"Oh, wow. So you know all about the Stars then?" Aspire was curious about Confident's experience with the Stars and why he tended to avoid them.

"Yeah, as much as I need to know." Confident seemed to have a little distaste for them. "I've overheard so many conversations creatures have had with the Stars, and I just think the Stars are weird and try to control everyone. I don't think they know what they're talking about all the time either. I mean, the Stars you know are kind of cool, maybe."

"Hm." Aspire was sad to hear negative talk about his Star friends. He liked them, but then he began to wonder if they were actually trying to control him too. No, he thought, they encouraged him and helped him. He shifted back to Confident, liking this open door to his life. "So you didn't make it past Liar's Loop and then chose to live in Trap Canyon? How long?"

"I don't know. A while, I guess. I like the challenges that are in Trap Canyon. It's fun there. It's not like Aimless at all. I actually have more to do."

"It doesn't seem fun to me though." Aspire thought it was weird that Confident liked Trap Canyon. There were so many threats in that place. He changed the subject. "What did the gnats tell you? Was it bad?"

"Well, you know, they're just 'lies,' I guess." Confident was silent for a bit then he let Aspire in. "They told me no creature would ever want to be in my tribe and that I would fail at being a king. I mean if my friends wouldn't be in my tribe, who would? I guess I didn't think the journey was worth it after that. Plus, those gnats were annoying and made me mad."

"Do you still believe them?" Aspire wanted to press further. He thought that Confident had potential and wondered if Confident thought the same thing.

"Ahhh…" Confident breathed a heavy and tentative breath. "I mean, maybe…"

"Why? The gnats only lie, right? I think you would be a good king." Aspire hoped Confident would embrace what he said. Confident seemed to sort of embrace the idea.

"Maybe. Thanks." Confident was quiet. Aspire was now sitting in the living room of his life. Confident still didn't seem to know how to respond to the fact that he even opened the door for Aspire at all.

"You're going on the journey with me, so you must believe a little bit that it's possible, right?" Aspire wanted Confident to have hope.

"True. I guess that means somewhere inside, I think it's possible." Confident stared ahead processing Aspire's words. They had seemed to sink nicely.

Aspire and Confident continued on the trails in silence again. Aspire took note that the scenery still had not changed. The more they walked, the more of the same grass, flowers, boulders, and birds he saw.

The sun was high showing it was past noon. Aspire and Confident agreed to take a break for food. They also wanted to rest to get some of the energy back that they were steadily losing. Aspire was comfortable with a break this time because he wanted to be sure he had a lot of energy for Mount Impossible, but this break had to be short.

After gathering their lunches, they met to lie down in the grass. This time a few puffy clouds were passing overhead as if on a slow-moving conveyor belt. After Aspire and Confident finished their meals, they enjoyed the varying shapes of each cloud passing by.

They both agreed the first one looked like a tasty ice cream cone. They couldn't decide on the flavor though. It had to be chocolate chunk according to Confident, but Aspire thought it looked more like cherry cordial. The next one left itself to question. To Aspire, it was in the shape of the lizards in Trap Canyon, but Confident thought it was a tiger ready to pounce. They agreed to disagree.

As another cloud passed by, Aspire sized it up, looked over to Mount Impossible, and realized the cloud and the mountain looked way too similar. This reminded him of what was ahead, shifting him out of feeling relaxed into feeling anxious to get on the journey again. There was silence until Confident questioned, "Does that look like Mount Impossible to you?"

"Yeah," Aspire agreed. "I'm ready to go."

"Okay. Yeah, me too."

Aspire took no time getting up and taking to the trails with Confident calmly following behind. When they got to the trail, they quickly aligned steps and continued at a fairly brisk walk. The scenery continued to repeat itself, and the sky took to its same clear, unchangingly vivid blue. The valley was obviously not a fan of much variety.

They pressed on with their goal to get the falls standing ahead before them. Silence was inevitable at this point. Until Confident decided that it was Aspire's turn to host a visit in his own life. To Confident's visible surprise, Aspire had no problem opening the door quickly and inviting Confident to stay a bit.

Aspire proceeded to tell Confident about his life in Mundane. He talked about his special invitation from the unicorn in the Ever After Mountains. He blabbered on about his important discovery about the falls. He also explained the decision to take to the trails and become what he had always dreamed of becoming, a Majestic, a glorious unicorn. Aspire also didn't forget to tell Confident about some of his conversations with the Stars and what he went through in Trap Canyon.

Confident told Aspire of his admiration for Aspire's strength to choose the journey and push through the struggles so far. Aspire was making it quite far for his first time. Aspire felt he could puff his chest high to the sky. He was proud of the fact that he was doing so well on the journey to the falls. But Confident hesitated like he knew something but didn't know how to say it.

"Aspire... I need to tell you something. I once heard that the unicorn, Complete, or something—you know the one in the magazine—didn't make it to the falls the first time. Honestly, I don't know if he made it his second time. It's actually not an easy journey at all. It's supposed to be really hard."

This information shocked Aspire. "Oh. Where did you hear that?"

"The Stars. They were talking to some creature who turned around quickly after that. The Stars said something about the fact that the unicorn didn't get it. What? I don't know."

"Oh." Aspire began to fear the fact that this journey was a whole lot harder than he thought, and he might have to face failure, maybe more than once. This caused his heart to sink.

"But I also heard that the Stars didn't like the unicorn at first. They seem to like you already. I bet that helps," Confident tried to reassure again.

"Yeah. They do!" Aspire found hope in the fact that the Stars did seem to like him. He was content with that. He was going to be different.

Aspire and Confident continued walking in the repetitive valley until dusk. They talked here and there about life, musings, and unimportant things that won't be mentioned here. They also began to talk about the day and spent a few moments in awe at how the valley never changed almost the entire day.

At this point, as the sun decided to turn in, the little dancing Stars began to show up in the night sky. Aspire didn't notice at first as he and Confident were busy laughing about the day and the weirdness of it. But amid a good laugh, Aspire turned his head up, and a glittering distant Star caught his attention.

"Ooh, Confident! The Stars are out! Let's find a spot to turn in for the night and talk to the Stars." Aspire immediately turned off the path and began looking for a cozy spot to stay for the night.

"That's fine. I'm just going to lie down." Confident didn't sound like he wanted to talk to the Stars again. He still seemed wary of them every time they came up. Aspire was beginning to understand though.

The Stars were different and liked who they chose to like. Aspire was almost sure that they didn't care much for Confident. He also knew that Confident had picked up on that from the beginning. Perhaps the Stars didn't like that Confident came across like he was too good for them.

Aspire and Confident finally settled down to a particularly soft grassy patch, according to Aspire's opinion. They began to fluff and pad their spots for sleeping. Once finished, Aspire sat up and began to search the sky for his four favorite Stars. Meanwhile, Confident curled up and tucked his head in his tail planning to start to sleep.

Aspire found his friends.

"Hello! Long time no see!" Aspire had intense excitement in his voice.

"Hello, Aspire," came an elegant chorus of four Star voices.

"How have your past two days been? So glad to see you on the trails still." Perchance sounded excited too.

"Oh, good! I have some stories to tell you!" Aspire began to describe to the Stars his past couple of days from the hurtful lies of the gnats to the weird repetition of the valley. He also wanted to bring up Mount Impossible. He wanted to know what the Stars had to say.

"Wow, what a couple of days for you!" Wistful awed.

"You're doing so well!" Believe exclaimed.

"Thanks!" Aspire was feeling good. "So we'll make it to Mount Impossible just fine, right?" He almost got serious for that question.

"Time will tell," Deferring said. "You still have a ways to go before you get there. You won't be ready for it until you pass through some other places."

"Oh." Well, if that wasn't rain on Aspire's parade.

"Don't worry! Many creatures don't make it this far!" Believe tried to lift Aspire's spirits.

"So do you know how to get past Mount Impossible? It's on the trails, right?"

"It is on the trails. You'll know what to do when you get there, Aspire," Perchance said this so elegantly and understandingly that Aspire found it hard to feel upset about her unhelpful answer.

"Okay." Aspire then wondered more about the valley he was in. "So are we almost out of here?"

"You're making good progress, Aspire!" Believe encouraged.

"You should be out in no time!" Wistful chimed in.

"But am I going to get out soon? I can't even see past it." Aspire was getting frustrated because he was wanting a definite answer from the Stars but felt he was getting none.

"Don't worry, Aspire. You'll make it through," Perchance said it soothingly. "For every creature, it is different. But you'll only hurt yourself if you expect anything to happen quickly."

"What do you mean?" Aspire was already concerned about the journey taking longer than he wanted, and now the Stars were confirming his worries.

"This journey takes time, Aspire. It's not supposed to be short. For some creatures, it's not the obstacles but the time it takes to get to the falls that keeps them from pushing through to the end. Plan on that." Deferring was sweet but blunt.

This news felt like a hit to the gut for Aspire. This journey takes a long time? How long? If the obstacles he faced and the more that were to come weren't enough, an extended amount of time spent on the trails would be exhausting. He didn't want to be on the unknown trails forever. He liked comfort, and the trails were not that at all so far. He began to feel frustrated about the difficulty of the journey. He wondered, would he actually make it?

"What about that one unicorn, Complete, that I read about who took this journey. How long did it take him?" Aspire was wondering if the answer would give him an idea of what was to come.

"Well," Believe said tentatively, "he did make a couple of long stops and got turned around a couple of times."

"A couple of years, right?" Aspire turned to see Confident sitting up and looking at him. Ah, Confident was eavesdropping on the Stars again. Confident's curiosity about the conversation with the Stars obviously took over as he joined the discussion this time.

"Wait, a couple of years?" The words processed in Aspire's mind, and he quickly and worriedly turned to the Stars to get the right answer.

"Yeah, a couple of years sounds about right," Deferring said plainly.

"If you don't get sidetracked and walk off the trails, you could make it sooner!" Wistful offered.

Aspire could feel his heart sink. He began to think a couple of years was way too long, and how did Confident know that?

Aspire strongly made up his mind not to get sidetracked.

"Where did he go?" Aspire was now curious about what could distract a creature from getting their dream.

"Oh, a little here and a little there. The island is beautiful, and some obstacles can throw you off. It also depends on how badly you want to get to the falls," Perchance said this so lightly that Aspire didn't fully understand the gravity of the distractions.

"Okay." Aspire made it up in his mind that he wanted to get to the falls quite badly. Clearly a lot more than other creatures, and he would not let himself get distracted from his dream.

"Confident, you made it past Liar's Loop! Congrats!" Believe was such a cheerleader.

"Uh, yeah, thanks." Confident did not seem to like this attention from the Stars.

"It helps to not go through it alone," Wistful stated.

"Yeah." Confident looked like he wanted the Stars to stop talking to him now.

"That is definitely one thing you both have that other creatures don't. A travel partner," Perchance stated. "You will find that helpful most of the time!"

"Most of the time?" Both Aspire and Confident were curious about that statement.

"Just be aware that sometimes hardships can affect relationships. The journey is not easy," Deferring warned. "Just be honest and faithful friends to each other."

By now Aspire was getting tired of the pills the Stars were causing him to swallow. The reality of the journey was hitting him hard. He didn't think he could take another comment from the Stars, and he was ready to turn in for the night to rest his heavy head. He looked at Confident who took note and seemed to be ready for the Stars to leave him alone as well, so he initiated the getaway.

"Well, if the journey is going to be long, we should get some sleep, Aspire," Confident stated it quite loudly for the Stars to hear. "Uhh, good night. From the both of us...Stars." Confident proceeded to lie down again, motioning to Aspire to do the same. Aspire sat too dazed to notice.

"Well, good night then, Aspire and Confident. Get good rest for the journey." Perchance graciously took note of the situation and felt it was good to let Aspire and Confident be for now.

"Good night!" the rest of the Stars chimed in, leaving Aspire heavy at heart. He felt too upset to say anything now that a naive daydream bubble of his had popped. The Stars were quite direct today.

After the Stars left to their own conversations, Aspire lay down in his bed. But his mind was too busy processing what the Stars had said to go to sleep anytime soon. Aspire turned away from Confident trying to avoid any interactions with any other beings for the rest of the night. He felt overwhelmed with disappointment and frustration and found comfort in silence alone. Soon the power of exhaustion grew too strong, and sleep finally took over.

5

"*A*spire. Aspire. Wake up." Aspire woke up squinting to the bright light of day and to Confident's nose in his face. Even after catching quite enough z's because of sleeping late into the morning, he did not have enough time to feel better.

He did not feel ready to interact with anyone. Plus, he felt more exhausted than even he thought he should be. He closed his eyes for a little bit, processing the fact that it was morning and the sun was already up high. He wished it was dark so he could sleep more. He didn't feel like facing the day nor did he want to face the reality of the journey again.

"Come on, Aspire. We should get going. We got a lot ahead of us, and it is late in the morning." Confident sounded surprisingly antsy to start up the journey for the day.

Aspire spent a few more moments still waking up to the day and trying to brush off the troubles of last night. Finally, he opened his eyes and slowly started getting up avoiding the brightness of the sun. It was too happy for him. Once he pulled himself up, Confident's obvious excitement for the day took him off guard as Confident began to prance around Aspire.

"Come on, let's go. Let's take on this beast of a trail!" Confident proceeded to hop right on over out of the field and onto the path. Aspire followed with a lot less energy and pep.

Aspire made it to Confident in time before Confident took to a brisk pace, and the two of them pressed on to their distant destination together. The only difference was, Aspire and Confident seemed to have switched places. Aspire's steps were slow and cumbersome while Confident practically bounced around on the trail with energy for the trek. Aspire lost excitement for the journey, but Confident must have picked it up somewhere.

The two continued on to the faraway goal embracing the fact that they both were clearly not themselves but still going forward just the same. In the meantime, Aspire scoffed while Confident practically chuckled as the valley still looked exactly the same as yesterday.

Aspire could not tell if they had made any progress at all the day before. He began to wonder if they walked backward in their sleep or if something lifted them up in the night and brought them closer to the beginning again.

Aspire was quite frustrated; the valley seemed to still stretch on for miles in either direction. Nothing was changing. Some bird flew by perfectly timed. The grass swayed perfectly synchronized, and the sky was the same blue as yesterday. However, one thing was different.

Mount Impossible looked wonderfully large before them. Mostly definitely larger than yesterday. The mountain even seemed to have more precise detail. The rock of the mountain looked sharper and more defined with dark green, red, and brown colors. The colors separated and blended with no discernible pattern. Aspire rolled his eyes at the threat of the mountain and walked on. Confident didn't seem to pay attention to the mountain at all.

Every now and then, Aspire would catch Confident glance back at him with concern. Aspire knew that he was not his usual bubbly self at the moment. The Stars never told Aspire that the journey was impossible. But they certainly made it sound quite challenging, and it made Aspire doubt his ability to make the journey. It was hanging over him like a dense gray cloud today even while the sun was shining brightly. This journey was turning out to be a lot less fun than Aspire thought it would be.

After a while, Confident broke the silence.

"So the Stars actually seem all right."

Aspire wondered if Confident was trying to cheer him up.

"Yeah. Are you actually changing your mind about them now?" Aspire turned to Confident talking for the first time that day. It seemed to give Confident assurance that he might be helping at least a little bit.

"I think so. The past couple of times that you talked to them, they sounded different, I guess. They are nicer to me than I thought too. I always ignored them before because I really didn't understand them. I didn't think they liked me either."

Confident seemed to be softening up toward the Stars, and it made Aspire feel better, but just a little. He had wanted Confident to like the Stars, and he wanted the Stars to like Confident. He figured they would. Aspire was sure of it.

"That's good."

Confident's attempt to encourage Aspire had helped, yet Aspire couldn't help but sink back in his sad shell again.

Confident seemed to try another way to pull Aspire out.

"Look! My paw is pretty much back to normal!" Confident showed Aspire his paw that did look a whole lot better than before. "Another day should bring it back to its regular size!"

Aspire looked over. "That's great. No wonder you have so much energy."

Aspire brought his focus back down on the path giving little excitement at the wonderful news. Confident, however, seemed not to want to give up on his attempt to pull Aspire out of his troubled spirit.

"Wow, how is it that everything has looked the same in this valley for miles?" He laughed. "This is a weird place."

"Yeah," Aspire agreed, but he still had a dead stare forward.

"So did the Stars bum you out or something?"

Confident clearly didn't want to beat around the bush anymore. What he was doing before obviously wasn't working that well, so he now tried to get at the root of Aspire's sadness. Aspire wondered if Confident was trying to be nice and helpful. He didn't know how to respond at first.

"No…well, maybe."

Aspire felt upset about what the Stars said. He just wanted encouragement from them, not a heavy dose of reality. He liked talking to the Stars because they always encouraged him and rooted for him. But now, they seemed to bring his hopes down. He did not want to talk about this to Confident, but he found himself doing just that.

"I guess I sort of knew that the journey would be hard and long. It's just… I guess the Stars made me actually realize it. I just don't want to think about it."

"So do you think you'll give up then?" Confident pressed further, and he had sadness in his voice.

"Uh…well, no." Aspire still wanted his horn. He had to have it, and he realized that he didn't like the idea of going back to his family having failed in his attempt to get to the falls. "Definitely no."

"Okay." Confident's tone brightened. He seemed to be more committed to the journey than Aspire was at the moment.

Aspire and Confident walked on in silence. This time, however, Aspire's mood was changing. It became more of a frustrated determination. He was not letting himself sink any lower. He did not want to give up on the journey, on getting his horn. He would not let his dream go; he was going to get it, no matter what. He would not be going home to his family with nothing.

However, everything else in the moment remained the same. This, in turn, gave Aspire and Confident more energy to speed up their pace and get out of the valley as quickly as possible. It was long and tedious, keeping them from getting where they wanted to go. However, Aspire and Confident couldn't tell if they were making much progress until they would look at Mount Impossible. They saw it gaining in height and width ever more steadily leaving the two, but especially Aspire, at a loss for how they would overcome it. They trudged on in the unchanging valley with the growing view of Mount Impossible for quite a time. Until Aspire couldn't take it anymore and burst out.

"I can't take this! Why is it all the same? I can't even tell where the valley ends. Does it?" Aspire's sudden outburst startled Confident causing him to step further away from Aspire, but he nodded with tired agreement.

"Yeah, this kind of sucks," Confident affirmed. "It's got to end at some point."

On they went, dealing with the fact that things were not going to change for who knows when. This definitely took away from the excitement Aspire had after making it through Liar's Loop. That was nothing to him now. At this moment, he just wanted out of the valley. He knew that there was a lot ahead that he and Confident still had to face. He just didn't know what lay ahead, which was the troubling part.

At this point, Aspire, and even Confident, began to get grumpy about their circumstances. It seemed as if so much was out of their control. The unknown of whether they would make the journey kept growing; it was the very thing that upset Aspire most of all. Aspire was also learning that when he first embarked on the journey, he believed that it would be no problem getting to the falls. He was strong and capable and would get there in no time. The interview he read made it seem so simple: take the trails, get to the falls, and ultimately get the desire, the dream.

Aspire wasn't bothered much by the struggles before; he was too excited about the falls to care. However, the time he spent in the valley caused him to realize more of what was ahead. He saw all that was at stake, and it was a lot more daunting and definitely not that simple anymore. There were a great deal more unknowns. The journey required a lot from him, and he didn't know if he could offer it.

"Hey, look at that."

Aspire turned to see Confident staring off into the grassy valley at a group of vultures circling high and low above something deep in the grass.

That was a different sight than what they had been seeing for quite some time. They both stared as they began to wonder what it was that interested the vultures so. Confident spoke his idea first.

"Do you think it's another creature?" He said it with such concern that Aspire began to feel entirely concerned himself.

Questions ran through his head. What if it was another creature? Could they still be alive? What should he and Confident do?

"Should we…go see?" Aspire felt concerned about the situation but was tentative about getting involved.

"Yeah, probably." Confident began to tread slowly off the path toward the circling vultures, and Aspire followed with an even slower pace.

It didn't take them long to get to the circling vultures. But the tension of the situation was so strong that Aspire felt like he was walking in slow motion toward a concerning unknown. Confident arrived first and scared off some of the lower flying vultures.

Aspire held his breath as Confident paused at the scene quite still. Suddenly he responded with a question that Aspire knew was not for him.

"Hey, are you okay?" Confident was his calm, cool, and collected self.

Aspire was curious about to whom Confident directed his question. He wondered what the scenario looked like, and his heart began to race. He walked as quickly as he could to get to the scene.

When he arrived, lying in the grass was a small horse. He was chestnut brown with a jet-black mane. The little horse looked alive but had an obviously injured back leg stretched out behind him.

The leg had a long jagged gash surrounded by a fair amount of dried blood; it also seemed semi-infected. Aspire directed his attention back to the horse's face. The horse's eyes were wide-eyed to the situation, but he surprisingly didn't seem scared or concerned about the vultures. He looked surprised to see Confident with Aspire following behind.

However, his face changed, to Aspire's surprise, as he spoke in quite a nonchalant tone.

"Uh, I'm fine! These vultures catch sight of blood and think I'm dying or something. I just wanted to take a nap." The little horse motioned up to some vultures which were still circling high ahead as he was talking. He definitely seemed fine despite his uncomfortable-looking wound.

"Yeah, they do that." Confident seemed to say that from experience. "Do you need anything? I'm Confident." Confident proceeded to put his paw out.

"I'm Searching!" The little horse held out his hoof. "I don't need anything."

"I'm Aspire." Aspire held out his hoof wondering if Searching even knew how bad his wound appeared to be.

"Hi!" Searching seemed genuinely excited to see other creatures in the valley with him.

"What are you doing out here? How did you hurt your leg?" Confident wanted to get straight to the point.

"I'm going to Contentment Isle!" Searching seemed very excited about his destination. "I have friends who have been there. They told me that it's the nicest place to live, and you can be someone there. They weren't there long before they already had fans!" Searching seemed quite interested in his own information as his eyes grew wide with excitement over the idea of having fans.

Aspire felt a slight curiosity about the isle. He wondered if it was along the trails. Maybe they could stop by. But he realized that they couldn't get sidetracked. He and Confident had a mission.

"Wow. That's cool," he said, still slightly wondering if the place would be worth the stop.

"I know," Searching agreed. "I can't believe I'm going to have fans!"

It was as if he had already planned to succeed. Aspire admired Searching's assurance of the possibility. He also felt slightly bothered by the fact that Searching might be too sure of his success. Aspire's faith to make it on his journey had seemed bruised, and he was envying Searching's apparent faith. Aspire wondered how Searching could be so sure of his outcome.

"So how did you hurt your leg?" Confident didn't seem to care to acknowledge Contentment Isle or the fans. Searching's leg needed more attention.

"Oh, uh, I went to catch the view of the ocean over there." Searching motioned across the valley. "I guess I leaned over too much. I slipped and almost fell off the edge! I'm fine. I just hurt my leg. It's healing, I think." Searching looked at his wound.

"You might want to take care of that." Confident looked concerned at Searching's wound.

"Yeah, probably." Searching didn't seem to care too much, however. He must not have known how bad it looked. "Where are you two going? I haven't seen any other creatures yet besides you two now!"

"Oh, we're going to Destiny Falls!" Aspire tried to take a turn at expressing excitement about his destination. He didn't feel right about his attempt.

"Yep," Confident agreed coolly.

"Oh, that's cool! I heard about the falls! I heard it's past Contentment Isle on the trails! Oh! We should go together! At least until I get to the isle. I think I'm a lot closer."

Searching's excitement made him seem like a wild little thing to Aspire. He didn't know how to respond.

"Okay, uh, sure." Aspire wondered if he liked that idea. Maybe it would be fine. *The more the merrier on this crazy journey, right?* he thought. But he wondered if Searching had just jabbed passively at the length of their journey.

"That's fine. We should go and get you something for your leg too." Confident was such a cool creature to Aspire. He acted as chill as when Aspire first met him, interestingly opposite of Searching who seemed to get excited about everything.

Searching excitedly stood up, with some struggle as his leg seemed to be hurting him quite a lot. Then, the three of them headed to the path to take the journey together, at least for the time being.

As they continued on again to their goal, Aspire and Confident found Searching to be quite a talkative creature. He had a lot to say about a lot of things, and most, if not all of it, pertained to himself. Aspire and Confident didn't mind Searching's rambling, at first. It was quite entertaining because Searching was comical, in addition to being excitable. Yet just like the unchanging scenery around them, Searching's gabbing got old.

Aspire and Confident spent quite a few hours walking, stopping for lunch, and ignoring the size of Mount Impossible with Searching in tow talking their ears off. Aspire and Confident could barely get a word in as well. The only funny part of it all was that Searching clearly had a fair amount of pain in his leg which caused him to walk with a ridiculous head bob.

This gave his sentences a wavelike intonation as the words he said when his head moved up had more emphasis than the words he said when his head went down. It left him with interesting-sounding phrases. Searching also didn't seem to notice, maybe because he was excited not to be alone anymore. This comedy kept Aspire and Confident from becoming entirely annoyed.

One thing was for sure, Aspire was beginning to forget about the previous issues from the day. Even the long process of the journey was slipping out of the forefront of his mind. He found himself merely walking forward and listening to Searching fling the door to his life wide open as well as all the windows and the back door. Aspire and Confident could learn about Searching from every angle. They practically learned about his entire life from the first day he entered the earth to the present.

Sifting through paragraph after paragraph, they learned he had a small but lovely family. He had a tranquil life living in the bay near Liar's Loop; Common Bay, he called it. Most of his life he kept himself busy and entertained by obsessing over well-known and popular creatures. He, of course, knew of the Majestics. His goal now was to be popular himself, and he figured if he could live on Contentment Isle and get fans, he would be living the dream, so to speak. He would be what he always admired, and that was all he ever wanted in life.

There was a moment in Searching's long spiel that caused Aspire and Confident to give each other confused but semi-interested looks. Searching seemed to brush over the fact that he didn't mind spending time around the gnats. The gnats, they heard, not only lingered very heavily outside his town, they also spent time in his village as well.

Aspire wondered if the gnats actually followed Searching around throughout his day-to-day. After their experiences, Aspire and Confident absolutely hated the gnats. It was so miserable for them to pass through Liar's Loop. Aspire could never imagine living with the gnats. He also could never imagine getting used to what they would say. Those gnats seemed to really enjoy utterly discouraging creatures no matter who they were.

Aspire and Confident both said nothing during that time. They left that topic alone exchanging surprised glances. Neither of them obviously cared to hear Searching's "secret" or way of surviving the gnats as they both had no desire to go back there.

As the hours passed, Searching still carried on chatting with every door and window flung wide open to his life. Aspire and Confident found many moments to exchange glances in reaction to Searching's babbling and even shared a few words here and there in reaction. They also exchanged some eye rolls as they weren't the biggest fans of the situation, but they couldn't leave him to fend for himself in his state. So they succumbed to walking the path and to simply listening.

In the process, they didn't notice that over time, the path had taken a turn, and the view of Mount Impossible had moved behind them. However, at this point, it was getting dark, and it was hard to see much of anything. It was also growing steadily darker in a strange way on the path ahead, so they decided to find a spot to sleep and call it a night. It turned out to be a nice change of pace as it quieted Searching down at the same time as Aspire and Confident took charge of the conversation figuring out what they would do for the rest of the night.

They found a nice grassy spot near the path and made up their respective beds. As they began to settle down in them, Confident walked up to Aspire and asked in a quieter tone as to not get Searching's attention, "Do you want to talk to the Stars tonight?" He sounded surprisingly open to doing so, but this time, Aspire was not. Aspire didn't want any more hard news from the Stars. He was already exhausted from the reality of the valley and spending a good portion of the day with Searching in tow. He hesitated to answer, lay down, and voiced his decision with a yawn.

"Nah, not tonight. I'm tired, and I think I just want to sleep now. We still have to get out of the valley."

"Oh, okay. Good night then." Confident kept his quiet tone and went back to his bed. He spoke up a bit. "Uh, good night, Searching."

"Good night! You know this is my third night out here. I never really slept outside before except for this one time—"

"Good night!" Both Confident and Aspire were officially done with Searching's talking.

"Oh, okay." Searching must have gotten the memo and proceeded to tuck his head in his body to go to sleep.

"Sleep well!" Aspire happily said the last words of the night as sleep fell over the three creatures not too late after.

*A*spire was the first to wake up. It was a cloudy morning, but the sun was starting to peek through the clouds on the horizon without care, even though it seemed as if the clouds were intentionally blocking its light. Aspire yawned and stretched and took a gander at his surroundings.

What immediately caught his attention was that everything looked new today. The mountains were a great deal closer; they stood right before him now. Aspire had a hard time at first trying to find Mount Impossible, which he soon discovered was in the other direction behind everything else.

Aspire viewed his new surroundings again, and that's when he saw it. There was a blue, sun-washed, wooden sign not too far off poking out of a rocky wall. It read, "Now leaving Reality Valley," and below it read, "Entering Mirage Jungle."

"What?" he said aloud.

Then he started thinking. Were they finally at the end of the valley? He looked beyond the sign to see that just a little farther down the trail lay a beautiful, viny entrance to a lush and thickly planted forest. He figured that it had to be the jungle from what he had learned about them.

The opening made the jungle quite inviting, and since it was proof that they were at the end of the valley, the jungle also looked like an exciting change. Aspire processed these sights for a second and then couldn't contain his excitement any longer.

"Yessss!" He got up, did a celebratory hop, and ran to Confident. "Confident! Wake up! Wake up! We're out of the valley!"

Confident was already in the stages of waking up but was not the happiest to be on the receiving end of Aspire's energetic outburst. Nonetheless, he had to take in the scene for himself. As he took it all in, all the glory, Aspire motioned Confident's attention to the sign. When he saw that Aspire was right, he began to show Aspire's excitement as well.

A smile spread across his face as another obstacle was officially completed. It was another victory that both Aspire and Confident shared. Another moment they would play back in their minds with fondness. A moment no one would understand but them.

"Let's get going! We're getting closer with every step!" Aspire was still full of excited energy.

"Yeah. But don't forget, you know." Confident motioned over to Searching, who was still sleeping.

Searching lay sprawled out on his back with a leg twitching. He looked to be dreaming about something interesting. Both Aspire and Confident walked over to Searching, observing the situation trying to figure out what to do. That's when Aspire pulled out his hoof and nudged Searching.

"Searching, time to get up. We're out of the valley now!" Aspire tried his best to be nice, but he wanted Searching to get up, so he decided to be a little annoying as well.

Searching responded by opening his eyes for a second and then rolled over to go back to his dream. "Mmmm, okay…" He snuggled right back into a happy sleep. His dream must have been good.

Aspire looked at Confident, whose shrug told Aspire that he didn't know what to do either. So Aspire turned his attention back to Searching.

"Uhh, Searching, we should get started on the journey. I don't know about you, but we have a lot ahead of us." He was frustrated with Searching now because he did not want to wait very long on this silly creature.

Searching did not respond this time. Aspire waited for a moment, then he looked to Confident. "Can you get him up?"

"Uh, okay." Confident didn't seem to want to attempt to wake up Searching but accepted that it was his turn to help. He nudged

Searching with his paw. "Searching, hey, it's time to get up. You can rest later if you want to. Let's go!"

Searching responded first with a yawn and then rolled over toward them. "Morning!" He yawned again, still trying to open his eyes. He was taking more time than Aspire wanted him to take.

"All right, come on!" Aspire tried to say it cheerfully. He started walking away to give Searching the hint that it was time to go.

Confident joined him, and they made it all the way back to the path when they finally heard, "Hold up!"

They stopped and turned to see Searching running, trying to catch up with them. When he arrived with a bashful smile, they shook their heads with a growing smile at his silliness. Then they began to walk to the entrance of the jungle together.

Searching was quiet most of the way. He read the sign's announcement out loud and commented on the view of the jungle entrance. However, it was not much compared to the day before, and it was a relief to Aspire and Confident. Aspire was beginning to wonder, though, if Searching's leg was bothering him more than yesterday. It still did not look good. If anything, it looked worse as Searching limped along.

"Hey, Searching, how is your leg doing?" Aspire looked at Searching's leg wincing.

"It's fine. Well, it hurts a little. Maybe a lot." It seemed like Searching was taking a bit to admit even to himself that his leg was not in the best condition.

"We'll probably find something to soothe it in there. Let's keep an eye out." Confident motioned to the jungle growing before them.

"Yeah!" both Aspire and Searching agreed.

The three of them kept their eyes straight on the jungle entrance that was getting taller and taller the closer they got to it. When they made it to the entrance, they paused to embrace the magnificent view. Moss-covered boulders and knotted roots lined the path. Thick vines draped heavily from the countless trees on either side of the way forming a canopy above them. It was a beautiful sight.

As they began to walk under the canopy, cool air flooded around them, and a bridge revealed itself. All three of them clearly had never seen anything like this before in real life, so they spent a fair amount of time oohing and aahing at the sight.

As they crossed the bridge, they found no choice but to stop and view the river gently flowing below. It looked as crisp and refreshing as anything ever could possibly be. They spent a fair amount of time on the bridge, drinking in the view of the jungle as well. They had a more unobstructed view of the forest on the bridge with its dewy treetops, long dripping vines, and leafy and flowering plants every-where. Once they got out of their mesmerized trance, they remem-bered their goal and started pressing forward.

Another aspect of the awe-inspiring jungle that caught their attention was the various noises of their surroundings. They could hear water flowing and dripping in almost every direction. Little creatures would chirp their hellos, and bugs with wings liked to make their presence known. The three of them, but especially Aspire, who never knew a place to be so magical, found themselves enjoying the experience a great deal. What a place for their adventure to take them.

They continued to enjoy the sounds of the jungle. But as Searching walked through a leafy plant, it brushed against his wounded leg irritating it, thus causing him to shout, "Ouch!" He stopped to look at his leg.

"Are you okay?" Confident stopped, which caused Aspire to stop as well. They looked at Searching, who was stretched around in an awkward position to get a better view of his leg.

"Um, yeah, I guess. That plant touched my leg." Searching motioned to the plant that he had walked through. He turned to look at his leg again. His brow furrowed at the sight of his leg. "Maybe we should start looking for something to help my leg."

"Yeah, okay. I've heard that there is a tall tree in here with weird white flowers, and its bark helps with cuts and infections and stuff. Look out for something like that." Confident seemed to take on the mission with pride of his knowledge.

The three of them now placed their attention on looking for this tree as they walked through the amazing jungle. It took them longer than they thought, especially since none of them had seen one of these trees before. Because of that, they may have passed a couple until Searching shouted with excitement at the hope of finding one.

"I found it! Look at that tree!" Searching pointed to a reasonably sized tree with white flower clusters clinging to the trunk.

Confident walked up to the tree, inspected its appearance for a second, tested the bark, and then stated with full knowledge, "That's not the one." He then left the tree and continued walking forward on the path.

Aspire and Searching exchanged glances that seemed to say, "All right, I guess he knows what he is doing." Then they proceeded to follow him until Aspire thought he saw one.

"Hey, is this it?" Aspire asked Confident with excitement while looking at the tree with curiosity.

Confident walked over to this tree. It was kind of tall, and it had big white flowers. He followed through the same process he had done with the previous tree and gave the same response. "Nope, that's not the one." Confident was sure. Aspire felt let down though.

They pressed on until Confident stopped and exclaimed, "Ah!" Then he walked right up to a very tall tree with long, pointy leaves and clusters of small white, odd-looking flowers. "This is it!" He was clearly proud to have found it. He began to dig in the trunk of the tree making a collection of juicy bark on the ground underneath.

Aspire and Searching watched with amusement. Once Confident got as much as he wanted, he summoned Searching over and made Searching sit down beside the pile of bark that he had gathered. Confident took the juiciest pieces of the bark and placed them on Searching's leg until there was a layer completely covering the wound.

"Let that sit for a bit."

Even though Confident said that he had never been in the jungle before, he somehow knew what to do. After that experience, Aspire undoubtedly believed that Confident would make an amazing king of a tribe, and he never doubted it since.

The three rested in the middle of the jungle for a full twenty minutes enjoying the wonder of the scene. Meanwhile, the bark of the tree soothed Searching's wound. At this point, Searching was showing immediate relief as the discovered bark hugged his leg with its healing properties. To prove his returning health, Searching started to express his original energy. This was the kind of energy that made his mouth and tongue move at a pace that Aspire and Confident could not keep up.

After the twenty minutes had passed, Searching's talkative energy had been fully recharged, and the rambling began. Searching started by noting the trees and the differences of each; he proceeded to try and count how many different trees there were. He followed his tree documenting by noticing the various insects that came across his path.

While he sat there, he thought it fun to count each one as well, all out loud. When he became bored with counting, he decided to switch gears and moved to the fact that the different sounds of the jungle were quite hilarious to him. Then in a natural Searching kind of response, he began to imitate all the various sounds he heard. He was clearly happy to be feeling better again.

This, however, began to drive Confident crazy as he began to groan and complain under his breath. Aspire exchanged weird looks with Confident over Searching's attempts to imitate the sounds of the jungle. It was time to move on.

"Okay, Searching." Confident jumped to his feet. He spoke slowly, obviously holding back irritability that was still peeping through his words. "I think that's good. We should get going now. Your leg should be able to heal up on its own. We can put more on your leg tonight too just to be sure. And…how about we respect the creatures in the jungle and be quiet as we walk?"

"Okay! I really like that stuff! My leg feels so much better. I could run for miles!" Searching jumped up and didn't even think to take the bark salve off his wound. In the process, Aspire couldn't help but laugh as Searching began to skip about with bits and pieces of the bark falling off his leg everywhere.

Confident's irritability slid into amusement without him knowing. Now he too was chuckling at the strangeness of Searching. Nonetheless, he reminded Searching again to settle down. He requested that Searching respect the tenants of the jungle when what he actually wanted was for Searching to keep from talking his ear off.

The three of them once again took to the trails. They remembered how much of a different place they were in on the journey and how exciting it was. Aspire thought that they had to be getting so much closer to their destinations. He felt so much closer to reaching the falls.

As they walked, they saw a couple of monkeys swing by high up in the canopy. They seemed to be chatting and laughing, not even catching sight of the three below in awe of the monkeys' ability to almost fly at that height. Aspire also caught sight of a chameleon and frustrated Confident in an attempt to find it.

Meanwhile, Searching had been obviously trying to hold in a lot of words, following Confident's orders, by holding his lips together. But that made his cheeks balloon with the air that he was holding in order to keep from talking. He had to stop every now and then to gasp for a breath causing Confident to roll his eyes.

Thankfully, the sights and sounds started to distract him, so he wasn't talking as much as they continued farther on the path. At this point, Searching mostly uttered a lot of sounds in his awe of each new thing that crossed their path on the trails.

Gradually, the three travelers grew more accustomed to the sights of the jungle and realized their hunger. They decided to stop, look for food, and meet up by the tall tree that looked like it had a scraggly arm pointing down to the trail.

When Aspire and Confident split ways, Aspire stopped and watched as Searching looked back and forth from Aspire to Confident. Confident continued walking farther away, so Searching decided to follow Aspire and ran to catch up with him.

"Hold up, Aspire!"

Aspire waited and shook his head laughing at the sight of Searching as he ran, almost tripping on the plants in his way. When Searching caught up, the two walked together off the path in a search for a tasty meal. Aspire tried to keep an eye on the tree that the three were to meet at when they found food. He was doing an excellent job until he noticed a sign that caught his full attention.

It sat posted by a wall of rock covered in greenery. Next to it was a curtain of falling, twisting vines. The sign read "waterfall."

At the sight, Aspire's heart skipped a beat. A waterfall! He looked in hope at the sign for a second and then felt the need to make sure he was reading it right.

"Searching, does that say what I think it says?" Aspire had excitement but uncertainty in his voice.

"Mm, yeah, if you think it says 'waterfall,' you'd be right. But if you thought it said 'wafertall,' you'd be wrong." Searching said this plainly. He was quite serious about what he said, but he seemed pleased with himself when Aspire burst out laughing at his observation.

Aspire couldn't contain his excitement now. "Confident! Confident! We found a waterfall! Confident!" Aspire left the scene for a second running to find Confident. When he finally found him, Aspire couldn't take any time to explain the situation. He breathlessly told Confident to come and quickly follow him right away.

When Aspire led Confident close enough to see the sign, he exclaimed, "Look! A waterfall!"

Confident, who was clearly unsure of what was happening, squinted his eyes at the sign. When they got closer, Confident understood. Yet he didn't seem to join in on the excitement Aspire had.

"It's just a waterfall, Aspire," Confident said unenthused.

Aspire didn't understand why Confident wasn't as excited as him. It was a waterfall! At the sign, they found Searching standing where Aspire had left him. But he was stretching his neck toward something beyond the sign. A closer look revealed to Aspire a nicely sized tarantula. He had a black body with orange cuffs on his eight legs that held him in a nook on the wall. The spider turned from staring at Searching to looking at Aspire and Confident who were breathing heavily from rushing to the entrance. His beady eyes blinked calmly.

"Well, hello and welcome," the tarantula said with a relaxed tone through his furry lips. He spent a few seconds staring and blinking at Aspire and Confident, who were still catching their breath. Aspire tried to process what exactly was happening.

Aspire finally gathered his breath. "Hi, thanks. So is there really a waterfall? Where is it?"

"Ah, yes, it's in this cave." The spider tapped the wall he was resting on and blinked at Aspire.

"Oh! How do we find it?" Aspire was not going to waste any time.

"Walk through these vines over here, head through the cave, and you won't miss it!" The spider sounded playful with a twist of excitement this time as he pointed to the curtain of vines.

"Okay!" Aspire felt excited. "Let's go check it out, guys!" He started walking to the vine curtain with the hope of what could lie before him. When he got to the veil of vines, he parted it and turned looking at Confident and Searching with nervous excitement, but they weren't following him. "Hey, come on! It's a waterfall!" Aspire did not understand why they were not going with him. He figured it probably wasn't the actual Destiny Falls, but it was worth checking out!

"I…don't know about that, Aspire. I don't like this." Confident was exhibiting not even the slightest ounce of excitement about the discovery. It dampened Aspire's enthusiasm. Confident furrowed his brow at the spider; he seemed to find the tarantula and the entrance to the waterfall to be questionable.

"But…it's a waterfall!"

Aspire had to see it.

The spider butted in.

"No doubt you'll find what you are looking for at the waterfall. Only good things come from the waterfall. When you walk in, just keep going. Don't worry about anything. Keep your eyes on the water."

The tarantula said this with a funny and creepy-looking smile on his face this time. It wasn't Aspire's favorite response, but he let himself forget it because his excitement for the waterfall was too high.

"How about you go in, and we'll wait here, Aspire." Confident was clearly not wanting to see what the waterfall had to offer. "I want to see what this tarantula is all about. What does he really mean when he says the waterfall will give you what you want?" He turned and looked at the spider quizzically.

"Um, okay." Aspire didn't want to go alone, but he also knew he had no choice at this point. Confident was not budging, and Searching chose to stay with Confident this time. Aspire looked through the veil of vines a second or two and finally walked through.

The cave was dark, so Aspire's eyes took a bit to adjust. When they did, he could see before him a little way was a blue light, and then he could hear the sound of flowing water. This caused him to feel jittery excitement, which made him walk faster.

In the process, he heard a strange plopping sound and soft scurrying. He began to look at his surroundings, which he could see better now. The walls blended with the ceiling, which was low. It also seemed oddly dark and bumpy, but Aspire paid no heed and moved on.

He walked toward the blue light, and he could begin to make out the colors and ripples of water, so he moved steadily forward with his eyes on the prize.

When he finally made it to where the light and sound was coming from, it was anticlimactic for him. The cave had opened up to a reasonably sized room, and light came from a hole in the ceiling where water was flowing down into a glowing pool. It was a pretty sight but not really a waterfall to Aspire's standards. The cave also started to give him an eerie feeling.

He was ready to turn around until he began to wonder if he heard whispering. It wasn't quite audible, so he leaned in to figure out what it was. Then he heard something clear its throat.

"Mhmhm. Welcome to the waterfall! Uhh…what do you want?" Aspire could not figure out where the voice was coming from, but he decided to answer it and spoke to the water.

"I, uh, don't know." Aspire began to wonder if he should get out of this scenario. Immediately, he felt that he wanted to be out of the cave and back with Confident and Searching.

"Uh, yes, but what do you want to be in life?" the voice returned before Aspire could leave.

Aspire knew the answer to that, so he stated. "I want to be a unicorn."

"Ahh, yes, you came to the right place. I just need you to do a couple of things first." The voice couldn't quite convince Aspire though.

"I, uh, I think I might go..." Aspire started to back away. He didn't entirely trust the voice, wherever it came from.

"No, no, uh, stay. You'll get that horn. Trust me. You'll be what you always wanted. The unicorn! This is your time! Don't miss it!" The voice was strangely promising and a little tempting to Aspire. He began to wonder what this place was. If he had heard wrong about Destiny Falls. Was this the place? He let go of the tension in his muscles and poised himself ready to listen to what the voice had to say next. Aspire heard whispering again then the voice cleared its throat.

"So first we'll—I'll—have you step into the water."

Aspire hesitated then decided, why not, what's the worst that could happen? The pool looked safe enough, so he stepped into it. The voice proceeded with more instructions.

"Now spin in a circle."

So Aspire spun around in a circle.

"Don't stop! Faster! Faster!" the voice shouted, and Aspire obeyed but was not sure if he wanted to do so. He spun and spun and was beginning to get dizzy, so dizzy that he fell off balance into the water, and it went up into his nose. But the voice still kept shouting, "Faster!" so he got up and kept spinning. He was beginning to feel frustrated until the voice gave another command.

"Okay, you can stop now. Um, dip your head in the water and blow bubbles."

Aspire thought this was a strange command, but he did it anyway. He spent about half a minute trying to snort bubbles in the water when the voice gave another command.

"Now, stand under the waterfall."

Aspire looked at the water rushing down. He did not want to get wet. He realized that he did not think this through.

"This is your time! Come on, unicorn!"

Aspire let go of all reason and obeyed stepping right under the falling water. The water was heavy and was pushing a lot of the hair of his mane over his eyes. It was hard for him to breathe. He was not enjoying this.

The voice came again. "Okay, you can step out of the water now."

Aspire stepped out from under the water and walked out of the pool dripping wet but relieved to be able to breathe and see again.

"Okay, now get down and roll around on your back," came the voice again.

Aspire questioned this command wondering how that would get him his horn, but he did it anyway. He got down on his back and began to roll around but half-heartedly.

"Yay, you did it! Now here is your horn," the voice shouted with celebration.

Aspire stopped, hooves in the air, confused at the sudden celebration. He didn't feel any different. Then he felt something drop on his stomach. He lifted his head to see what it was. As his eyes focused, he realized it was a leaf rolled up to a point with two thin, stringy vines poking through two sides of the bottom.

At first, he didn't know what to think. Then, he got up and sat there in shock staring at the leaf cone that had rolled off his stomach and stopped at a nearby rock. What had just happened?

The voice started laughing and tried to speak through stifled laughter, "Put it on! We'll help you tie it! You're a unicorn now!"

Suddenly, Aspire started to hear laughter all around him. His face felt hot with growing embarrassment, disappointment, and confusion. The laughter increased and was now coming loudly from every possible direction. If that was not enough, little black blobs began to drop around him everywhere.

Suddenly, a discovery sent Aspire in shock. These laughing creatures were spiders, and they were laughing so hard at the trick they collectively pulled on him that they couldn't keep their grip on the ceiling of the cave. Aspire saw and felt spiders fall to the ground all around him like rain. Suddenly, one of them landed on Aspire's nose, and he let out a loud shriek breaking himself out of shock. Tears flooded to his eyes, and he darted out of the cave shaking off spiders all the way through.

When he burst through the vine entrance of the cave, he stopped before Confident and Searching, who had run to the opening at the sound of his yell. They looked at him with deep concern. His eyes had filled up with so many tears he could barely see at this point. Confident's gentle question asking Aspire if he was okay broke the floodgates. Aspire sat down and, for a good minute, let loose the tears that had built up, trying to explain what happened to him.

"They...they tricked me...the tarantulas. They were...they were falling on me everywhere." Aspire managed to get some words through his deep sobs. But his crying cut short when they heard a chuckling to the side. It was the tarantula that convinced him to go to the waterfall in the first place.

"What are you laughing about? That's my best friend you hurt!" Confident sounded quite angry. The spiders had hurt and humiliated Aspire, and the king in him was coming out again as he defended Aspire, his friend.

"Ahh, nothing." The spider laughed. "That was just a good trick! The best one yet! It was definitely so worth it!"

"Worth what?" Confident stormed over to the tarantula demanding information.

"The tricks make a lot of us lose our grip from laughter, and we generally don't survive those falls. But it's so worth it! This one especially!" The spider was laughing harder now.

Confident made a disgusted face at the fact that the spiders were so willing to risk their lives at the humiliation of another creature. This time it was at the expense of Aspire. His best friend. He didn't have anything to say after that.

Aspire was still processing the situation. He slipped into a speechless shock, and Searching, for the first time, also had no words. He seemed to not know what to think. The situation seemed unreal to Aspire for a moment, and the tarantula was still laughing hard. Confident was now fuming; if smoke could pour out of his ears, it would.

"Come on, guys, we're getting out of here." Confident walked over to Aspire and tugged at him to get up. He started leading Aspire and Searching out of the area back onto the path. "Let's just get out of here now, the whole place. This whole jungle."

As they walked away, they could hear the spider laughing harder and harder until, rather abruptly, the laughter stopped. Searching looked back to see what happened. Aspire looked too. The spider wasn't there.

"Guys! He's gone! What happened?" Searching hadn't followed the previous conversation very well enough to know what had happened.

"He fell, Searching. Come on, let's go." Confident didn't even look back, but he started walking faster. He mumbled under his breath. "Serves him right."

Searching, who still seemed clueless, followed behind Confident and Aspire as they found the path and pressed forward.

Aspire was still sniffling, and his head drooped low. He wanted out of the jungle quite badly, so he walked a fast pace with Confident. The previous wonder of the jungle was wholly diminished. It was no longer an awe-inspiring place to him.

At the same time, Confident began blaming himself.

"Serves me right. I didn't listen to my bad feelings about that place. I should never have let you go alone. I should have protected you. That's what a king would do." He had been showing responsibility for both Aspire and Searching and was trying to be a leader for them that day but seemed to feel that he had failed.

"It's not your fault," Aspire whispered. He knew it was his, and he learned that day to not flit and float to whatever sparkled. He had to be wise.

Searching, well, Searching remained oblivious behind them.

They pressed on until it got dark. By this time they had made it near the end of the jungle, which began to reveal intimidating silhouettes from the darkening foliage. When Aspire saw the outlet, he started to run and run until the jungle was a dark, black hole behind him, then he stopped. Confident and Searching tried their best to keep up.

They were all relieved to be out and gave deep sighs after trying to catch their breath. They were also exhausted now. Aspire took no time to crash off to the side of the trail to rest as the exhaustion of the day struck him. They didn't make beds for themselves that night as Confident and Searching snuggled up close to Aspire. Soon enough, the three fell to a heavy, defeated sleep, never waking until the sun urged them up.

7

*A*spire woke to the warmth of the sun on his face. It was a familiar warmth reminding him of how the sun would shine through his bedroom window at home. It was a good feeling, but as he woke up to the full reality of the day, he remembered the events of yesterday, and his heart sank. He was still embarrassed. He should have left when he thought to, but really, he shouldn't have gone in the cave at all.

He released a heavy sigh trying to let go of the feelings from yesterday that kept building. He lifted his head to see where he ended up after scrambling out of the jungle and found Confident and Searching sleeping right beside him. Confident lay curled up with his face in his tail, and Searching lay sprawled out, probably dreaming again, impeding quite a bit in Confident's space.

Aspire gave a soft chuckle at the sight as it was the one time that Confident did not seem bothered at all by Searching. At that moment, the sun was coming up over the mountainous horizon. It seemed to understand his pain somehow and offered its hopeful light gently. Aspire could feel it working.

It's a new day, Aspire thought.

Aspire still couldn't let go of the memories of yesterday and looked over to the jungle off to the right. It rose to the light of day, oddly silent and distant. He tried to release emotions that were slowly building up again with another exhale. He was glad to be out of the jungle and even more glad that he did not have to spend the night in there. But now he had his fill of processing the memory and turned his head away.

For a moment he forgot everything because off in the distance, golden sand, sun-washed brush waving in the wind, and sparkling blue water spread out like a display case of something expensive. He never knew how close to the coast they were the whole time. He felt peace as it was such a warm and welcoming sight. As he looked farther, he could see a mass of land floating on the water proudly.

Ah, Contentment Isle, it has to be, he thought.

It was quite a sight even from a distance as it sat on quaint waters decorated with tall palms with coconuts and big shady trees. Aspire stood up to get a clearer view but woke Confident up in the process.

"Hey, you feeling better?" Aspire turned to see Confident squinting in the morning light at him. Aspire could see the concern in his face.

"Yeah. I think." Aspire turned to look at the beach. "Confident, look. I think that's Contentment Isle over there." He looked back at Confident, glad to change the subject but also excited to have potentially discovered the place.

Confident stood up as well and looked with Aspire at the vivid view.

"Yeah, that has to be it." Confident soon fell in a trance at the sight still waking up to the day. His eyes seemed to be fixed on the gorgeous, peaceful scene. Aspire joined him.

The scene was mesmerizing. The ocean waves tumbled foamy white on the shore, and birds flew over the water pronouncing their good mornings. Aspire had never seen such a pretty sight. The light of the scene emanated so warm and inviting.

"It's pretty, huh?" Aspire smiled at Confident, breaking the silence after a few minutes.

Confident clearly had no desire to pull out of his trance, but he responded to Aspire with his eyes on the rolling waves. "Yeah."

They spent a few more moments giving into the strong pull of the coast until they heard a voice behind them.

"Woah."

Searching, for once, had woken up on his own this time. He now seemed to be pulled into the same trancelike wonder at the view of the sand, water, and island off in the distance. Aspire wondered if this beautiful sight actually had power and woke Searching up itself. He broke the silence again.

"Searching, do you think that's Contentment Isle over there?" Aspire looked at Searching, whose eyes were glittering at the view.

"That's it!" Searching's eyes seemed to glitter a little more, if that was possible, as a huge smile spread across his face. He had made it to his destination. He visibly could not wait; he was ready. He jittered and started making his way to the beach skipping and dancing along. He followed the curving path with intense excitement. He took absolutely no notice of what was around him, the fact that he was leaving his new friends behind in the dust and that there a few flowery bushes that he almost trampled. His mind seemed straight on his goal that grew closer before him.

Aspire and Confident shared a laugh as Searching skipped away, and they followed behind him curious to see how Searching's dream would come true. As they continued to follow Searching and falling farther and farther behind him every minute, they couldn't help but enjoy the walk to the coast. Although, Aspire began to wonder what it would be like to finally make it to his destination. He wanted to feel the joy that Searching was showing.

Nonetheless, the scene was still beautiful with the waterfront awfully cool and inviting in the hot morning sun. Birds were conversing sweetly in the cloudless sky over the jewel-blue water that glittered under the sun. The sand looked like a warm blanket stretched out before the water. Aspire felt that if the lapping water could talk, it would say a warm welcome.

The smell in the air was delicious too. It was salty fresh with sweet notes, and it was so thick Aspire and Confident could almost taste it as they looked at each other in wonder. It reminded Aspire of the saltwater taffy his dad would buy him on special occasions. Aspire couldn't help but close his eyes for a second on the walk so he could take in more of the sounds and smells of the atmosphere.

It didn't take them long to get to the entrance of the beach. Right off the path stood a sign. Carved in a beautiful cursive were the words "Belle Vue Beach welcomes you." Beyond it was another sign in the same font that said, "Contentment Isle this way," with an arrow pointing in the direction of the beach.

Aspire and Confident had stopped to slowly read the signs, but they quickly took the path together that diverted from the main trail in the direction of Belle Vue Beach. They slowed when they stepped into the warm sand, and the ocean breeze enveloped them almost immediately upon doing so. They both couldn't help but take a couple moments to stop, raise their face to the sky, and drink in the fresh ocean air.

As they moved closer, they saw that Searching had already made it to the water. They leisurely walked to the slow rolling waves staring out at Contentment Isle, which looked so lovely and grand from this viewpoint. They moved next to Searching and found him mumbling to himself.

"So how are you going to get there?" Confident had very quickly connected the dots of the issue at hand. There was a fair amount of water between them and the isle, and there was no boat or raft anywhere along the water, let alone any kind of visible bridge.

"I'll… I'll find a way." Searching was still staring at the isle with so much longing in his eyes that it made Aspire feel bad for him. He wondered, what if he had no choice but to swim that distance? Would Searching make it?

Aspire and Confident looked at each other. It looked like Confident was thinking the same thing.

"Should we do something?" Aspire asked Confident quietly so Searching wouldn't hear.

Confident shrugged his shoulders and stared at Contentment Isle with a bit of a puzzled look. "I have no idea."

So they continued to stare at the problem along with Searching. Aspire turned to Confident and could see him soon begin to look around and brainstorm ideas for Searching. Then, he finally spoke up.

"Well…we could find all the big leaves and stuff we can and make a raft. Or, better yet, we could wrangle up some bark from the trees, and you could use one of those big leaves as an ore!" Confident seemed excited as he pointed to a tree with very wide, thick leaves.

Searching didn't seem to like the idea as he turned and frowned at the tree.

"Yeah, maybe. You really think we can do that?" Searching looked at Confident, semi-curious about the idea.

Just then a voice spoke up.

"You're trying to get to Contentment Isle, huh?" This new voice caught Aspire off guard. He turned and immediately began looking around. Confident and Searching seemed just as confused as they were looking for the owner of the voice too.

"I'm right here." The now unamused voice came louder from below them, and Aspire soon discovered a little crab. It was blue with a white belly and claws. It looked up at them with blinking uninterested eyes at the fact that they could not find it at first. They all stared for a second until Searching broke the silence.

"Yeah, I am going there! Do you know how to get to it?" Searching suddenly had renewed hope in his voice.

"Yep, I do." The crab stared at him with the same unamused face. "But first, you gotta pay up."

Aspire was interested in the crab and its weird character, but he looked over to Searching at the advent of this new obstacle. Confident did the same.

"Uh, but I don't have anything." Searching's tone and head lowered. He was clearly unprepared.

"Ah, well, I guess it's all right. Just put in a good word for me."

Aspire turned back to the crab who now seemed somewhat kinder than before. Searching perked up. Confident looked interested.

"I can do that!" Searching seemed quite willing to do whatever he could to get to the isle.

"Okay, so here's how you gotta do this," the crab began. "First you need to get the fans, the Winglets. They'll help you get there." He nodded his head and started to scoot away.

Searching needed more information though.

"Wait, but how do I do that?" Searching started to urgently follow the crab. Aspire looked at Confident who shrugged his shoulders and started to follow too. Aspire joined.

The crab kept walking but replied, "Yeah, so you need to get the Winglets to like you. That's them over there."

The crab pointed with his claw and, consequently, a whole side of his body to a group of conversing birds flying overhead. They congregated together and landed on the sand a ways away.

"First you gotta get their attention. Then you gotta get them to like you."

Searching looked over at the birds seeming to process the challenge of his next mission.

"Okay, easy, thanks!" With those words, Searching was off to a location of the congregating birds in the sand.

"And don't forget to put in a good word for me!" the crab shouted out to Searching as he continued to leave, making sure that Searching followed through with the promise.

"Yeah, yeah!" Searching shouted as he trotted away not even looking back.

Aspire and Confident looked to each other with amusement at the scenario. Confident nodded over to Searching, and they decided to see how Searching was going to get these fans, the Winglets.

"Thanks!" Aspire looked over to the crab to see him scurrying far off somewhere further down the beach.

With that, Aspire and Confident left to catch Searching's show. As they began to catch up to Searching, they watched as he proceeded to move from a trot to a run when he got closer to the Winglets. Then, he announced his presence with a loud "Hi!"

This startled the Winglets and caused them to collectively disperse and fly off much farther away. This didn't stop Searching though. He turned his attention to another group that was closer now to win over. But he ran to them the same way as before, causing the very same reaction. He couldn't even get a word in this time. He tried again with them for the third time, and even a fourth time, this time a little slower, but they just flew up to the sky, leaving Searching to watch them flying above. He began to look discouraged and slumped to a pouty pile in the sand.

Aspire and Confident walked up to Searching. Aspire didn't know what to do, and Confident wasn't offering any input. This looked like a much more difficult task than it had seemed before. The three sat there for a moment in silence.

"Maybe you should do something funny. That gets attention." Aspire looked at Searching with hope, trying to offer his help.

"But I don't know what that would be." Searching was whining now. He obviously didn't want this to be so hard.

"Well, you've got to do something to get their attention besides charging at them," Confident said this calmly but with annoyance at Searching's whining and lack of creativity at how to get the Winglets' attention.

"But what would I do?" Searching whined with frustration, stomping his right hoof.

"Geez, I don't know. Go slower to them. You're just scaring them off. Try to be their friend. Do something funny like Aspire said." Confident was getting more irritated by Searching, and his tone showed it.

Searching huffed. He seemed quite upset at the difficulty of the situation and stared off at a group of Winglets that just landed in the sand not too far off. Aspire watched as Searching's mind twisted and bent to come up with a solution to get fans.

Aspire looked at the Winglets and then at Confident. Confident gave Aspire a look that was equally curious over how they could win the Winglets over.

After a bit of time, Searching gasped. Aspire saw Searching's eyes widen as he exclaimed his sudden joy in having come up with an idea.

"I got it! Come on, guys! Watch me!"

Off Searching went to the group of congregating Winglets. In his excitement, he started to run but remembered Confident's advice and slowed down to a relaxed walk. Aspire and Confident followed with interest. Aspire was so curious as to what Searching was going to do.

When Searching was about ten feet away from the Winglets, he slowed his pace even more. Then he tried to talk to the clique tentatively.

"H-hi, guys. D-do you want to hear a joke?"

The birds collectively turned their heads in his direction. They looked at Searching with blank, blinking eyes. Searching paused and waited for a response. Nothing. Yet the birds were still looking at Searching, so he took this opportunity to begin another and hopefully final attempt at winning them over.

"Okay, uh. What is brown and sticky?" Searching paused slowly.

No response, only blinking eyes.

Searching waited another second for a response. When the birds still did not respond, he burst out the answer with laughter.

"A stick!"

Searching started to laugh hard. He couldn't even hold himself up from his laughter, so he fell to the ground rolling on his back.

Aspire and Confident watched as, even though Searching greatly enjoyed his joke, the Winglets could not have cared less. They gradually turned their heads away.

After a couple of minutes, Searching stopped. He seemed to notice that he was the only one laughing and looked over at the Winglets from his place on the ground. He saw that he didn't have their attention anymore. This was clearly not what he wanted.

This visibly frustrated him a great deal. He got up to his feet and huffed, looking defeated again. He looked over at Aspire and Confident for help. Aspire looked at him and then to Confident. They both shrugged their shoulders.

The joke was sort of funny to Aspire, but the Winglets clearly did not think so. Aspire didn't know any better jokes. At this point, it also looked like that was the only joke Searching had in his repertoire, so being funny didn't seem like an option for him anymore. Searching turned and started to walk away from the Winglets.

"This is not fair. I don't know what to do," Searching was whining again.

Aspire had a new idea and tried his best to help. "Maybe tell an embarrassing story? Those tend to get attention!"

"I don't have any." Searching slumped and huffed next to Aspire and Confident. Suddenly, he perked up as if a light bulb lit up in his head. "But you guys do!"

Without any consent from Aspire or even Confident, Searching hurried back over to the Winglets and proceeded to offer "one of the best embarrassing stories ever."

This got the Winglets' now unblinking attention, and a few more even flew in to hear the story as well. Searching began to tell of Aspire's mishap at the waterfall with the spiders in the jungle. In the process, he shed a horrible light on both Aspire and Confident who fell to "the greatest prank of all time."

Searching did not forget to tell of the tarantulas that so willingly risked, as well as sacrificed, their lives for the best prank ever. When Searching finally finished the story to Aspire's great dismay, there was a moment of silence. Then, in a burst of amusement, the Winglets fell to full out hee-hawing laughter. They obviously liked this story, maybe too much.

Searching stood puffing his chest with pride and accomplishment. He seemed to believe that he had won the Winglets over. This had to get him to his destination.

However, Aspire sat frozen in pure horror as he and Confident relived that very uncomfortable experience, and it was anything but fun for them. The horrible, embarrassed feeling washed again over Aspire, and he sat there utterly humiliated once more.

His face felt hot, and he drooped his head down holding back tears, trying to swallow the knot in his throat. Confident, on the other hand, growled low with anger. Aspire and Confident had been humiliated at the expense of Searching's desire to get fans. Aspire looked at Confident to see what he would do, and his face looked hot too but with burning anger at Searching.

"So you liked that story, right?" Searching tried to speak over the Winglets' laughter. He needed to know for sure if he had won them over.

They kept laughing, but then some of the Winglets shouted their affirmations in the middle of their laughter.

"Really! What losers!"

"Seriously, what a good story! I'd hear that again!"

"Those tarantulas! What a sacrifice! Worth it!"

"It's so funny I'm telling the rest!"

This put a smile on Searching's face, especially since some flew off to retell the story. But suddenly, a question from a Winglet wiped the smile off his face almost immediately.

"Are they actually your friends?"

Searching looked over at Aspire and Confident, and the birds' eyes followed. Aspire didn't feel so good with this kind of attention after the embarrassment he felt. He tried to look away but caught the torn look in Searching's eyes.

He began to wonder, was Searching trying to decide if he actually was his and Confident's friend?

Searching straightened his face, seeming to make his choice, and turned to the Winglets. "Haha, no! You think I'm dumb? I wouldn't fall for that prank. I knew the whole time."

Aspire turned and saw Confident's jaw dropped. Aspire looked at Searching in the same kind of shock not even knowing what to say or how to respond.

Searching had the Winglets hooked, and they gave their replies.

"Of course!"

"Yeah, you're smart!"

"And funny!"

Quite a few Winglets agreed with the other Winglets' responses.

If this alone wasn't enough, Searching seemed to want to make sure he had the Winglets even more secured as his official fans. He proceeded to make fun of Aspire and Confident even further. He told the Winglets of what he knew of Aspire's and Confident's journey to the falls.

He mentioned how silly he thought they were to believe they could make it, let alone get a horn or become a king or whatever. Searching finished with a sentence that burned in Aspire's mind for a while. "They are so dumb! They should just give it up now! What a hoot!"

The Winglets laughed hard again at the expense of Aspire and Confident. Then the Winglets offered it, the phrases Searching seemed to be striving to hear. Aspire and Confident stared at Searching in disbelief as the Winglets celebrated Searching.

"You're so funny! What's your name?"

"Yeah, you're great!"

Many Winglets nodded in happy agreement.

"I'm Searching!" Searching seemed so proud of himself at that moment that he lifted himself high on his toes at the announcement of his name.

"Searching!" all the Winglets stated his name with awe. "You should come with us to Contentment Isle!"

"I'd love to!" Searching was clearly jittery with so much excitement and jumped up high.

"Come with us!" The Winglets flew up together and surrounded Searching. There were so many birds that Aspire could barely see Searching at first as the Winglets directed him off to a place farther up the beach, closer to the isle. Then, suddenly, they drew in closer, lifted him right up, and flew him straight over the water to the isle.

If Aspire and Confident were in a better mood, they would have been laughing at how ridiculous Searching looked flying with the Winglets. To carry Searching over the water, the birds gripped any part of him they could. They held onto his front legs, his mane, and his tale.

Searching flew in wild excitement with the Winglets, stretched out with his behind high in the air, his head pulled back, and his arms stretched out. On top of it all, he had the cheesiest smile on his face in anticipation of what was before him.

Then suddenly, Searching was gone as he disappeared behind some trees off to enjoy his little dream on Contentment Isle. No goodbye. No thanks for how, ultimately, Confident and Aspire had helped him get there. Aspire didn't think that Searching would even remember the little crab who wanted a good word put in for him.

Aspire and Confident sat in silence a moment.

Aspire felt quite hurt, and it went deep. He felt his identity and dreams had been sucker punched by Searching, just so the little horse could prove his worth for what he wanted. It was a low and heavy blow. In his wounded state, Aspire began to doubt if he could make the journey. He began to think that maybe he should let it go.

He looked at Contentment Isle again. That place wasn't going to be an alternative for him. There was no way he or Confident could win any Winglets over after that episode. This moment hit Aspire the hardest. He couldn't move. The world around him blurred and unblurred. He felt dizzy and had to lie down.

"Aspire, you all right?" Confident looked at him with concern.

"Yeah…maybe…are you?" Aspire continued to stare off at Contentment Isle then down to the sand below him. He didn't feel like looking Confident in the eyes at the moment.

"I'm fine. Let's just get out of here. Forget it all happened." Confident sounded bitter and angry. He stood up. He seemed ready to move on and forget the little aloof, fan-pleasing Searching. "We don't want to lose time, right, Aspire?"

"I… I don't know. I don't think I can do it." Aspire looked at Confident then broke his stare and looked to the ground.

"You can't let Searching's opinion mess with you! Seriously, what does he know! He just wanted the Winglets to like him!"

Confident was still burning strong with anger. He looked off at the isle shaking his head. He had never before shown such great dislike for Searching.

"I'm just so exhausted now." Aspire didn't want to try to get up. He couldn't.

"Come on." Confident urged Aspire up. "We can walk slowly along the beach a while."

"Okay," Aspire gave his consent quietly.

The two strolled along the beach for a while as the sun began to set.

It became rather soothing. The sand was warm and soft, and the waves rolled gently to the shore with a comforting sound. The setting sun painted the sky and clouds with muted colors of burnt orange, wine, and violet. The environment was peaceful.

Aspire's eyes settled on the sky as they walked, listening only to the sound of the waves and the distant voices of birds sending out their goodnights.

Aspire and Confident walked far until they came up to cliffs rising high in the evening light before them signifying the end of the beach.

Over here the beach was different. The sand was even whiter and fluffier. The water was a deeper blue. The rolling waves were large but not treacherous. They seemed to welcome Aspire to stay. Aspire and Confident both agreed to stay the night there and made spots in the sand to sleep. Before Aspire laid down, he had to walk up to the water and be closer to the waves.

He sat before the waves. It was dark now, but the moon was unusually bright reflecting off the water. It was so bright Aspire didn't even pay attention to the Stars that were visible above him. They had a good view of him and watched sorrowfully as he released stress into the ocean, wave after wave. Aspire closed his eyes soaking in the peace of the moment. Then a soothing, comforting voice spoke.

"You'll make it, Aspire. You'll get there."

Aspire opened his eyes. He didn't recognize that voice. He looked around. He could see no one, and Confident was already asleep on the sand in the distance. But that wasn't Confident's voice anyway. It was strong but kind and soothing, so different from what he had ever heard before. It seemed to come from all around him but also from inside him at the same time.

He sat before the water wondering who owned the voice. It didn't scare him. The voice had given him hope and peace. He suddenly felt a strange assurance that he was going to make it.

He was going to get his dream. He spent a few more moments soaking in the peace and serenity of the night scene. All of a sudden, he felt healthy for the journey again. He hadn't felt that in a while. Soon enough, the waves started to lull him to sleep. As his eyes began to close, he decided to retreat to his bed with his newfound hope.

*A*spire woke to the bright sun on his face and the sound of the ocean's waves energetically charging to the shore. Though he was still waking up, he felt refreshed. It was a new morning, and he had new energy for the remainder of the journey. He didn't know how much of the journey he had left, but he felt so close to the finish line. He lifted his head to view the ocean and saw Confident out by the waves staring into the vast horizon. Aspire decided to sit up and gather in his surroundings.

This side of the shore was beautiful, quite possibly more beautiful than the side across from Contentment Isle. Bright green trees and plants of all kinds, some with red flowers, sprouted everywhere. So many more trees cast a perfect shade on the sand, and the cliffs in the distance added an elegant dimension. Aspire stood up and stretched. Then he slowly walked toward Confident and sat down by him looking out at the water too, soaking up the serenity of the scene.

"Ah, you're awake," Confident said, still staring at the water. After a couple minutes, he turned to Aspire with a hopeful question. "Do you still want to go to the falls?"

Aspire looked at Confident and smiled. "Yes. Definitely."

Confident turned back to the water with a smile on his face too. "Good."

They sat before the water reveling in the moment. It seemed as if the energy from the waves was being released in the air as the waves crashed to the shore. Aspire caught it and felt it course through his veins. He felt excited for the journey again and almost couldn't wait to leave, but the beauty of the beach still had him captivated. So he sat still staring at the water a little longer with sparkles in his eyes.

Aspire also began to feel great appreciation for Confident. He and Confident had already made it quite far on the journey. They had chosen to overcome so much together, and because of that, Aspire felt a bond with Confident so much stronger than he had ever experienced with any friend before.

After he had taken in all he could of the peace and energy from the ocean, Aspire felt jittery with excitement for the journey and turned to Confident. "You ready?"

Confident looked back at Aspire and smiled. "Let's go."

With that, they both stood up and began to walk away from the water. Aspire took a couple glances back ensuring that he would remember that moment always. When Aspire and Confident got to the end of the beach, they found the path with an arrow sign pointing them straight back to the Adventure Trails. On the other side, there was a sign that read in a lovely cursive font, "Thank you for visiting Faith Beach. Come again for your refreshment." They stared awhile at the sign understanding its truth.

"Faith Beach." Confident sounded to be processing thoughts. "That sounds so true. I really feel like I have faith again. That's so interesting."

"Yeah, me too!" Aspire agreed. "That's cool."

They pressed on to make it back to Adventure Trails walking in silence. While on the trails, Aspire tried to process the past experience and suddenly remembered his experience with the voice last night. He had to tell Confident.

"Oh! Confident! Last night, I don't know where it came from, but when I was sitting at the ocean, a random voice came out of nowhere and told me that I'll make it. I think it was talking about Destiny Falls. It gave me so much hope after everything that happened."

"No kidding, I thought I heard a voice this morning tell me the same thing when I was sitting there!" Confident seemed surprised at this information. "I thought I was hearing things before, but now I don't know. Who was that? Where did it come from?"

"I don't know." Those questions circled Aspire's mind too.

They ambled on the main path of the Adventure Trails in silence with no answers to the questions in their heads but assurance of the choice to keep going just the same.

It seemed to be a promising day as the sun was bright and happy. Both Aspire and Confident expressed to each other that they were feeling energetic and ready for anything.

Suddenly, they stopped as a way before them stood a tall, looming forest of giant twisting trees. It was dense, so dense that it wouldn't let in much light causing it to look quite dark inside. To make it worse, they could see Mount Impossible poking its head out from over the forest to stare them down and remind them of its size. Aspire stared back sheepishly.

This could have been an exciting place for Aspire and Confident to be. They had finally made it closer to Mount Impossible. But before they could get to that obstacle to overcome it, they had to walk through this strange, dark forest. It was quite intimidating as the path to it seemed to disappear inside, swallowed up by the gnarly, knotted trees.

They looked at each other, took a deep breath together, and pressed forward. In the meantime, to make the whole scene even more intimidating, the wind started to blow. Aspire tried to walk a steady pace with Confident, but he could feel himself slowing down as he would look at growing clouds above. Gradually, the wind pulled a veil of gray clouds overhead entirely covering the bright light of the sun.

Aspire paused and slowly asked Confident. "What…is happening?"

Confident stopped and looked up, shaking his head, and he replied, "I don't know."

"Do you think it will rain?" Aspire looked up at the sky again. The clouds were thick and threatening above him.

"I hope not." Confident started to walk forward again.

Aspire followed.

When they made it to the edge of the forest, they peered inside. It looked eerie as the clouds overhead made it appear even darker inside. Then, droplets of rain started to fall, forcing Aspire and Confident under the cover of the forest. With no other choice, they began to slowly trudge through the woods.

They stuck to the path, though, here, and there they had to hop over a fallen tree and brush aside branches intruding on the trail. There was even one moment when Aspire got distracted by a rather large tree. It looked like it had a gnarly old hand with long, slender fingers reaching over the trail waiting to grab anything that passed under it. What he didn't notice, however, was a slim leafy branch that crossed over the trail before him.

As Confident passed under it, Aspire followed behind but found himself with a mouthful of the branch and leaves while he was gaping at the threat of the tree above. This immediately scared him and caused him to jump. He let out a muffled noise with a surprised look and a mouthful of the tree.

Confident quickly turned with raised eyebrows to see what had happened. He scrunched his eyebrows at the sight of Aspire, but his almost immediate laugh quickly broke some of the tension in the air. Aspire joined him in the laughter spitting out the branch, trying to walk very far around it.

Still laughing, Confident proceeded to walk forward while Aspire attempted to catch up.

"Whew, that scared me." Aspire caught up and tried to calm some nerves that had built up by releasing a long breath.

"That was hilarious." Confident chuckled again. "This forest is nothing to be afraid of. It's fine. It's just a bunch of tall trees. Plus... they are keeping us from getting wet." Confident sounded like he was trying to convince himself of this as well.

As Aspire walked, this time much more aware to avoid any more scares or surprises, he could see and hear a strong wind begin to blow through the top of the forest. It sounded like the rain was pelting down harder on the trees as well. It was coming down so heavy now that every once in a while, Aspire would feel a heavy drop of water land on his back.

Nonetheless, he was still grateful to be under the cover of the trees. Yet as the wind grew, the trees began to sway, creak, and groan. Aspire began to fear that at any second, a tree could fall over and block their way or, worse, land on them. Confident seemed to feel the same as he would also flinch at any loud sound.

The trees didn't seem to be handling the wind well at all. It was coming in big gusts and was causing some leaves to break off the trees and flutter around them. Additionally, because of the heavy rain, a mist was growing in the forest making it foggy.

The mist made the trees look even more dark and sinister as they swayed and creaked with arms reaching out to snatch up Aspire and Confident at any second. Aspire imagined the trees walking toward him and Confident, scooping them up, and then he didn't want to think about what they would do next. It all seemed too scary.

Aspire and Confident looked at each other wide-eyed and shrunk low in response to the trees' intimidating movement. They exchanged glances with fear that this could end very badly. Aspire wondered out loud if this would be how he died. Confident wouldn't let him talk that way. He believed that they were going to be all right.

In the distance, birds cried out, then suddenly, a big group flew to a tree not too far off, chirping with what sounded like frustration over the wind and rain. Aspire figured the birds must have been trying to take cover from the storm. The trees creaked and moaned some more, and it was uncomfortably creepy in the dark, misty forest with the cries of birds.

Suddenly, Aspire and Confident heard a boom! And a crack! Not too far up in the path, a tree had fallen over. Even from their distance, they could see it smoking. They walked closer to see that the tree had been struck by lightning, and the electric shock to the tree had split it in half sending the other half in another direction. Now there was a hole in the canopy above, and their path was largely obstructed by the part of the tree that landed there.

Aspire peered up and saw a light flash in the hole of the canopy where the tree once stood. Thunder came not too long afterward. It was a big thunderstorm, and it began to bring back the memory of the experience Aspire had in Trap Canyon. He remembered the intense thunderstorm that had woken him up and how scary it was to be in the canyon in the storm.

Oddly enough, he felt safer in the forest now even though he feared a tree would fall on him at any second. He wondered if it was because he wasn't so drenched like he was the previous time. As he processed the memory, he remembered the colorful sunrise and rainbow that followed after the storm. It was so peaceful and beautiful after the messy storm. This began to give him hope.

Aspire stood close to Confident. "We'll be okay." He tried to sound excited. "And we should look for a rainbow after!"

Confident looked at Aspire. "Let's hope." He sounded less sure about the situation.

Aspire and Confident assessed the fallen tree on the path trying to figure out how to get past it. Confident quickly located a part where they were able to climb over.

When they made it to the other side, a ways off stood the gladly welcomed end of the forest. The rain was still falling down hard, but there was more light in the distance, and though they had to push through some other fallen branches in the way of the path, relief came. They were closer to the end of the forest.

As they pressed forward, pushing branches out of their way and hopping over some small fallen trees, the winds began to die down. The sound of thunder gradually disappeared, and the trees began to quiet down as if they weren't so afraid anymore. Aspire noted it.

"The trees are kind of quiet now. I wonder if they were afraid of the storm too."

"Maybe." Confident's eyes were steady on the path ahead. He seemed very ready to leave the place.

When Aspire and Confident finally made it to the end of the forest, they stopped and breathed a sigh of relief together. They had made it out alive. Plus, the storm was still showing signs of calming down. There was just a steady rain now with occasional gusts of wind.

"Let's stay here until the rain stops." Confident sat down at the edge of the forest still under the canopy.

"Okay." Aspire decided it was a good idea and sat next to Confident.

They rested, calming tense nerves from the storm while watching the rainfall for a while. Aspire took a look back at the forest and shivered at the threat of the trees. He wasn't going to do that again. After Aspire began to feel calm again, he looked at the world around him outside the forest. Immediately, his attention settled on an expansive lake off to his right.

As the rain slowed to a stop, a gentle breeze began to pull the clouds away to another location. Now the lake was sparkling from the sun. It drew Aspire and Confident out of the forest to take a closer look at the vivid sight. They walked closer and stopped right before a fence surrounding the lake.

"Wow!" Aspire felt overjoyed to experience such beauty after the storm.

"Yeah, this is beautiful." Confident sat in awe of the sight, and Aspire joined him. The water looked fresh and glittery, and the mountains in the distance gave it the perfect backdrop. They reflected their image across the water.

Again, Aspire remembered the rainbow he saw in the canyon and began to look for another one. After scanning the skyline, he stopped where Mount Impossible was now in full view. Then he saw it. Stretching out from behind Mount Impossible, as if to say, "Your destination is here!" stood the rainbow bright and bold.

"Confident, look! It's a rainbow!" Aspire was giddy with excitement to see it again. He needed Confident to experience this sight with him.

Confident looked over and paused in awe at the sight. "Wow. I've never seen one like that before!" Then he paused and nodded toward the mass that stood before them. "That must be Mount Impossible, huh?"

It stood tall and looked as impossible as ever.

"Oh. Yeah." Aspire felt his joy diminish a bit at the reality of the mountain. It looked daunting, and he still had no idea how they would ever get over or around it. He wanted to get his mind off it for a second and turned in the other direction. "This lake is beautiful! It makes me thirsty. Do you want to check it out?"

"Yeah, sure. I've never been to a lake before." Confident seemed eager to discover this new thing.

"Me too." Aspire had only seen pictures of lakes and was anxious to experience it as well. Plus, Aspire was nearly aching to get a taste of the fresh and sparkly water after the scary hike through the forest.

Confident quickly found an opening in the fence where a path led directly to the lake while Aspire followed. They almost missed a sign off to the side, but Confident caught it and read its warning out loud, "Lake is negative, avoid water."

"Avoid the water?" Aspire did not like the idea of that one bit, so he looked over to the water glistening under the sun. It didn't look dangerous in any way. In fact, it looked tempting and mesmerizing instead. "Why?"

"I don't know what that even means." Confident stood puzzled at the sign. He looked to the lake. "The water looks fine."

Aspire looked at Confident. "Well, we can still go over there, right?"

"Hm. Yeah, we'll be fine. If the water looks bad, we can just leave."

After some hesitation, Confident made the final decision to continue walking to the lake. Aspire happily agreed with it.

They walked quickly to the water and soon came upon the rocky waterfront. It was a new sight to both of them. The beach area consisted of small smooth rocks instead of sand, and it gave the lake a crisp and fresh look. It was so inviting now that the sun was beginning to heat everything up quite quickly.

Aspire now felt hot and thirsty. He could tell that Confident was feeling the same way, but they walked over to the water slowly inspecting it for anything that looked alarming. When they came to the edge, they stared for a couple minutes.

"Looks fine to me," Confident broke the silence and shrugged his shoulders.

Aspire could see nothing but clear, fresh water as far as the lake stretched as well.

"Yeah, me too." Aspire was tempted to jump in and enjoy a good long drink right then.

"I'd say we're fine."

"Yeah, me too."

Aspire stooped to the water and took a sip. Confident joined him. It was as fresh as Aspire had imagined.

"Oh, this is so good!" Aspire went back to the water for more.

"Yeah, I needed this!" Confident went back for seconds as well.

Then, they couldn't stop themselves. After they got their fill of water, they stepped right in the lake and immersed their whole bodies. They lay on their backs basking in the coolness of the delightful lake for some time.

"Ah, this is great," Aspire said after a while.

"What a great choice." Confident was staring at the views of the birds and clouds in the sky from his position. "So we're finally at Mount Impossible."

"Yeah." Aspire's mood changed a bit. He felt his joy dampen at the thought of the mountain. "It's big."

"Sure is." Confident didn't seem to care too much about it at the moment.

"How are we going to get past it?" Aspire began to mull over options but couldn't quite figure it out. "Are we ever going to get over it? Is it even possible?"

"I don't know." Confident seemed to think about it too. "Do you know of any creatures that completed it?"

"Just the one in a magazine I read. But I don't know if I believe him anymore." Aspire began to feel upset at the prospect of the situation. "He didn't even mention Mount Impossible."

"Hmm, that's weird." Confident stared at the sky with a muddled look on his face, and Aspire joined him.

After a bit of time, Aspire and Confident discovered that they had floated to the middle of the lake and decided to swim back to the shore to dry off. But in the process, their swimming kicked up a dark green, murky substance that sat on the floor of the lake. It was not pretty as green flecks started to float around and behind them fogging up the once clear water.

Soon enough as they neared the shore, dark green, swirling clouds swarmed around them in the water. At this point, they couldn't even see through the water anymore. Aspire found himself very much displeased by what was happening. He paused and looked at Confident with a disgusted face. Confident returned an even stronger one. They proceeded to quickly jump out of the water and try to shake themselves clean of the murk at the shore.

"What was that?" Aspire stared back at the water in disgust.

"I have no idea." Confident looked at the water with the same distaste. Then he turned to Aspire, and his face showed to remember something. "Maybe that's what the sign meant." He looked at the water again. "Yuck, we drank out of that water."

"Bleh, don't remind me." Aspire's happy mood from before had slipped away, and now he was sulking. "That stupid lake, tempting us with its fake clear water."

"Seriously. Let's get out of here. I don't want to see this lake anymore." Confident started to take the trail back to the main path.

Aspire followed.

After both Aspire and Confident expressed feeling very upset with the turn of events, Aspire began to feel a tad irritated. It seemed as if Confident was as well considering his reaction to the plants that tickled his legs or got into his face on the way to the main path. Aspire didn't appreciate the brush either. Needless to say, the intruding plants didn't stand a chance against Aspire and Confident that day.

When they made it to the main path of Adventure Trails again, they stood in the direction of Mount Impossible and tried to continue forward. Aspire was going to face this thing and defeat it, so he picked up his pace. The mountain could not stand a chance against him and Confident.

Mount Impossible stood looming before them growing in massive intimidation the closer they got to it. They pressed on a while, but slowly the situation began to look worse and worse until Aspire could not take it anymore. He stopped and blurted his frustration in a whine.

"It's just too big! What are we going to do?" Aspire sat down in the middle of the path and sulked.

Confident, who hadn't been the biggest fan of whining, was beginning to show a lot of frustration with Aspire now. He stopped, breathed out a frustrated sigh, and turned to Aspire. "Well, don't be like Searching. He was so annoying with his whining and complaining."

"I'm not whining! I just want to know how to get past this thing!" Aspire turned his frustration to Confident.

"Well, don't turn into Searching. I'll gladly leave you on some island somewhere." At this point, Confident had started walking forward on the path again and was giving Aspire a sort of "talk to the tail" vibe.

Aspire huffed and was very unhappy that Confident would even think to compare him to Searching. Searching was a dull and mean creature to Aspire now. Aspire got up and started following behind Confident. He replayed his experience with Searching going over what Searching did to get to Contentment Isle. Now that Aspire had some time to process the experience, he began to grow in bitter anger toward Searching until he burst out.

"Searching! Gah, I hate him! He's *so*…he's *so*…" Aspire stopped because Confident had stopped.

There they stood at the entrance to Mount Impossible. The self-explanatory words on a nearby sign read in all capitals: MOUNT IMPOSSIBLE.

The mountain loomed and stood heavily set. Confident rolled his eyes at it. It was dusk at this point, and the sun was disappearing behind Aspire and Confident. It ducked behind the forest. The mountain was beginning to look more like a tall looming shadow than a real rock structure now.

"Well, there's no use in trying to get past it now!" Aspire was still upset about everything.

"Geez, calm down," Confident huffed. "Let's just…let's just figure it out tomorrow. I'm going to look for a place to sleep for the night." With that, he began to look for places off the path to cozy up for the night.

Aspire tried to calm down and started to follow Confident in his search. When Confident found a spot, made up his bed, and laid down in it, Aspire followed suit close to him. But Confident didn't seem to be happy with the situation.

"Uh, you're sleeping there?" Confident looked at Aspire with disapproval.

"Um, yeah." Aspire looked at Confident wondering what exactly he meant.

"I think I'll just move then." Confident got up and found a spot farther away, made his bed, and curled up in it.

"Fine."

Aspire lay still in his spot, upset over the whole day. He was upset about the lake, about the mountain, about Searching, about Confident, and mostly about his life thus far. However, he found himself more upset with the fact that Confident didn't want to be near him. Aspire rolled to his back to see that remnants of cloud from the storm were covering most of the Stars for the night.

Though the moon was still able to peer through brightly, Aspire felt alone. There was no one to talk to. He tried to go to sleep, but it wasn't working for him. As he tried to embrace the silence, he heard a strange noise and felt a breeze past him.

Aspire immediately lifted his head up to try to find what caused the sound and the breeze, but it was too dark. He heard the noise again on the other side of him, and this time he felt scared. He felt alone and was afraid that whatever was out there might take advantage of him.

"Uh…Confident?" Aspire whispered loudly to see if his friend was still there. "Do…do you know what that noise is?"

"I don't know…" Confident sounded almost as scared as Aspire.

Aspire stood up and met with Confident who was now walking toward him too. "Um, Confident, I'm a little scared."

"Yeah, me too."

"Also, I'm sorry for my bad attitude." The situation was sobering to Aspire. His actions and outburst from earlier felt silly to him now, and he just wanted Confident's company.

"Yeah. Me too." Confident seemed to be in the same boat.

"Can we find a different spot to stay the night?" Aspire was hoping to get away from whatever was making the noise and to be closer to Confident.

"Yeah, that's a good idea." Confident began to move to the other side of the path looking for a place to stay the night.

Aspire followed.

Confident found a spot. Aspire joined him as they hastily made their beds and settled down in them for the night. This time, quite close to each other.

Aspire was feeling a little better now. "Good night, Confident!"

"Good night, Aspire!"

Aspire, and even Confident, seemed to feel safe and content now that they had fixed the tension growing between them; plus, they were keeping each other safe in the fright of the dark. Soon they fell asleep, entirely unsure of how the next day would play out.

9

*A*spire opened his eyes. The sun was up and taking on the day with positive energy, but Aspire was not ready for it. He groaned, closed his eyes, and tried to go back to sleep. He heard Confident rustling next to him.

"Hey, are you awake?" Aspire opened his eyes slowly to see Confident lying beside him. Confident faced him looking sleepy and disheveled but ready to get up.

"Ugh, no." Aspire couldn't keep his eyes open for long and rolled over facing away from Confident trying to hoard as much sleep as possible.

"Do you know what happened yesterday?" Confident yawned loudly to express his sleepiness.

Aspire rolled toward Confident and tried to remember the events of the day before. Nothing was coming yet. All he knew was that he was utterly exhausted, and he wanted to sleep longer.

"I don't…remember." Aspire didn't want to think about the day before, so he closed his eyes again.

Aspire felt Confident stand up and leave, so he opened his eyes slowly. He watched as Confident walked to the path and took a good look at his surroundings.

"Oh, right." His words were slow and pensive.

Now it had Aspire's interest. Aspire sat up slowly and took in a 360-degree view of his surroundings. When he caught sight of the forest, he was immediately reminded of the events of the day before.

He remembered the storm in the forest, the strange lake experience, and most of all, the seeming impossibility of Mount Impossible.

It hit him like a ton of bricks, and he had to sit still to process all that happened the previous day.

Aspire also thought about the happiness he felt from seeing the rainbow, but then he remembered how his mood went downhill after the lake experience. He had to chuckle at how silly he and Confident acted afterward.

Confident broke Aspire's concentrated silence. "Do you think the lake did something to us? Since the sign said to avoid the water because it was negative and all that?" He had been sitting on the path seeming to process the previous day as well.

Aspire connected the dots of the sign and the events that followed. "Oh…that was so strange. It was like it gave us negative energy or something."

"Really. I'm glad we were able to stop it though."

"Me too." Aspire remembered what happened before he and Confident fell asleep. "Also, what was that noise?"

It was that minor scare in the dark from whatever that thing was that had caused Aspire and Confident to recognize that they needed each other despite being mad at one another.

"I really don't know." Confident shook his head. "It didn't come back though."

"Yeah." Aspire looked at Mount Impossible. The sinking feeling returned. They had overcome so much, but this prominent obstacle remained, and it was standing unobstructed.

Confident walked over to sit by Aspire as they sized up the rocky beast. Aspire still had no idea how to defeat it. The mountain was massive. It was so tall and reached high up into the sky tickling clouds with its peak. It was also broad standing bold with a sturdy base that spread out and halted to a stop into the lake in the distance. It made the prospect of going around it not look like an option at this point.

At this point, it looked as if there was no choice but to climb it. Questions ran through Aspire's mind. How were they going to get over? Would they make it?

"Well, we're not going to get over it if we just stare at it." Confident sighed. "Let's go."

Aspire took a deep breath and released it slowly. "Okay."

They walked together toward the mountain side by side. Their eyes were steady on it. If it wasn't such a roadblock in their way, they would have found this mountain quite beautiful with its crown of clouds. The sun shining over it revealed its vibrant greens, browns, and speckles of purple and red. It was quite elegant for a mountain. But they did not want to give the mountain the benefit of being glorious in any way. It was currently their enemy.

They timidly walked closer, gathering what they could of their courage, trying to hold their heads high in the face of adversity. They each had moments where they would glimpse off to the side at the lake sparkling fresh under the sunlight. It seemed to be tempting them again, almost as if its negative energy was drawing them back into its murky clutches. But each time, they would give each other a look as if to say they would not be repeating the events of yesterday. They had to remain positive.

When they made it to the mountain, they could see the path halt and diverge in the direction of the lake. It was as if the path also felt that the mountain was too impossible to get over and retreated to the lake, giving in to the cool but negative water.

Aspire and Confident looked at each other after taking in the event of the scene. Aspire did not want to be like that path. He would not give in to that disgusting lake again. He looked forward at the mountain knowing that their only way out of the situation was over. But the question remained: how would they get over this mountain?

Mount Impossible seemed even more high and mighty, and its walls looked impenetrable. Right away they couldn't find any nearby spot to climb. The foot of the mountain was steep and oddly smooth, even though it looked sharp and jagged the higher it went. Aspire kept trying to push past the doubt that he could ever make it over.

"Let's look over this way." Confident began to walk to the left scanning the side of the mountain for any possible way up. Aspire followed.

Yet the more they looked, the more Aspire found himself trying to fight his ever-growing doubt.

"Oh, here's a spot!" Confident found a small ledge on the wall and hopped up on it. He looked up to find the next place to grab. Aspire watched him as he struggled to reach for another one. Once he reached that one, he looked for another spot to grab. Aspire looked too. Nothing.

But Confident was not giving up yet. He reached out with his paw to find something to grip. He circled over the wall with his paw feeling for a spot to grip onto next.

"Ah!"

Nope. It was a false hope as Confident's paw slipped with the pressure of his weight. There seemed to be no moving up from that spot no matter how hard Confident tried.

"It's fine." Aspire wasn't happy with the prospect and was ready to move on. "I wouldn't have been able to climb that anyway."

Confident hopped down. "Well, we'll just find a better spot."

Confident kept searching for a place to climb, but any other possibility wasn't the easiest for him and would not have worked at all for Aspire. Aspire started to welcome the idea that there was no way he would be getting over the mountain. Confident stopped. He looked beyond as the mountain blended in with another mountain and another in the distance.

Aspire viewed it in frustration. It all looked the same, and it never ended. Aspire slumped along the wall sliding down to the ground. The reality of the situation was sinking in, and he was not feeling good. What little hope he had was slipping away, and he began to face the possibility of having to go back home. This made him even more miserable. Confident sat down next to Aspire expressing defeat with a heavy breath out.

"Well, I guess that's it then, huh?" Confident looked down at the ground. "I didn't want to let my hopes up. I didn't think the falls were magic or anything, but I guess I started to believe that my dreams could come true or something."

"I just can't believe I made it this far to end here." Aspire hid his face in his body. "All that for nothing." Aspire laughed at himself. "I'm so stupid!"

"You're not stupid, Aspire. You just...didn't know." Confident tried to console Aspire but seemed to not know what else to say.

Aspire looked at Confident and offered a weak smile at his gesture. "Yeah, clearly. Ahh, why did I do this? Why did I leave home to just fail?" Aspire started to tear up, and he faced the sky as if to let it know of his discouragement. "This was not how I pictured it ending!"

His eyes filled up with tears to the point that he couldn't see. He blinked and let the tears roll down his face. He had already cried in front of Confident and was not ashamed of these tears this time. They were full of hurt, frustration, and anger at himself, at the mountain, and at life. He was utterly disappointed.

Aspire had tried before to think about the possibility that he wouldn't make it to the falls. His parents had advised him to do so, but he had never accepted that idea until now. Aspire looked at the forest far off in the distance. There was no way he was going through that again, let alone the jungle, and especially not Liar's Loop. Also, he couldn't face all his family and friends and tell them that he didn't get to be a unicorn after all.

Aspire thought about Searching and how his journey was so easy. Searching was injured and a bit lost when they found him. But he got what he wanted soon after. That was not fair to Aspire. Aspire wondered if he should go back through the forest and try to live on Contentment Isle instead.

Maybe the Winglets forgot his embarrassing story. He knew how to win them over this time. But even if they did forget, he remembered that he would have to live on the island with Searching. Aspire couldn't do that. Even if he could muster up all the forgiveness he could, Searching would be too much of a painful reminder of his failure to make it to the falls.

Aspire thought about the peace and serenity at Faith Beach. Maybe he would settle there instead. He liked that place a lot. Then Aspire imagined living on the beach, but without his horn, without accomplishing his dream. The beach where a voice told him that he would make it, where his hope for making the journey and becoming a unicorn was reignited.

He imagined feeling stuck at the beach with a burning desire to be a unicorn and never being able to quench it because of the dumb mountain. No, he would have to go home. It would be easier to forget his desire to become a unicorn there. He would simply shove his dreams in the closet and become a gardener with his family. He would be the best gardener ever. His family would be so proud.

Aspire closed his eyes and leaned his head on the rocky wall behind him. *Well, that's it. That's the end,* he thought. Confident breathed heavily next to him and sounded just as defeated.

Aspire and Confident sat a while in silence resting from the wound of defeat. If they were to go back home, they had a long road ahead of them. They might as well gain as much strength as they could before heading out on the journey again.

After trying to brush off his defeated thoughts, Aspire began to wonder about Confident and what he would do.

"So what do you think we should do? Should we head back?" Aspire slowly looked to Confident wondering if he had any ounce of hope left in him.

"Yeah, probably." Confident sat up beginning the process of getting himself ready to face the road back.

"Yeah." Aspire felt his heart sink a little lower as if it wasn't already low enough. They settled it. They were giving up. Going back home was Aspire's present reality because Confident was ready to do the same. "Where are you going to go?"

"I don't know. Maybe back to Trap Canyon. I can't go back to my hometown. Those creatures bore me to death." Confident seemed quite all right with going back to that treacherous canyon, despite its dangers.

Aspire began to open up to Confident's plan. "Yeah, maybe I'll join you." Aspire looked at Confident hoping for a positive answer.

"Sure, that'd be cool." Confident leaned back on the wall looking off at the forest.

Despite the disappointment, Aspire didn't feel like leaving yet. Apparently Confident didn't either as he sat still with Aspire in silence for quite some time. In the meantime, Aspire began to notice the beauty of the space around them.

The world around was pretty with the sparkling lake and the green forest that didn't look so threatening from this distance. The mountain range he could see was awe-inspiring, the field before him was fresh and grassy, and there was an occasional tree here and there for shade. This spot really wasn't so bad.

Aspire wondered what it would be like to live here. He had everything he needed, at least he thought so. Then he laughed to himself at the silliness of that idea. He realized he would have to live right next to the very thing that stopped him from getting to his dream. That would be a horrible reminder, he thought.

"I'm hungry." Confident broke Aspire's train of thought.

"Yeah, me too." Aspire looked back at Confident.

"I'm going to find some food. I'll be back." Confident got up and left to find some food.

Aspire thought it was a good idea and left to do the same.

When they both found the sustenance they wanted, they met back at their old spot along the mountain wall. They enjoyed their food together in silence, and though they felt that they had no other option but to go back home, they took their time.

There was something noticeable in each of them that would not entirely give up on the journey to the falls just yet. After all present hope had seemed lost, Aspire noticed that something had been growing in him through the tough journey. Now, it was happily living on its own despite the circumstances. Aspire wondered, was it faith? Desire? Or stubbornness? He couldn't tell.

After they finished their food, they sat against the mountain wall to let their bodies digest. Aspire and Confident began to reminisce about the day they first met each other and laughed over the silliness of it. They talked about their first impressions of each other and the moments that began to change those impressions.

"I remember the first time we laughed so hard we were crying." Confident started to laugh at the memory. "You were super thirsty and drank out of my water spring like you never had water before, and you were soaking wet. You kind of seemed different than other creatures, so I started to like you. All the other creatures that passed by before had been mean or weird."

Aspire laughed remembering that moment. "Yeah, I remember that. You seemed different than other creatures to me too. At first, I was kind of intimidated by you, but that moment we laughed so hard together changed everything." Aspire laughed again at the memory too.

The two went on to reminisce about their experience on the Adventure Trails together and the many obstacles they overcame with each other's help. They agreed that they would not have made it this far without one another. There was no doubting that.

The subject of Searching came up as well, but now they didn't care much about it anymore. Aspire and Confident hoped Searching had gotten what he wanted. They left it at that.

Aspire and Confident found themselves in a wonderful friendship, a bond that they never once had before. One that could only have formed by going through every single obstacle that they overcame together.

"You know, if I hadn't chosen to go on this journey with you, Aspire, I would have missed out." Confident smiled at Aspire. "I'm glad I went even if we have to end here."

"Actually, me too, Confident." Aspire smiled back at Confident.

At this point, with all their talking and reminiscing, they didn't notice that the entire day came and went. The sun was setting now disappearing behind the forest giving it an orange halo. The sky was darkening but was quite clear tonight.

As the sun left and light blue faded to dark, the Stars began appearing one by one dancing in their chosen place in the sky. Aspire and Confident continued to talk and laugh together this time at their ridiculousness from the night before. While in mid-laugh, Aspire caught his four Star friends smiling at him from above, catching him off guard.

"Oh, hi, guys!" Aspire straightened up as he greeted the Stars. He smiled at Confident inviting him to join. Confident nodded with a small smile and straightened up looking at the four Stars who were smiling at him now too. He smiled back.

"We're so glad you have made it this far, Aspire and Confident!" Believe was shivering with her excitement over the fact.

"I'm sure you have stories to tell!" Wistful seemed excited to hear them with her bright smile.

This made Aspire smile. He felt proud of himself, forgetting that he and Confident were about to quit and turn back. Aspire and Confident then began to tell the Stars about their adventures thus far. They talked about how they helped each other along the way through the many obstacles and troubles. They brought up Searching but moved on to explain what they learned and how they grew as friends along the way. They decided then and there that they would be friends for life, no matter what.

"Well done, Aspire and Confident. You're so close!" Perchance's words were encouraging to Aspire, but then he remembered the mountain.

"Yeah, thanks. But…we can't get past this mountain. We actually decided to go home. Tomorrow, I guess." Aspire's mood dropped low remembering the difficulty of the mountain.

"Nobody can get past it on their own." Deferring was quite frank about this statement, and it made Aspire curious.

Confident sounded just as curious. "Wait, what do you mean?"

"No creature has ever made it without help," Deferring said plainly.

"So…there's help?" Aspire pressed further.

"Yes! Every creature has to have help to get over Mount Impossible. That is why it's called Mount Impossible," Perchance sounded quite positive.

"Oh." Aspire began to slowly process what this meant. "Will you help us?"

"No." Deferring was quite blunt today.

"But we know one who can!" Believe shimmered brightly with excitement. "You'll get help, and you'll get over that mountain in no time!"

Aspire leaned back against the wall, and though it was dark, it was as if new and brighter colors were appearing in his world. His dreams were reviving from their deathbed like a rising sun. His eyes brightened up. He *was* going to make it to the falls after all! Excitement began to grow in him, and he turned to Confident.

"Confident, there *is* a way over!" he whispered with excitement as a huge smile grew on his face. He began to embrace his dream to become a unicorn all over again.

"You sure they are serious?" Confident didn't sound quite sure about it yet.

"I know they are!"

Aspire's smile was so big and hopeful that it spread to Confident as well.

There was a renewed energy in the air. Aspire felt ready to take on the mountain because now there was help! Aspire couldn't contain his replenished joy, so he jumped up needing to celebrate the change of events with a leap in the air. Confident laughed at him but remained calm and relaxed leaning against the wall like his usual self.

Aspire knew the Stars would get him help. He trusted them as their advice and suggestions had proven trustworthy thus far. Aspire calmed a little and sat down next to Confident.

"So who is going to help us?" Aspire questioned the Stars now, very curious again.

"Artist is going to help you," Perchance said this as if it was already set in motion.

"Artist," both Aspire and Confident said the name out loud.

"I've heard of Artist. Didn't you mention the name before? Who is Artist?" Aspire thought he remembered the Stars mentioning Artist at some point.

"Artist has been the one rooting for you on your journey!" Believe seemed very happy to give this information.

"I love Artist." Wistful seemed to be in her own world at the moment.

"You'll soon find out who Artist is, Aspire." Perchance smiled at him.

"Yes, and we must leave you now. You need to sleep. Artist will help you tomorrow." Deferring reminded Aspire of his mother at that moment, as her gentle but firm tone caused him to obey her orders immediately.

"Okay, good night!" Aspire waved to the Stars.

"Uh, yeah, good night!" Confident chimed.

The Stars sang "Sleep well!" in unison and left to their own conversations.

"Wow, I didn't expect that!" Aspire looked at Confident with so much joy and hope in his face.

"No, me neither! I am so glad we could talk to them tonight!" Confident returned the joy but yawned. "I think we should get rest for tomorrow."

"Good idea."

"Good night, Aspire!"

"Good night!"

Aspire and Confident slid from leaning against the wall of the mountain to lying beside it. They each got comfortable, curled up, and gradually fell asleep. Aspire fell asleep with a smile on his face and excitement playing in his head like good music. He and Confident were about to overcome another obstacle, and it was the biggest one of all. Better yet, they were going to make it to the falls.

10

*A*spire awoke right before the sun began to rise. It felt like a morning of possibility. He instantly remembered his conversation with the Stars the night before, and excitement flooded in his heart. He couldn't and he wouldn't go back to sleep because he felt so ready to get past this giant mountain that he woke up beside. In his mind, he was already over it. Aspire looked to the sky. He could see a couple Stars beginning to tuck themselves in for the day as it was now their bedtime.

He smiled at them. At this point, he appreciated the Stars, all of the Stars, a great deal. They had always treated him so well and gave him hope and much to think about. Now, they were connecting him with the help he most needed.

Aspire began to feel jittery with anxious excitement. He needed someone to share his enthusiasm with so he didn't explode. He looked to Confident who was comfortably sleeping curled up away from him. Aspire wondered for a second if he should let him sleep. But he couldn't help himself.

"Confident, hey, are you awake?" Aspire spoke softly but earnestly and tried to stretch his neck farther to see if Confident would respond.

Nothing.

"Confident? Confident!"

Aspire stopped as Confident started to move. Confident slowly lifted his head and looked at Aspire with his fur ruffled up and his eyes in squints.

"Good morning!" Aspire smiled brightly at Confident.

"Mm, yeah, you too." Confident closed his eyes and laid his head back down. He clearly wanted more sleep. But Aspire didn't think that Confident remembered what was going to happen that day.

Aspire continued talking as if Confident was still listening. "You ready to get over this mountain today? I'm excited! I wonder how it will happen."

Confident responded with a couple inaudible words muffled by his fur.

Aspire continued talking.

"The Stars said Artist was going to help." Aspire paused to consider who exactly Artist was. "I wonder when we'll meet Artist. I wonder what Artist looks like."

Confident didn't respond this time. Aspire looked over to see Confident peacefully asleep. Aspire sat comfortably against the mountain wall behind him and began to imagine how Artist would help them get over that mountain.

He let his brain go wild with ideas and imaginations of Artist out loud. Maybe Artist would show them a secret cave in the rock somewhere that led to the other end. Maybe Artist would reveal a hidden staircase up and around the mountain. Or perhaps Artist would give them superpowers to be able to get over the mountain themselves. Oh, the possibilities were endless.

Aspire was anxiously anticipating the arrival of Artist's help. As minutes passed and Confident snoozed late into the morning, Aspire got bored of daydreaming and wanted things to progress. He felt ready, but he also wanted Confident to be ready for when Artist comes. Aspire tried waking Confident up again.

"Hey. Confident." Aspire wasn't speaking so quietly this time. He figured Confident got enough sleep and would want to be awake when help came anyway. "Artist is helping us get over the mountain today. We should be ready."

Confident rolled over opening squinty eyes at Aspire and yawning. "Oh, yeah. When is Artist coming to bring help or something?"

Aspire began to think. He suddenly didn't remember. He started to think over the conversation with the Stars last night. He realized that they didn't mention when Artist would help except that it would be today.

"I-I don't know actually." Aspire began to deeply wonder when Artist would show up.

"Okay." Confident stretched to his feet. "I'm hungry."

"Okay, hurry back." Aspire watched Confident leave, wondering how long it would take for Artist to come and help them. He hoped that it would be soon.

Aspire started to feel antsy. He wanted Artist to show up right then, but he also was feeling hungry. But he was concerned that after he left, Artist might show up. He didn't want to leave his post just in case if Artist were to show up at any moment. The last thing Aspire wanted was for Artist to arrive and not find them. Aspire didn't want Artist to think they didn't need help and thus leave without helping them.

Minutes later, Confident came back and sat in the shade of the mountain next to Aspire to enjoy his meal.

"Are you going to get some food?" Confident looked at Aspire with a mouthful, contentedly enjoying his food.

Aspire looked at Confident and realized that Confident could hold the post while he went to get food. "Um. Yeah. Just stay right here, okay? And just yell for me if Artist comes."

"Okay." Confident chuckled a little. "Don't worry, I'll be here."

Aspire took that as confirmation to trust Confident, even though he noticed that Confident didn't seem to take him very seriously. So he left to get his food.

He searched quickly, found what he wanted, and rushed back to the same spot along the wall next to Confident in the cool shade. He hoped that this would be a good spot to stay and wait and that the Stars told Artist where to find them.

After finishing their food, Aspire and Confident sat in silence. Aspire had eaten quickly and sat upright by the cool, rocky wall anticipating Artist's arrival at any moment. He was ready.

But slowly time began to pass. Minutes took forever but soon turned to hours. Artist was still nowhere in sight. At this point, the sun had crept around the mountain and was shining semi-harshly onto Aspire's neck making him feel uncomfortably warm.

Aspire grew impatient and worried. He turned to Confident. "Do you think we missed Artist?"

"No." Confident was calm and relaxed per usual. He didn't seem to care too much about the wait. "I'd say we're in the right spot. Don't worry, Artist will come."

"Okay." Aspire tried to calm his nerves, but then another fear jumped into his mind. He looked nervously at Confident. "But what if the Stars were supposed to tell Artist we needed help and they forgot?" His heart began to pound over this fear.

"I don't think so." Confident was as calm as ever; nothing seemed to be worrying him.

Aspire took a deep breath and tried to take Confident's word for it.

"Yeah, they wouldn't do that." He knew the Stars were too kind to do that, so he decided to wait a little longer.

Yet as time continued to pass slowly, Aspire felt more and more frustrated with the waiting. It was now early afternoon, and Artist was nowhere in sight. Aspire tried to fight away thoughts that the Stars or Artist forgot that he and Confident needed help over the mountain that day. However, it was getting harder for him.

Now, his brain seemed to be swimming in fears, doubts, and frustration. He tried to tread water with hope reminding himself of what the Stars told him. But the longer he sat there waiting for help, the more he had to fight drowning in fears and doubts.

But even so, the spirit deep within him that would not give up continued to give him strength to stay above water and dream about the possibilities of overcoming the mountain. In his head, he arrived at the glory of Destiny Falls. It was a beautiful moment, and he wanted it. He wanted his horn.

Aspire closed his eyes. He shook his head as if to disrupt and get out of the deep worries and fears in his mind. He wondered if there was a plug somewhere in his head that he could pull to drain out the bad thoughts. But he couldn't find one. He felt stuck in murky thoughts.

Furthermore, the sun was getting hot on his back causing him to sweat, and the ever-present reminder of the difficulty of the mountain behind him was making him feel stir-crazy. He couldn't take this kind of waiting any longer.

Aspire stood up, and with frustration, he tried to shake and stretch the worries and anxiety out of his mind. He didn't feel that was enough, so he began to jog in short distances back and forth to release the nervous tension the whole situation was causing him.

Meanwhile, Confident watched in a relaxed position with an eyebrow raised and curiosity in his eyes. Aspire caught him and slowed to a halt but then returned to his pacing jog. Confident might have been feeling bored but certainly seemed amused now.

"Uh, Aspire, are you all right?" Confident still had the same look on his face, but a little concern began to show.

Aspire didn't want to respond until he felt calmed down. But breathlessness got to him first, so he plopped heavily down next to Confident in slight defeat.

Confident repeated his question: "Are you all right?"

Aspire spent a moment trying to catch his breath, and then hesitantly responded, "I think, yeah." He wasn't exactly sure if that was true.

"What was that for?" Confident furrowed his brow at Aspire. "You're weird sometimes."

"Um, to release some energy." Aspire let a heavy breath go but then started to get worked up again. "Oh, when is Artist bringing help?"

"I don't know." Confident looked at Aspire, semirepulsed by his attitude. "Do you need to go for a long walk or run or something?"

"No, I don't want to miss Artist." Aspire slumped and pouted along the mountain wall. "I wish I knew when Artist was coming to help."

"Artist will be here." Confident returned to his usual cool and relaxed self, but he had a slight thread of annoyance in his voice. Aspire could tell Confident thought he was acting impatient, but he didn't care at the moment.

Confident laid his head on his paws and seemed to find the waiting time relaxing. Aspire did not understand. He needed to get over this mountain.

After five minutes passed, Aspire worriedly asked again, "Do you think Artist forgot? What if the Stars were supposed to tell Artist, but they forgot?"

"Well, we'll just have to get over the mountain by ourselves then." Confident turned his head up to Aspire, clearly tired of the questions he kept repeating. His tone sounded short and annoyed.

"Haha, funny. You know that's impossible," Aspire whined as he did not enjoy Confident's answer one bit.

Confident looked at Aspire plainly and shrugged his shoulders. There was no answer.

Aspire began to wonder what they would do if Artist never showed up to help. The Stars had given him a dose of hope the night before, but now it seemed to be leaking away as time slowly crept along and no help was coming.

Aspire and Confident sat under the heat of the sun in silence as Aspire stewed in his anxious thoughts. It was late afternoon, and Aspire felt mad at this point. He couldn't help but express his frustration through a heavy sigh. Confident responded with a slightly less heavy sigh. Aspire didn't know if it was at him or at the impossible situation before them.

Suddenly, a wind started to blow. It grew stronger and stronger sending in thick gray clouds rolling and swirling above Aspire and Confident. Aspire looked up to see the sky begin to threaten what looked like a giant rainstorm.

"Oh, great. Just great. Now it's all getting worse!" Aspire was quite upset with the situation. He looked around. There was no cover along the mountain to hide from the rain. Some small trees littered the field in front of the mountain, but Aspire didn't want to leave his post in case Artist showed up to help. Aspire took a breath to try and calm his deep frustration.

Aspire turned to see Confident staring up at the sky. Aspire joined him watching the clouds swirl and move from the wind with no bit of blue sky in sight. Confident looked at Aspire with a bit of alarm, and his face told Aspire that he knew they could be in trouble.

Then suddenly, a strange sound came from the sky. It caught Aspire's attention. He and Confident immediately looked up at the sky to discover a massive eagle soaring high against the dark, swirling clouds. It gave another sound as if it didn't make its presence known before.

They continued to watch as the eagle circled high a while gradually moving in closer and closer to them. Before Aspire could step out of his awestruck wonder, the eagle circled down to twenty feet above them. It caused Aspire and Confident to look at each other with alarm. When they turned back, the eagle quickly swooped down ten feet away. It landed gracefully, touching the earth with an expansive wingspan and a bow of its head.

They watched in awe as the eagle, in royal elegance and strength, stood up tall pulling its wings back and lifting its head. Now, it looked directly at them. Aspire felt slightly intimidated and could feel his body pulling back.

As he and Confident stood a second in awe, the eagle assessed them, looked to the sky, and cawed with authority. Soon, another eagle appeared above, circling amidst the wind and cloud. It repeated what the previous eagle had done. It too landed gracefully in the same royal drama next to the first eagle.

The eagles stood tall before Aspire and Confident. They looked absolutely magnificent with the dark and threatening backdrop of the stormy sky. Aspire and Confident sat speechless until the first eagle broke the silence.

"You are Aspire and Confident? We got the word you needed help." The eagle spoke with command that partially intimidated Aspire.

Confident was the first to reply.

"Yes…are you Artist?" Confident looked so small compared to the eagles.

The first eagle gave a sophisticated and relaxed laugh. "No, Artist sent us. How can we help you?"

Aspire found his words again, and he practically shouted out, "We need to get past this mountain to the other side!"

The first eagle nodded its head as if it had done this very thing before and knew exactly what to do. "We'll help you."

Aspire grew jittery with excitement, completely forgetting his frustration from before. He looked at Confident, and they both shared a smile that expressed relief and anticipation for what was going to happen next. Aspire looked back at the eagles who had suddenly disappeared. He frantically looked around and saw them rising up in the sky again.

For a moment, Aspire began to feel betrayed. He questioned with anger, "What are they doing?"

However, as soon as the question came out of his mouth, Aspire saw the eagles shoot straight up and suddenly dive directly down to the ground. Aspire's upset feelings quickly switched to fear as the eagles flew in fast, aiming straight for him and Confident. He had no idea what the eagles were going to do, and he was immediately imagining a painful collision.

Before he had any more time to think, the eagles swooped in, grabbed Aspire and Confident around the waist, and pulled Aspire and Confident straight up into the air with them.

The shock knocked Aspire's breath away for a second. As he tried to catch his breath, the eagles slowly circled him and Confident up to a higher altitude. Gradually, Aspire's shock switched to pure enjoyment as he viewed the shrinking world below.

The eagles soared effortlessly, cawing with strength and command. As they lifted Aspire and Confident higher and higher, they flowed with the stormy winds reaching closer to the swirling gray clouds. Aspire looked over to Confident. Confident seemed to enjoy flying with the eagles, although he was gripping tightly to the legs of the eagle carrying him.

Aspire laughed a laugh he never knew he could. "Confident! We're flying! We're flying!" he shouted over the sound of the wind with pure excitement.

Confident looked over to Aspire and smiled a toothy grin. He nodded with happiness, face blowing in the wind, and showed his teeth to the world below. Aspire never expected such help would come. It was a glorious surprise. He and Confident were flying with eagles!

The eagles gradually moved up into the clouds and stronger winds making it hard for Aspire to see among the wisps of cloud.

Soon, the eagles reached a desired height and took to simply gliding and riding the wind. Aspire looked forward and saw the tip of Mount Impossible appearing in and out through the clouds.

There it was. The very thing that had seemed to frustrate and defeat him. Now, he was going to overcome it with the help of the most magnificent creatures, the eagles.

Aspire's stomach suddenly tightened as the eagles quickly pulled up higher through and above the clouds. The sun shone brightly here over the whipped cream puffs of cloud. It seemed to share the same hope and excitement that Aspire felt.

The whole scene was quite beautiful. Rolling puffy clouds of white and cream spread out as far as Aspire could see, and splashes of sunshine appeared around the clouds like golden lining everywhere. It was a moment never forgotten. Aspire looked at Confident in awe, and Confident seemed to share the same emotion. Aspire couldn't help but close his eyes and feel the wind rush past him. He couldn't help but love his life in that moment.

The eagles soared for a time gliding steadily ahead until they suddenly dipped low. Aspire's stomach tightened again from the drop. Both Aspire and Confident couldn't help but express sounds of surprise and pleasure as they flew back into the mix of gray clouds again. Aspire tried to look for Mount Impossible, but he couldn't see it through the clouds.

Gradually, the eagles began to circle Aspire and Confident down below the clouds. Aspire could see the ground again. He felt another rush of excitement as he realized that it was the ground on the other side of the mountain. He and Confident had made it! They were officially past Mount Impossible.

As Aspire could see more detail of the world below, his excitement grew, and he began to squirm with joy and anticipation. Aspire had never felt such pleasure before. He had made it past, what was to him, the biggest obstacle on the journey to the falls. He felt such relief to have Mount Impossible on the other side of him.

As the eagles circled Aspire and Confident closer and closer to the earth, they neared a fresh and bright patch of grass until they were able to gently release Aspire and Confident to the ground.

The grass all around them was thick and vivid green and spread out far. There were many lush trees speckled around the area, and they were covered with bright fruits of different colors. Aspire looked up to see the eagles flying up to the sky again. The eagles continued to soar and glide in the strong winds and thick clouds until they disappeared. Aspire and Confident looked to each other with bright smiles, seeming to not know what to say at first.

Finally, Aspire couldn't contain his happiness.

"We made it!" Aspire jumped for joy. He landed and immediately started rolling with contentment in the soft grass.

For a moment, he laid still and stared with wonder at the cloudy sky. He realized once again that they were in fact on the other side of Mount Impossible. Even though he had wanted so badly to get past the mountain, he could never have imagined this incredible experience. This was almost too good to be true for him.

Confident laid down next to Aspire and stared at the sky with him. "Wow, I never expected that!"

Both Confident and Aspire lay there to process what had happened. Aspire began to rub his eyes wondering if it was all a dream. No, this was reality. However, he remembered that he and Confident still had to get to Destiny Falls. Aspire had no idea where they were or how close there were to Destiny Falls. He assumed they had to be super close. Now that they were past the mountain, the rest of the journey had to be easy from here on out.

However, at this point, the sky was clearing, and the sun was motioning its start to descent for the day. Aspire began to feel tired too from all the excitement and adventure he and Confident had gone through. All he could do was revel in the moment and remember the fantastic experience of flying over that giant mountain with the eagles as he stared at the smalls puffs of cloud littered across the sky.

Aspire and Confident lay in the grass in complete and rested silence for a while. The sun began to set behind the mountain making its border burn with bright orange. Meanwhile, the dusty blue and mauve sky slowly faded with the orange to deep indigo.

The Stars began to wake up in the process, dancing their hellos to the world in the sky. Aspire slowly sat up, and Confident joined him to look for their four friends who soon gladly announced their arrival.

The four Stars cheered all together in a pleasing chorus with their excitement for Aspire and Confident.

"Aspire and Confident! Overcomers of Mount Impossible!"

The harmonies of the four Stars tickled Aspire's ears. Aspire smiled from ear to ear soaking in the wonderful words of the Stars.

"You're on the other side of the mountain! I'm so proud of you!" Believe exclaimed her excitement immediately.

"We're so happy for you." Perchance smiled brightly at Aspire and Confident.

"We told you help would come!" Wistful was practically bouncing with excitement.

"How was the experience?" Deferring asked with a happy smile.

Aspire and Confident looked at each other not knowing what to say first. They turned to the Stars and exclaimed together, "It was amazing!"

"I never imagined anything like that would happen!" Confident sounded like he was still caught in awe.

"It was so fun!" Aspire smiled brightly at the Stars. At that moment, he had a great appreciation for the eagles who gave him the experience but realized that he never did thank them.

Aspire and Confident began to tell more of their experience with the eagles and how it began with the big winds and heavy clouds. They told about the beauty of the eagles and the wonder of flying above the clouds.

"I'm glad you had that experience!" Believe responded, seeming to share their happiness over the experience.

"What a good adventure!" Wistful chimed in.

However, Deferring changed the mood with a question directed to Aspire.

"Aspire, we heard what happened before the eagles arrived." Deferring's tone caught Aspire by surprise.

"What do you mean?" Aspire felt confused.

"What we mean is you didn't trust us," Perchance explained with brutal honesty. "Why?"

Aspire felt taken aback.

He began to think about his impatience before the eagles arrived. His face suddenly felt hot. He had let his mood get sour, and it even affected Confident's mood. He immediately started to feel bad for not trusting the Stars and waiting well. He lowered his head.

"I'm sorry." Aspire glanced at Confident, who was sitting by him.

Confident shrugged his shoulders as if to say he wasn't bothered by what happened.

"You can learn from this though! You'll do better next time!" Believe made the situation feel lighter. It caused Aspire to feel better.

"Yeah!" Aspire began to think. "Wait, so how did you find that out?"

"Artist told us," Deferring spoke plainly, and it caused Aspire to raise his eyebrows at the thought.

Who is this Artist? he thought, *And where was Artist this whole time?*

"Artist wants you to learn from this so you can be ready!" Wistful broke Aspire's thought process.

"Ready?" Aspire didn't know what that meant.

"Ready for the falls, Aspire. Ready for what you want," Perchance explained.

"Oh." Aspire began to think, why did he need to be "ready" for the falls? What exactly did being "ready" mean? "So do I need to know something else before I get there?"

"No," Deferring stated.

"Just keep learning!" Believe smiled.

"Okay." Aspire decided to not question the Stars anymore. It seemed they only left him with more questions, and he was too tired to think.

Confident yawned. "I'm tired. I think I'm ready to go to sleep."

"Yeah…" Aspire stated this hesitantly as his mind began to try to process what the Stars said. But he was ready to end the conversation with the Stars.

"Get good rest!" Perchance sweetly stated.

"Sleep well!" the rest of the Stars chimed their goodnight melody.

"See you tomorrow!" Confident seemed to be enjoying the Stars more as his tone was growing much nicer toward them.

With that, the Stars pulled away to talk amongst themselves. Aspire's mind darted back to Artist. He still wanted to know who exactly Artist was, and questions raced in his mind. How did Artist know what happened? Where was Artist the whole time? He decided to leave it alone for the night since he had no answers. He looked over to see Confident contentedly rolled up and falling asleep.

"Good night, Confident." Aspire lay down to try to fall asleep.

"Good night." Confident yawned and soon fell to steady breathing signifying his slumber.

However, Aspire still couldn't get Artist out of his mind. He wondered, why did Artist need him to be "ready" for the falls? What did that mean? Eventually, Aspire fell asleep with so many questions still in his head.

11

*A*spire woke to the sound of birds singing. The sun was up and cheerful, and the world around was drenched in golden sunlight. Aspire immediately remembered where he was, and that he and Confident were finally past the mountain. He suddenly felt bubbles of joy rise to the surface in his body, and he yawned happily.

He sat up to soak in the beauty of the scene. It was such a pleasant atmosphere with soft green grass stretching out far into the distance. Wildflower patches swayed in the breeze, and fruit trees covered in a variety of delicious fruit spread out everywhere.

Aspire saw apples, cherries, and pears, and he instantly remembered their sweet flavors. Then he noticed Confident off in the distance enjoying his early breakfast in the cool shade of what looked like a pear tree. Aspire thought the tree looked like it would make a great structure for a tree house. Aspire felt so much warmth and joy. It seemed like the perfect place to celebrate overcoming Mount Impossible.

Aspire lay in the grass for a time soaking up the moment, until his stomach grumbled, and he knew exactly what he wanted. He excitedly hopped up and searched for the nearest apple tree. He found the juiciest, most colorful one and brought it over to enjoy next to Confident. Confident was enjoying the warmth of the sun that peered through the pear tree onto his face.

"Good morning!" Aspire was cheery and already had a bite of apple in his mouth. It made Confident chuckle slightly at Aspire while he remained in his relaxed position.

"Morning, it took you a while to get up. When did you go to sleep?" Confident continued to enjoy his spot under the pear tree with his eyes closed now.

A wind blew gently by carrying with it the fresh scent of what Aspire began to think was ripe peaches. It was such a peaceful, happy environment, and it pulled Aspire into its serenity.

"Not too late, I guess." Aspire began to think about the questions that kept him up late. "Who is Artist?"

Confident opened his eyes slowly and looked at Aspire. "I have no idea."

Aspire turned his head down to the ground at his half-eaten apple and quieted his voice a bit. "What does Artist want me to learn?"

"Well, you did get kind of impatient out there...and a little dramatic." Confident was frank, but he continued to enjoy the warm sun and gentle breeze with his eyes closed.

Aspire felt his face get warm and kept looking at his apple, finishing a bite. "Oh, yeah. Sorry."

"You don't have to apologize to me. Just learn to trust and... wait a little."

Confident glanced at Aspire like he genuinely meant what he said. Aspire looked up at him sheepishly, but the two then shared a smile. Aspire was all right. Confident understood. Aspire would simply learn from this experience.

They spent quite a few more minutes silently enjoying the heavenly space. Aspire tried to embrace all the peace and tranquility it provided. Eventually, Aspire felt ready to continue on the journey. He still had his goals at the forefront of his mind.

"Are you ready?" Confident turned to Aspire to show a glimmer of excitement.

Aspire smiled big. "Yes!" He got up and began to look around him and suddenly realized that he didn't know where to start. "Uh, where is the path?"

Confident stood up and began to search with him. In all their excitement of flying with the eagles, they didn't pay attention to where they landed. They had no idea where the Adventure Trails started up again from the other side of the mountain. Aspire wondered, *Did the trails even continue on the other side of the mountain?*

Aspire and Confident began to spread out looking harder for any sign or path anywhere. The many fruit trees were not making the situation easy. They blocked a lot of the view around them, and some of the fallen, sticky fruit littered underneath the trees were creating obstacles. Aspire began to feel nervous.

Several questions started to float to the surface in his mind. What if they couldn't find the trails? What if they got lost and won't ever make it to the falls? Aspire could feel fear and impatience shoot through his veins. He needed to find the trail now.

Then he remembered what he should have done the previous day. Confident's words rang in his ears: "Trust and wait a little." Aspire decided to try his best to trust that they would find the path and to not rush the process.

After ten minutes of searching and searching, Aspire caught sight of something promising. Not too far ahead lay a path stretching away from the mountain. When they ran up to it, about ten feet ahead stood a big sign proudly labeling it as the Adventure Trails.

Aspire felt relief wash over him and then excitement bubbled up again. Aspire knew that Confident felt the same emotion as the two shared a wide smile. Then they set off on the path walking side by side to Destiny Falls, completely unaware of what was ahead but with the mountain behind them.

Aspire continued to enjoy the scenery as they walked. Luscious fruit trees gathered on either side of the path, and birds were singing happy tunes. It all added to the excitement that Aspire had to reach the falls. He felt on top of the world.

As Aspire and Confident walked, they talked about the Stars and how the Stars seemed to know everything. Both Aspire and Confident wondered if the Stars kept tabs on them during the day or if the Stars slept at all, but they each agreed to feeling safe when the Stars were out, as if the Stars guarded them against danger somehow.

They also took the time to express their growing excitement for reaching Destiny Falls. They dreamed together about what it would feel like to finish the journey and reach their goals. Then they started to think about what they would do after they made it.

"When I become the king of a tribe, the first thing I am going to do is throw a big celebration party. For any creature too. They don't have to be a part of the tribe." Confident's voice was filling evermore with excitement over the idea. He seemed to be fully embracing the fact that his dream could be a reality. "But my party will be so good that everyone is going to want to be a part of my tribe. Everyone."

"Cool! I'll be there…that is if you invite me." Aspire smiled at Confident.

"Of course! You can even host with me if you want." Confident smiled back at Aspire.

"That would be awesome!" Aspire liked the idea a great deal. He began to think about what he would do exactly after he got his unicorn horn. "When I get my horn, I am going to…I don't know exactly." Aspire began to think hard. He had so many ideas about what life would be like as a unicorn. But he never thought realistically about what he would first do when he got his horn. This began to send him in full daydreaming mode.

Aspire pictured himself on the Ever After Mountains. His horn glinting, mane blowing in full view of everyone. He imagined his family and friends standing awestruck at the sight of him. His parents would be so proud that he made it, and his friends would be so impressed by him in all his unicorn glory.

"I think I'll go live in Ever After but visit my family for a little bit to show them that I made it. I'll tell everyone the story and maybe get interviewed for magazines. They'll put my picture in it too, like that other unicorn. I'll have a really cool place in Ever After and of course be at all your parties. Maybe we could have them where I live too!" Aspire really liked this idea.

"Did anyone believe you could make it? To the falls?" Confident switched the tone and seemed genuinely interested in Aspire's response, and his question hit a soft spot in Aspire.

"Well, yeah." Aspire looked at the ground as they walked. "They said it would be really hard for me. They doubted I could make it, I know it." Then Aspire straightened up and looked ahead. "But I made it this far, and I am going to make it to the end. I'm going to get my horn."

"Cool."

Confident accepted that answer well, which gave Aspire relief. He didn't want to think any more about other creatures' opinions at the moment. The journey had been hard, a lot harder than he thought. But he was still going, and he was going to make it.

Aspire and Confident walked on the path for a time in silence. Aspire was still processing what it would be like to make it to the falls and get his dream. At that time, the only sounds in the area were the songs of birds and the wind in the leaves of the fruit trees. Occasionally, a piece of fruit would fall from a tree to the ground, sounding when it landed.

Aspire and Confident had gotten used to the rolling succession of the peaceful noises. So their ears immediately perked up when a different sound floated on the breeze to them. Aspire thought it sounded like laughter. Confident looked at Aspire with curiosity in his eyes, and they picked up their easy pace on the path to find where the noise was coming from.

As they got closer to the sound, Aspire could tell it was coming from a large group of creatures. It sounded like they were having a lot of fun together, almost like they were having a party.

As Aspire and Confident rounded a small curve in the path, the sound instantly drew their attention to just beyond through the fruit trees, an open clearing full of animals.

There were dogs, birds, cats, an elephant, lizards, rabbits, raccoons, and they *were* having a party. Green and blue balloons and streamers decorated the clearing. A table that looked covered in treats stood off to the side, and it looked as if the animals were enjoying themselves as they sat grouped together on blankets spread over the grass in the middle of the clearing.

Immediately, something else caught Aspire's eye. It was a deer. The deer had a beautiful, shiny chestnut coat and dainty antlers. He stood before the group of animals, appearing to lead the gathering. But what drew Aspire's attention the most was a pearly, blue horn that stood on top of the deer's head. After he blinked, Aspire's eyes widened at the realization that the deer in fact had a unicorn's horn! However, he was most surprised that it was a deer, not a horse.

Aspire felt a mixture of wonder and confusion. He thought that only horses could be unicorns. He even felt a slight twinge of jealousy at the fact that the deer of all creatures had one, but he did not.

This unusual sight had grabbed Aspire's attention so much that he didn't realize he was staring quite intently at the deer until the deer caught sight of him and called him over to join the party.

"Hey, you! You two! Come on over!"

This caused the whole party of the animals to turn their attention to Aspire and Confident. Aspire felt taken aback and found himself feeling suddenly quite shy. He didn't respond but looked at Confident instead.

"Looks fun, let's see what they're up to."

Confident was calm and collected as usual. He started walking toward the party of animals.

Aspire wasn't so sure if he wanted to get involved, but his curiosity over the deer led him forward. He followed slowly behind Confident. When Aspire and Confident made it to the clearing, the deer led the introduction.

"Welcome! We were just starting a game." The deer gave them a closer look. "I haven't seen you two around these parts. I'm Perfect! Who are you?"

"I'm Confident." Confident sat down outside the party facing the deer with his chest puffed up with self-assurance. "And this is Aspire." He motioned toward Aspire with a nod of his head.

Aspire still did not know what to say, so he sat down next to Confident but ever so slightly behind him as Aspire felt intimidated by the whole scene.

The entire party of creatures welcomed them with friendly "hi's" and "hellos," which helped Aspire to feel less intimidated as he looked around to see lots of warm smiles. He began to wonder what the party was for and if someone was being celebrated.

There weren't any signs signifying what kind of party it was. But amidst the balloons and streamers, Aspire saw glittering confetti everywhere. He looked over to the table of food, and his mouth began to water.

There were chocolate and vanilla cupcakes, large trays of ripe fruit, endless varieties of cookies, and cake. The cake was vanilla, and it had four layers. Huge globs of creamy white frosting stuck each layer together while all sorts of sugared berries dripped down from the top of the cake. The cake stole all of Aspire's attention, but Perfect called him back to reality.

"You can join our game if you want. We were just playing King of the Orchard."

Aspire saw this information instantly catch Confident's attention as his ears perked and his head tilted. "King of the Orchard… how do you play?"

Confident seemed eager to jump in.

"Here, I'll show you. Just sit down here."

Perfect motioned toward the rest of the animals sitting comfortably on the blankets. Confident followed Perfect as he walked over and sat down on the edge of the blanket in the front. Aspire followed slowly behind looking for space for himself closer to the back. He sat down next to a small rabbit.

"Hi! I'm Cordial! You're Aspire, right?" The rabbit smiled warmly, making more room for Aspire on the blanket.

"Yeah. Nice to meet you." Aspire smiled back and felt some timidity slip away.

Perfect gathered all the creatures' attention as he explained the game for the new players.

"I'll host the game this time."

He went on to explain that his job was to choose the "king of the orchard." He had already chosen who the king was to be for that round, so he told everyone to close their eyes while he nudged the chosen king on the shoulder.

Then, Perfect commanded everyone to open their eyes. Aspire felt surprised at how fast and silently Perfect had notified his chosen king. Perfect proceeded to explain directly to Aspire and Confident that all the creatures had to race the clock to discover the "king of the orchard." They had seven minutes to ask the host questions about the character and qualities of the chosen king. Perfect showed them the timer he had ready beside him.

However, the limitations were that they could only ask yes or no questions. Plus, the king had the choice to veto. This meant that the host had to refuse to answer a specific question if the king so decided. Perfect also explained that the king would want to be very discreet when vetoing; otherwise, creatures could easily find out.

Perfect finished by saying, "If no one finds who the king is in seven minutes, everyone has to follow the king's orders for another seven minutes. And the king can order whatever they want, just as long as it doesn't harm or offend anyone."

From the back, Aspire could see Confident stand up with excitement.

"Okay, I'm ready." Confident sounded calm and collected, but he seemed very, very anxious to play, maybe to be king.

"Aspire, are you ready?" Perfect looked right to Aspire.

"Uh, yeah, I think so."

Aspire didn't speak very loudly, but Perfect heard, and the game began.

The creatures began asking numerous questions that would either get a head nod or a head shake from Perfect. They wondered if the king was small, and Perfect shook his head. They asked if the king was athletic, and Perfect nodded. They questioned if the king's favorite ice cream was chocolate, and Perfect nodded his head.

They asked many other questions while Aspire spent the time observing. Confident, on the other hand, chimed in by asking questions about the king's appearance. He stared down the creatures around him to see who matched the answers. He was quite into the game from the get-go.

Suddenly, Cordial, the little rabbit sitting next to Aspire, got excited and sweetly piped up with a big smile. "Oh! I know! I know! Is—" But as Cordial was finishing the sentence, the timer rang.

All the animals responded with defeated sighs and shouts.

Cordial piped up less excited, "Is it Daring?"

"Yes, it is Daring, but you didn't ask in time, so he is the 'king of the orchard' for seven minutes!" Perfect responded.

All the animals responded by playfully "booing" while a leopard stood up to get crowned by Perfect with a golden wreath of leaves.

"Thank you, thank you!" Daring, the leopard, exclaimed, bowing before all the creatures. "For my first decree, I say that everyone should eat chocolate ice cream!"

Perfect proclaimed, "The king decrees we eat chocolate ice cream!"

All the creatures shouted their excitement while they stood up and followed Daring to the table of food. Aspire and Confident watched together from behind the group.

The creatures pulled out a cooler from under the table and sifted through it, finally lugging out a tub of chocolate ice cream. Daring helped all the animals get a spoon, and everyone took turns scooping a big bite of chocolate ice cream. Confident joined in grabbing a spoon. This seemed fun to Aspire, so he joined in too.

As the creatures were happily licking their spoons, Daring gave his following proclamation. "Now, since you all have fattened yourselves up, I decree that we all go for a light jog to burn off those calories."

Perfect shouted, "The king decrees a jog!"

All the creatures moaned and groaned but followed Daring's orders and jogged in a circle around the edge of the clearing. Aspire and Confident looked at each other, smiled, and followed the creatures in the jog.

After they jogged around in a circle a couple times, Daring gave his final decree. "Now that you have gotten your exercise, I say that we all get a drink of water and take a nap!"

Perfect shouted in response, "The king decrees a drink of water and a nap!"

All the animals breathed sighs of relief, ran to the table, and gulped down water from a large pitcher. They proceeded to lie down on the blankets to rest their eyes until the timer rang again. Aspire and Confident were the last in line. When they finished drinking water, there was no room on the blanket anymore because all the creatures spread over every inch.

Perfect walked up to them before the timer rang.

"So do you like the game?" He smiled at Aspire and Confident.

"I do." Confident smiled brightly. He seemed to still have the energy he had since the beginning of the game.

"Yeah, it seems fun." Aspire smiled back at Perfect.

"Good." Perfect looked back at the creatures who were now laughing with Daring over his commands. He looked back at Aspire and Confident. "I don't know if you caught it, but they asked if Daring was athletic and if his favorite ice cream was chocolate. Since it was true, he used those two specific things as a theme in his seven-minute reign. You don't have to do it exactly that way, but it makes the game more fun. We all like to do it."

"Oh, cool. I'd like a shot at that." Confident observed the other creatures, and his mind seemed to be buzzing with plans. Aspire could see in Confident's eyes that he was ready to have a seven-minute reign over these creatures himself.

"I like the game," Aspire stated. He looked at Perfect but felt intimidated by Perfect's eye contact and turned away to observe the fun that the creatures were having together. He began to feel a desire for a group like that. They seemed to have so much fun together. He thought maybe he would get one when he got his horn, and all the creatures would want to be his friend. He'd go to a lot of parties like this one. "What is the party for? Is it someone's birthday?"

"Eh, no. It's just for fun." Perfect was quite nonchalant as if this was a usual thing. "I throw a lot of parties for my family. Usually every week. This is actually nothing compared to some of the parties we throw around here."

This caught Confident's attention. "So you throw the parties? Like, is this your tribe?"

Perfect tilted his head and seemed to think a moment. "I guess you could say that. I mean, I am the leader of this group. But we're all just family. No one greater than the other." Perfect sounded so normal as if the fact that he had a horn and a tribe wasn't a big deal to him.

Aspire and Confident glanced at each other with surprise and slight jealousy in their eyes at this amazing creature.

Confident whispered to Aspire, "And he has a horn."

Aspire was strongly aware of the fact. Boy, did he know, and he was even a little annoyed at Perfect's, well, perfection.

Perfect laughed at their reactions. "So are you two headed to Destiny Falls?"

"Yeah, how did you know?" Confident looked at Perfect with an eyebrow raised.

Aspire looked at Perfect with the same curiosity.

"Usually, there aren't other creatures besides us out here. When there are, they're headed to the falls. I just took a wild guess." Perfect smiled.

"Oh." Aspire smiled a small one back.

"Good luck on your journey!" Perfect kept his smile.

"Thanks." Aspire smiled a little bigger.

"Yeah, thanks." Confident smiled too.

"Are you ready to play again?" Perfect offered the question to the whole party.

The response was a resounding "Yes!"

"You two want to keep playing?" Perfect looked at Aspire and Confident again.

Aspire and Confident looked at each other and agreed to keep playing. Perfect and his life was now too fascinating to leave at the moment. Aspire wondered if any life could get better. Perfect had everything. He was also nice about it and didn't make it a big deal. It was refreshing.

Confident hopped back to his first spot on the blanket looking quite ready to play again. Aspire started to walk over to the blanket, and he felt a gentle nudge. He looked over to see Perfect discreetly lean over to him and whisper, "You're the king."

Aspire looked around him. Not a single creature noticed, but Aspire felt like a spotlight stood right over him. He didn't know if he wanted to be the king at the moment. He didn't feel ready. He sat back down next to Cordial not knowing how to respond to being the "king of the orchard." He was still processing the previous conversation with Perfect. Aspire had already felt intimidated by Perfect from the beginning. Now, Perfect seemed even more above him for some odd reason.

Perfect proceeded to get all the creatures' attention and told them to close their eyes. Aspire did too until he realized that he was the king this time, and he slowly looked up. Perfect winked at him as if to say, "You got this." Perfect then commanded the creatures to open their eyes, and the game began.

At first, all the questions the creatures asked received "noes" from Perfect. They seemed to struggle in their attempt to discover Aspire. Aspire was beginning to warm up to the fact that he could have a seven-minute reign. Until one of the creatures asked if the king was shy, to which Perfect nodded yes. Another asked Perfect if the king had a mane.

Then Cordial piped up pointing right to Aspire, "It is Aspire?"

Cordial looked to Aspire quickly after and whispered, "Sorry," as if she already knew it was him.

"Yes!" Perfect responded. "Sorry, Aspire! No seven-minute reign." Then the timer rang.

"It's all right!" Aspire weakly laughed it off feeling a little disappointed. But what bothered him most at that moment was the fact that all the other creatures thought he was shy. That didn't seem like a good thing to him. He was on a difficult journey to get his dream, and he had already come so far. He wasn't shy; he was brave, he thought.

"Let's play again!" many creatures shouted in unison.

The party played King of the Orchard many more times and experienced the seven-minute reign of a few more kings until it was early in the evening. Then, the group migrated to the table of food and chatted in small groups while they ate.

Aspire and Confident found each other and walked to the table together to find some treats. Aspire took some of the delicious cake while Confident found the biggest chocolate chip cookie. Then they sat under the cool shade away from the other creatures.

"That was kind of fun," Aspire spoke first with a mouthful of cake and frosting.

"Yeah." Confident's brow had been furrowed since Aspire found him, and it remained the same as he bit into his cookie.

"You seemed to really get into the game. Did you like it?" Aspire began to wonder what was so heavy on Confident's mind as it was causing his forehead to wrinkle.

"Mostly." Confident sat for a moment as if he had something else to say but wouldn't let it out yet. Then he burst out, "I never got to be king." He sounded a little annoyed.

"Well, I never did either." Aspire was beginning to understand the problem, so he tried to help ease the weight.

"Yeah, but you at least got chosen to be one. You had a chance. I didn't even get chosen." Confident almost pouted.

"Oh. That's true." Aspire didn't know what to say after that.

Confident proceeded to sound frustrated. "I'd be a good king. I'd be a fun king. Just give me a chance. I'll show you. They might even like me more than those other creatures, like Daring."

"I think you'd be a good king. You don't need a seven-minute reign to show that. It's just a game." Aspire could see now why Confident had been so invested in the game when they first began. It was more than a chance for a seven-minute reign. Confident seemed to want to prove to everyone, and maybe even himself, that he would make a great king.

"Meh. Maybe." Confident sunk down. He seemed to really want to be "king of the orchard."

Just then, Perfect walked over. "Hey."

He sat down next to them with some watermelon. He looked at them. "Is everything all right?"

"Yeah, it's fine." Confident didn't make it sound like he was fine though.

Perfect looked into Aspire's eyes, and he caved under the pressure. "Uhh. He just wanted to be 'king of the orchard.'"

Aspire looked sheepishly at Confident, who was clearly not pleased that Aspire had given that information to Perfect.

"Oh." Perfect chuckled. He looked at Confident. "We can play again and give you a chance if you want."

"No, I'm fine." Confident sounded like he was completely over the fact that he wasn't chosen as "king of the orchard."

"Okay, well, let me know if you change your mind." Perfect smiled and left to talk to some creatures who were laughing very happily together.

"Change my mind. Yeah, sure. I'll let you know," Confident said gruffly under his breath. But Aspire heard well enough and could catch Confident's annoyance toward Perfect. Aspire didn't judge Confident. He felt a bit similarly.

Aspire and Confident spent time in the shade wallowing in their feelings for a time. They talked a bit about the game but mostly how Perfect had everything they could ever want. By now, the sun had begun to set, and the animals started to clean up after their partying from the day laughing as they did it.

During the party, Aspire pushed to the back of his mind why he and Confident were there on Adventure Trails to begin with. When Aspire saw the sun melting into the earth like ice cream, he remembered his original mission.

"Oh no! The sun is setting, and we haven't made any progress at all today. Darn it." Aspire slumped into more frustration.

"Well, there's no use now." Confident rolled his eyes.

"We should at least try." Aspire got up to look for the path, stretching his neck to find it. It was hard to spot the trail in the dusk light as darkness was sneaking up quickly. He slumped back down. "Never mind."

"You two need a place to stay for the night?" Aspire could see Perfect walking up to them. Perfect stopped before them and looked down at their sorry state. "I've got some space for you guys. That way you don't have to travel in the dark."

Aspire looked at Confident, and Confident shrugged his shoulders. Aspire looked back at Perfect. "Okay."

Perfect led them out of the clearing through the trees using the little bit of light left from the day. He brought them to another opening. Many animals were already making their beds on soft piles of leaves and brush under the light of the rising moon.

"We've got some extra over here." He pointed to a spot where a large pile of leaves stood. "Make yourselves comfortable!"

Aspire and Confident each pushed some leaves from the pile off to the side a bit of a distance from the rest of the group and made them into comfortable beds. As they laid down in their surprisingly soft piles, Perfect gave the nighttime announcement.

"Today was great everyone! Such a fun day." He then led the animals through a discussion of their favorite parts of the day and fun ideas for parties in the future. He finished with "Now let's say good night to our new visitors!"

All the creatures said sweet goodnights to Aspire and Confident. After some whispered conversations, they all began to fall asleep. Confident seemed too upset about the day to talk and had tucked his face in his tail.

So Aspire lay there for a time alone in silence thinking about the day. Questions spun around his mind like a merry-go-round. Who was this Perfect? How did he get his horn? Did he go to the falls too? Aspire decided that he would ask tomorrow. He slowly fell asleep as his unanswered questions settled in his mind for the night.

12

Aspire woke up to the sound of rustling and whispering. He opened his eyes and, in his waking blur, tried to remember where he was. He looked around to see creatures pushing piles of leaves into one big pile near a large tree. Then he remembered he was in the orchard with Perfect's tribe.

The sun was rising, and the creatures were getting ready for another day of fun. Aspire turned over to see if Confident was awake but found an empty bed of leaves instead. He had a quick moment of panic as his heart started beating faster. His eyes darted around until he discovered Confident and Perfect talking together in the distance. Relief flooded over him.

Other creatures began walking and congregating over that way too. Aspire could see a breakfast spread ahead of them. He felt hungry at the sight and decided to walk over to get food. He also wanted to know if he could join Confident's and Perfect's conversation. When Aspire neared Confident and Perfect, he decided to join the conversation first.

"Good morning, Aspire!" Perfect was immediately cheerful and welcoming. He was so likable to Aspire but also made him jealous at the same time because he owned up to his name. He was Perfect.

"Morning!" Aspire tried to return the cheer. "What are you talking about?"

"Oh, Confident and I were just talking about him being the king of a tribe! I think he'll be great." Perfect smiled at Confident.

Confident smiled back and looked at Aspire with the same smile. His demeanor was so different from the day previous. He and Perfect also seemed to be on good terms now.

"That's great." Aspire began to wonder what exactly Confident and Perfect talked about.

"So are you two hungry? If not, you should at least take some food before you leave for the falls." Perfect motioned toward the breakfast spread where all the animals were congregating.

"I could eat." Aspire stared at the food with his mouth watering.

"Yeah, I'm hungry too."

"Have at it!"

Aspire and Confident walked over to the spread, and a couple of kind smiling cats made room for them. Aspire and Confident picked out what they wanted and sat under a tree to enjoy their morning meal together. Perfect picked some food for himself and joined them.

"So, Aspire, Confident told me why he is going to the falls. Why are you going?" Perfect sat by Aspire and took a bite out of an apple he had and waited for Aspire's response.

Aspire paused, looked at Perfect's horn, and wondered how vulnerable he wanted to be in that moment. He decided to open up a tiny bit.

"I'm going to get a horn. I want to be one of the Majestics." He was curious about how Perfect would respond.

"Nice. I wish the best to you!" Perfect leaned back on the tree causing his horn to glint in the sun. For a second, Aspire found himself mesmerized.

"So...how did you get your horn?" Aspire's curiosity over Perfect's horn had peaked, and he needed to know how it happened. "You went to the falls too?"

"Actually, no."

Aspire looked at Perfect with wide eyes. This news surprised him; he had to know more.

"It was a gift." Perfect smiled at Aspire's response.

"A gift?" Aspire's mind was buzzing.

"Yes, when I was younger, I had an interaction with Artist. Have you heard of Artist? It was amazing. We talked for hours I remember.

Near the end, Artist asked if I wanted anything. I told Artist I didn't know except that I wanted to talk more. Artist laughed. Then suddenly, I was given this!" Perfect pointed to his horn.

"Wow, that's…wow…" Aspire didn't know how to respond.

Aspire remembered when the Stars mentioned Artist. He still wanted to meet Artist, especially after Artist helped him and Confident over Mount Impossible. He never knew that Artist could give him a horn, however. That changed everything. He began to wonder how he could meet Artist.

"So how did you meet Artist?"

"Ah, that part, I don't remember well, but I was walking in this orchard, and Artist just kind of showed up, I think."

"That's cool." Aspire felt a strong desire to meet Artist right then. He was so ready to get his horn. So ready.

"So cool," Confident chimed in. "Artist helped us get over Mount Impossible."

"That's amazing!" Perfect seemed to be reminiscing over his experience. Then his voice sounded sad. "It's been a long time since I have last seen Artist though. I really only recall meeting Artist that one time."

"Oh." Aspire's new hope diminished a little. "We didn't meet Artist either." He had another question for Perfect. "So how did you get to be a king of a tribe?"

Perfect paused as if he didn't understand the question for a second. "Oh, I like to call myself 'the fam's big bro.' It just kind of fell into place. Somehow I ventured over here, met Artist, and he gave me a horn. Then, I ran into a bunch of different creatures, and the family just kind of started. We have a lot of fun together."

"Oh, that's awesome." Aspire felt increasingly impressed with Perfect's life story. Plus, Perfect's completely beautiful dream life seemed more attainable because it was a gift. Aspire now felt more hope for his dream. It seemed more possible.

"Yeah. It's great." Perfect took another bite of his apple and watched as the creatures at the breakfast spread began to leave in groups laughing along the way.

"Do you have a party today?" Aspire began to wonder what the day would look like for Perfect and his family.

"No, it's a chill day. Everyone is doing what they want today. We'll meet together for dinner though." Perfect continued to rest, leaning against the tree as if that was all he had to do that day.

Aspire embraced the peace and the joy of the scene too. He liked Perfect's life. He even liked the idea of being a king of a tribe, or as Perfect termed it, "the fam's big bro." He decided Confident would be better at that though.

"Well, Aspire, we should probably get going. Perfect said we have to get through this orchard and then there is a little more to travel after that." Confident stretched as he stood up. He seemed ready to leave now. He looked determined and empowered as he looked for the trail.

"Yes." Perfect straightened up. "But you're getting close!"

Aspire felt the positive energy flow through him after Perfect said they were close. Aspire felt ready and energized to finish the journey, more than he thought he would. He stood up and stretched. Perfect followed suit.

"It was great to have you hang out with us, Confident and Aspire!" Perfect smiled and pointed beyond them to where they could see a ways off through the fruit trees a small path. "The trail will be that way. Take some fruit with you as you go, and after you get what you want at the falls, stop by again so we can celebrate with you!"

Aspire and Confident smiled back. "We will! Thanks for having us!"

They waved goodbye and headed off to the direction of the Adventure Trails. On the way, they plucked some plump peaches off a nearby tree for energy for the trip and because the scent was so tantalizing. As they enjoyed the sweet flavor of the peaches, Aspire couldn't help but feel giddy and full of hope to make it to his destination.

He also thought about the kindness of Perfect. Perfect made Aspire feel that he was worth his dream and that meant a lot to him. Initially, Perfect's life seemed so unattainable. Yet now, Aspire felt that anything was possible.

He felt much appreciation for Perfect and everything Perfect did for him and Confident. Not only did Perfect welcome them and share his food with them, but he also opened up his place to them for the night and treated them so graciously. Aspire's feelings overwhelmed him, and he had to express it to Confident.

"Perfect is just so cool." Aspire shook his head at the thought that Perfect was the complete package. "He has everything, and he's so nice and chill about it."

"I know." Confident joined in expressing awe over Perfect. "I didn't like him at first."

Aspire chuckled because he had felt the same way but was proven wrong about Perfect.

When they made it to the trail, they stopped and looked down at the direction Perfect told them to take. They could barely see the path through the trees ahead, but they pressed forward ready to get through the orchard to the next step of the journey.

"I had a good talk with Perfect this morning." Confident seemed to be thinking about the conversation Aspire caught the end of when he woke up. Confident was staring straight ahead. "I woke up to some creatures getting breakfast ready. I was still mad from yesterday, but I went over to talk with them, kind of about Perfect." Confident chuckled to himself. "Then Perfect showed up with his smiley self. But he asked me if everything was all right and if he had made me mad or something."

"He did?" Aspire felt surprised at the attentiveness of Perfect.

"Yeah, it kind of took me off guard. He asked like he was sad about that. So I said, 'Kinda,' and he asked why. I didn't want to tell him anything, but it all kind of poured out, I guess. You know, my dream and all. Why I want to be king of a tribe and stuff. He was really encouraging and apologized that he didn't give me a chance to play king."

"Wow, that is cool." Aspire didn't know if he could admire Perfect even more, but it was happening anyway.

"Yeah, I know." Confident shook his head. "He even told me some of the things he learned and experienced about leading a tribe. He gave me some tips and stuff too. Then, he actually said he was excited for me to be the king of a tribe. He said that he thought I would be a good one." Confident smiled.

"Wow, Perfect is awesome."

"Yeah. I know."

They walked in silence for a time. Aspire thought more about Perfect and decided that he would try his best to go back and visit when he got his horn. He wanted to celebrate with Perfect and maybe spend more time with him and his "fam."

"I just… I think it's cool that I talked about throwing parties when I become a king and then we show up at Perfect's. His family seems to really like him…and the parties. I'm definitely going to use some of his ideas and tips. He's…a really good king, well, bro…is that what he called it?"

Aspire could tell that it took a lot for Confident to admit that Perfect had it all right.

"Yeah, he has everything, but it's not a big deal to him. It's like he doesn't care too much about it. He just enjoys his life. And he doesn't put himself over the other creatures either. He's so humble."

"Yeah." Confident agreed with a big head nod. "I'm going to be humble. Everyone likes you better. I like him better because of it too. It's funny… I actually kind of want to be like him now."

"Yeah. Me too." Aspire nodded.

Aspire saw the importance of being humble too. He thought it was a good idea; after all, he also wanted to be liked. Nonetheless, he was beginning to see that good character was an essential quality to have in life. This way, he could be the best of whatever he wanted to be. Perfect had inspired him. He wanted to be the complete package too.

Aspire and Confident continued on in silence. Aspire embraced the views of the morning sun shining through the orchard and took deep breaths of the sweet, fresh, fruity air. It was a good moment. He felt more ready than ever for his dreams to come true.

Afternoon came, and Aspire and Confident found themselves at the end of the orchard looking out at a stretch of land before them. It was rather large and full of tall, dry grass blowing in a strange wind. They could see the path start to take a turn off to the left in the distance, but it was hard to see where it was turning as the sky was darkening with thick clouds swirling above and a loose, hazy fog was floating in blocking a good view of the path.

Even with the cloud and fog, they could see in the distance ahead of them a rocky and gloomy coastline. Upon squinting to get a better view, Aspire could see blue water right at the edge of the rock. It made him curious, and as the path began to tug him and Confident away from the coastal view, they ignored it and stepped off the trails to follow a smaller footpath leading them straight through a clearing in the tall, dry brush.

They came to the edge of the rock and stopped as it quickly dropped down to deep blue waters that stretched out to a textured gray horizon. Aspire took a step back. It was a beautiful but intimidating sight. Even from their distance, the water looked vast and powerful, even more so as the sky and wind threatened a storm that caused waves to crash hard on the small shore below hitting the rocky wall.

"Wow, this is quite a bluff." Confident looked impressed.

"Yeah, wow." Aspire had never seen a bluff before.

Aspire and Confident sat a while staring at the majestic sight.

Aspire slowly looked down the steep drop to a small section of beach. The water quickly covered and uncovered the sand, and then stretched far out to the horizon where the clouds had slightly parted to let in some light. Tall rock structures jutted from the sand below up high and mighty to the sky, and the heavy sound of the waves added to the grandeur of the sight.

Aspire took a deep breath. The air was thick but so fresh and clean. He took another deep breath. He could feel his spirits lift and almost soar over the water to the horizon. He felt ignited.

"I feel like anything is possible," Aspire whispered. "Like I can be anything."

"I feel…powerful," Confident responded with a smirk and sparks in his eyes still staring out at the waves. "I'm ready for anything."

Aspire agreed, "Me too."

It was as if they were on the threshold of something great; they only had to reach out and touch it, and it would be theirs for the taking.

They spent a few more moments sitting at the edge of the bluff, at the edge of greatness. Aspire tried to hold as much of the view in his mind as he could until he felt like his brain would explode. Confident sat beside him in the same wonderment. Then, before any brain could explode from the majesty, they looked at each other, stood up, and followed the small trail back to the main path, ready as ever. For now, it was their turn to go and take what was theirs; their dreams were waiting for them.

When they made it back to the path, they stopped and discovered that the fog had grown thicker and heavier making it even harder to see ahead. Aspire could only see up to five feet in front of him. However, after the moment of inspiration at the bluff, this didn't bring him down. He was energized and saw this as a challenge.

Aspire looked at Confident, and Confident looked Aspire. They shared a smile that said they each saw the problem, understood the struggle, but would take it on nonetheless. They were ready, and nothing would stop them now.

Aspire slowly started taking steps forward on the path along with Confident. They stayed close together occasionally warning each other of a rock, bush, or anything else that stood in each other's way. It was riveting at first. They were stepping into an unknown and had to depend on each other to see along the way.

Aspire found himself enjoying this bonding opportunity he and Confident had as they pressed further into the fog. They both kept aware of each other and what they could see of their surroundings. There was no way they would let the fog deter them from getting to the falls this day.

"This is crazy." Confident laughed after a time and looked at Aspire with excitement in his eyes. The challenge seemed to be invigorating him too.

"I know. I'm so glad we have each other." Aspire laughed with Confident.

"Me too." Confident turned his head back to the ground before him. "Watch out, there's a rock in your way over there."

Aspire caught sight of the rock and gingerly stepped over it. "Thanks!"

Aspire and Confident pressed on feeding off each other's energy. This was turning out to be quite fun for Aspire. But throughout the time, Aspire began to notice how the land around felt quite silent and empty, as if nothing was there at all besides rocks, plants, and the fog. He could almost hear his brain thinking in this emptiness.

However, there was one moment when he swore he heard an unknown voice whisper his name clear as day.

"Confident, did you just say my name?" Aspire stopped and looked puzzled at Confident.

"No." Confident stopped and looked confused at Aspire.

"Are you sure? I thought I heard my name."

"Well, I didn't. Seriously." Confident shrugged his shoulders.

Aspire furrowed his brow and wondered what had happened. But he continued to walk forward with Confident and dismissed his questions. As he looked to the ground far as he could see before his feet, he began to slip into daydreaming. He dreamed about reaching the falls, getting his horn, and he imagined the response he would get from Perfect and his family.

They would celebrate him and call him brave. He would tell them the story of his journey. They would feel bad for thinking he was shy and would say that he was the strongest creature they knew. Then, Aspire would join the Majestics and roam the Ever After Mountains in fierce glory.

He pictured himself for quite a time as the Majestic unicorn he wanted to be. He would also drop in on Confident's parties, and everyone would want him there. He would be something, something big. Even the Majestics would want him at all their parties.

Aspire remembered Confident and his dream. He thought Confident would be a great king. Confident would throw huge parties, and his tribe would be fun. Aspire saw himself hosting some parties with Confident imagining them being the talk of the whole land. Yes, they were going to be great.

Aspire snapped back into reality as he had stumbled over a plant in his way. He stopped and shook his head to rid himself of the dream to see where he was. He wondered why Confident hadn't warned him and looked over to tease Confident about it, but he wasn't there. Then Aspire realized that he wasn't even on the path anymore!

Aspire's heart started to beat faster. He frantically searched for Confident and the path, but in his sudden panic, he found himself all turned around and couldn't find either. He called out Confident's name.

"Confident." Aspire waited a few seconds. "Confident!"

A distant voice called out his name, "Aspire!"

"Confident! Confident! Where are you?" He waited again. "Where are you? Confident!"

No reply.

Aspire could feel his heart sink, and his nervous energy rose higher. He called out Confident's name again. Once again there was no reply. He felt a cold sweat. He also had a lump building up in his throat as he tried to hold back tears, but his eyes were filling up anyway.

Aspire stopped and tried to take a couple deep breaths, and then proceeded to look for the path again. He called out for Confident yet a couple times but still received no reply. Aspire searched and searched, but he couldn't find the path. It was gone, nowhere in sight. By now, it was steadily getting darker and darker to the point where Aspire could barely see anything ahead of him at all. As night arrived, it caused Aspire to feel even more panic.

"Oh no. Oh no, oh no, oh no."

He stopped for a moment and frantically tried to figure out which direction he was facing. He tried to listen for the ocean and, in a split second, thought he could hear it quietly off to his far left. He quickly picked a direction that he thought was correct, away from where he thought the bluff might be, and decided to make a run for it. He wanted to try and get out of the fog and find the path as soon as possible.

As he ran, he lost control of his tear ducts, and tears started streaming out of his eyes and down his face. He looked up to the sky to see if the Stars were there to help, but the fog was covering them too. He stopped, sat, and burst out crying. This was the last thing he ever wanted to happen. He didn't know where he was, and Confident was gone.

Worry flooded through his mind that he was truly lost, so he stood up and started searching for the path again.

After some time, Aspire started to slow down as his anxiety and worry were wearing his body out. He started to sniffle and tried to calm himself down. It was even darker than ever, and his head dropped heavy, close to the ground so he could try to see where he was going. He felt thankful for the light of the moon that was shining slightly through the fog.

As Aspire searched, tears started to flow from his eyes again. This was not fair to him. He wondered how this could have happened. As he walked slower and slower ahead, he could see through the blur of his tears something good. It was the edge of the path. Aspire felt a flow of relief rush over him. He had hope that he could find Confident now too.

He stood on the path and started to look around. Just then, the clouds parted above slightly to let some light of the moon shine through. This gave Aspire more hope. It would be so much easier to find Confident now. He pressed forward and caught sight of something; it was a little bit of light straight ahead in the distance, and it was moving.

Aspire looked harder to see what it was and found a familiar sight. It was water, and the moon had been reflecting its light off it. Aspire tried to catch sight of the surrounding area. He walked closer to the water and saw a familiar drop-off with scraggly, tall structures black against the water. Then he realized he had been there before. It was the same bluff he and Confident were at before.

Aspire slumped to the ground and cried. He cried and cried and cried. This could not be happening to him. He'd gotten lost and lost progress on the journey, but most of all, he lost his friend. He had no idea what to do, so he cried some more.

After Aspire thought that he probably cried out every tear possible, he lay his head to the ground and sniffled. He didn't know what he was going to do next. He felt like he was slipping out of his body into a weird dimension. It felt like the end. He felt like it was all over, but worst of all, he felt he couldn't do anything about it. He couldn't find his way out of the dark and had no choice but to sit in misery.

Aspire began to feel angry, upset that he was in this place. He was mad that he was stuck in the dark alone, and he also felt bitter. This was not supposed to happen. This was not fair. He was supposed to make it to the falls and get his dream. He has worked so hard, traveled so far, and even overcame Mount Impossible. He was supposed to make it. Just then he heard a buzzing and a familiar voice.

"You're done for. You won't make it to the falls. It's not for you."

Aspire didn't have the strength to bat away the annoying lie, so more came.

"You'll just have to deal with this kind of life. You're not good enough for any better. You're stuck here. Get used to it."

The buzzing disappeared as the insect flew off.

Aspire didn't have any more tears to cry at this point. He didn't even care about the lies anymore. He gave up. His frustrations had snuffed out like a candle, and he decided to let the darkness overtake him. He would simply disintegrate into the black of the night and let that be that. There was nothing more for him now.

He lay still for quite some time staring into the darkness before him. There was nothing else he could do or even think to do. This was it.

But sweetly, through the dark and silence, Aspire heard his name with a gentle breeze.

"Aspire."

Aspire couldn't lift his head, but he perked up his ears to listen if it came again. He had heard this voice before. He wondered if it was Confident.

The voice came again.

"Aspire." Then it proceeded to say with great comfort, "All is not lost, Aspire."

"Wha…who…what?" Aspire didn't know how to respond to this voice. He didn't even know where it was coming from. It wasn't Confident, but still it sounded familiar.

"Aspire, you can keep going. I'm here. I've always been here." The voice was gentle and kind.

Yet Aspire still did not know where it was coming from. He lifted his head.

"Who...who are you? Where are you?" He squinted his eyes in the dark.

"I'm Artist," the voice, Artist, spoke gently and steadily. "I'm here."

It gave Aspire a strange feeling of peace growing like a plant inside him.

"I...I can't see you. Where are you?" Aspire sat upright and stared more intently into the dark searching harder for Artist, but he could see absolutely nothing.

"It's all right. I'm here." Artist's voice was comforting even though it provided no answer to Aspire's question.

"Oh, okay." Aspire didn't know how to respond, but he suddenly remembered the moment earlier when he was walking with Confident, and thought he heard his name. "Wait...was that you earlier? Did you say my name earlier?"

"Yes, I have been here trying to help you."

"Help me?"

"Yes, I wanted to give you direction."

"Oh." Aspire sat still trying to process exactly what was happening. One thing he knew, he did need Artist's help.

"Aspire, do you still want to reach Destiny Falls?" Artist posed this question in such an exciting way that Aspire began to feel hope rise again. His ears perked up. He knew the answer.

"Oh, I do!" Aspire stretched his neck out still trying to find Artist. No attempt was working, so he settled back thinking about his answer. He still did want to get to the falls because he greatly wanted his horn.

Then he remembered what Perfect said about Artist. How Artist gave Perfect everything. Aspire's heart skipped a beat as he realized that maybe Artist could give him a horn now! He saw his opportunity and had to seize it. "So, Artist, do you remember Perfect?"

"The deer in the orchard, yes."

"Right, so...he said you gave him his horn, right?"

"Yes, I did."

"Okay, I was wondering if, well, I… I want a horn too. Could you…give me one? If it's not too much trouble." Aspire waited in tense anticipation for Artist's response.

Artist laughed a jolly kind of laugh. "I knew you would ask. I thought you wanted to reach Destiny Falls first."

Aspire did not know what to think of this response. "Um, yeah. But I wouldn't mind if you gave me a horn now." He waited deeply, hoping that Artist would agree to give him his horn.

"Don't you want to complete the journey first?"

Aspire didn't like this answer. "Um, yes, but I came for a horn."

"Let's go together to Destiny Falls. I'll give you your horn there. It's a much better place for you than here." Artist sounded direct and firm but still so kind and gentle.

Aspire felt frustrated. This was not the response he was hoping to receive.

"But…I tried! I tried and I failed. I'm not…good enough." Aspire started to tear up.

"Don't worry. I'm with you, and I'll help." Artist seemed to not let Aspire think otherwise. "Just listen to me this time."

Aspire sniffled. "But I can't even see you! I can't even see anything!"

"That's all right. You only need to listen."

Aspire wiped his nose and took a deep breath trying to process what he had to do.

"But what if I can't hear you all of a sudden and then I get off track and get lost again?"

"I'll just keep speaking to you. Remember what my voice sounds like and you'll find it. I know you can."

Aspire sniffled. It sounded like he had no other choice. Artist was offering him a chance to get to the falls. It was the only one he saw now as there was no way he was going to reach it on his own.

"Okay. I'll do it."

"I'm glad, Aspire. This will be so good." Aspire could hear Artist smiling. It sounded warm, like a summer breeze through his bedroom window. Aspire couldn't help but smile too.

"So where do I go?" Aspire felt ready to begin again.

"You should rest for the night. You'll need good energy for this last bit."

"Oh." Aspire didn't like this answer. He wanted to go; he didn't want to rest. Forget sleep, he thought.

"It's all right. I'll be here, and I will help you tomorrow. You will have more energy when you rest well."

This was not the first time that Artist had offered his help "tomorrow." Aspire realized that he wasn't the biggest fan of that answer. He didn't want to wait, but he saw that he had no choice. Plus, he began to realize his exhaustion, and now his eyes were starting to close without his control. He laid his head down.

"Good night, Aspire."

Artist's voice was soothing, and though Aspire still had questions, he felt at peace, and he couldn't fight the sweet sleep taking over him.

"Will you be here? The whole night?" Aspire yawned.

"I'm here. I won't leave."

"Oh, okay. Good night." With that, Aspire surrendered to sweet, sweet sleep.

13

"*A*spire."

Aspire opened his eyes. He lifted his head and tried to focus on his surroundings. He wondered who said his name and where he was. It felt like morning to him, but it was still dark and overcast. Aspire couldn't find even a hint of the sun. He looked over to his right and squinted his eyes. It was the bluff from the past two days before.

All the memories from the day before came flooding in his mind, getting lost, losing progress, and giving up. He began to feel sorry for himself when he remembered that he had lost Confident. Until Artist came to the forefront of his mind. He had found Artist! Well, Artist found him.

Aspire suddenly remembered that Artist was going to help him get to the falls. He thought about the thick fog that had ruined his progress yesterday and quickly turned to look at the path. He hoped that it would be clearer today or gone altogether.

No, the fog was still there, dense as ever. Aspire slumped back and started to think about Artist again. An unsettling thought crept into his mind. He didn't know where Artist was. Had Artist left him?

"A...Artist?" Aspire leaned his head forward to listen and began to look around.

Artist promised to stay the whole night, but Aspire felt doubtful that Artist actually did.

"Good morning, Aspire. I'm glad you're awake."

Aspire felt relief rush over him and let out the air he was holding in his lungs. He was happy that Artist hadn't left him. However, he still could not see Artist anywhere.

One thing left him puzzled as well. Artist's voice seemed to come from somewhere in the fog, somewhere in the unknown. Aspire couldn't see much from his position, so he stood up and stepped further into the fog.

Still nothing was in sight. He tried to search harder and walked farther in, but he still couldn't find anyone or anything. This confused Aspire, so he stepped out of the thick of the fog and stood next to the bluff again where he could see better.

"So…where are you?" Aspire felt a little frazzled.

"I'm here." Artist's voice was steady and even-keeled, but even though Artist's voice sounded close, there was no hint of anything in sight.

"But I can't see you. Where are you?" Aspire didn't like not being able to see Artist.

"It's all right. I'm here." Artist's voice was calm and steady.

He furrowed his brow thinking about what Artist could be and then he remembered the Stars. He couldn't see them but knew that they were still there.

"Are you a Star?" Aspire felt sure that he knew who Artist was now.

"No. I'm closer than a Star."

"Oh." He furrowed his brow again. "Oh! Are you the sun?"

Aspire had spoken to the Stars but had only watched the sun rise and set. He never thought about interacting with it. Aspire liked the sun; it was beautiful to him.

"Think closer," Artist said it simply and plainly.

"So…the moon?"

"Think closer," the answer came again.

Aspire realized he should have expected that one.

Aspire felt flustered again. He had absolutely no idea who Artist was.

"Okay, well, I don't know then! Who are you?"

"I'm the dreamer. The designer. Artist. I created this island." Artist spoke with a tone of wild adventure but also kindness and simplicity.

Aspire didn't get the significance of Artist's words at first.

"Oh." Aspire furrowed his brows once more processing the significance of Artist's words. "Wait, what? You mean you made this island?"

"I dreamed of and made this island and gave it everything it needs."

"Oh, wow." Aspire began to understand more who he was talking to and began to realize the greatness of this moment. "So you own the island?"

"It is my artwork, but I let it be its own."

"Oh." Aspire began to think about the island, his home, and all the places he had traveled up until now. He was reminded of so much of the beauty he had seen along the way.

His brow crinkled as he thought about all the places and events that he didn't like, such as Liar's Loop, the valley, or his experience in the jungle. He had a bit of a distaste for the lake too, and he still didn't quite like Mount Impossible even after being on the other side. He didn't like where he was either. In fact, he began to think that he didn't care for most of the island at all.

"Why did you make it the way it is? I mean, it's...well...not always fun."

Artist sighed. Aspire could hear sadness in it.

"I love this work of art. I loved the process of dreaming it. It is quite beautiful to me."

Aspire didn't know what to say in response. He sat in silence feeling bad for not appreciating Artist's craftsmanship.

Artist continued, "But this is not entirely what I intended it to be."

This had Aspire's deep interest, and he leaned forward and asked, "Really?"

"When I created this piece of land, I made it to be something of its own. To me, it is beautifully independent of me." Artist continued, "It would lose its significance if I tried to keep shaping it and controlling it. It would lose its purpose, its unique expression."

"I see..." But Aspire didn't fully understand.

Artist went on to explain. "I am a good artist. Any regular artist may finish their work but always find a fault in it and try to fix it.

But a good artist wouldn't try to control their work after it's finished. The work must stand alone, left alone to be what it was made to be from the beginning. A good artist finds no fault in the work when it's finished. It is beautiful. But sometimes, the work strays from what it was created to be."

Aspire began to understand. "So you didn't make the mean things or the hard things?"

"No, I didn't make anything mean or hard. I'm sorry you were hurt, Aspire," Artist's reply was gentle and sincere.

Aspire began to process what Artist meant. The idea sunk deep into his heart and soul. He admired it. Now he was starting to understand Artist a whole lot better.

The beauty of art, of a craft, is that once it is finished, it is free to be itself and all it was created to be. A good artist lets their work be independent of the artist. The work has the freedom of choice as all great art does.

"So does it make you sad?" Aspire wanted to know more.

"It does."

"So what was this island supposed to look like?" Aspire was very curious about Artist's response.

"If I told you, it would take too long. Do you still want to get to your destination?"

Aspire had gotten so lost in this eye-opening conversation with Artist that he completely forgot what he had set out to do.

"Oh, yes. Yes, I do!"

"All right, listen closely and I'll lead you now." Artist's tone was firm but gentle.

"Okay." Aspire might not have taken Artist's words as seriously as he should have.

"You should have some sustenance for the trip today. You'll find some behind you near the bluff's edge."

Aspire turned to discover a very supple, green plant right where Artist said it was. He hadn't noticed it before. He spent a couple seconds staring in shock.

"Oh, wow. Wait, where did that come from?"

"I put it there." Aspire could hear a smile in Artist's voice. "I've done it lots of times for you."

"Wait, you've done it before?" Aspire was even more shocked.

"Of course. I have been rooting for you, Aspire. I want you to make it."

Aspire began to think of all the times where something had shown up when he needed it most. The plants and water in Trap Canyon and all the good and unexpected discoveries he had made along the way. Even Confident was a gift. Confident. Aspire realized how much he missed him, but then, he remembered another moment.

"Was that your voice at Faith Beach?"

"Yes. I wanted you to know that you will make it."

Aspire thought about it. He did need to hear that. But then he was immediately reminded of Searching.

"What about Searching? Did you want him to do what he did?" Aspire knew the answer, but he wanted affirmation.

"No, I wanted him to go with you too. He would have made a great unicorn as well. I had ideas for him."

"Oh." Aspire did not expect to hear that. "Do you have ideas for everyone?"

"I do."

"Do you have any ideas for my mom and dad? My friends?"

"I most certainly do." Aspire could hear a big smile in Artist's voice. "I want everyone to have a dream and to accomplish it like art."

Aspire did not know what to say. His mind was opening up to a new world where everyone he knew or even didn't know could be something more, like what he wanted for himself. Even Perfect's family. They all could be something more as well.

"That's...wow. Crazy." Aspire began to realize his smallness in it all.

"It's beautiful."

"So that's what you had in mind?"

"Of course."

"Do you root for everyone?"

"Of course, they are all important. But, Aspire, you are important. You understand something. When you get your horn, I want to tell you a secret."

All at once, Aspire felt the excitement of his dream coming true fill his entire being. *When* he got his horn, Artist wanted him to know something. He liked to hear that.

He also liked that Artist made him feel significant even amongst the significance of others. Aspire felt special even while Artist was rooting for everyone else too. But most of all, Aspire felt even more energized to get his horn.

"Okay, I'm ready. What's next?" Aspire stood up prepared to hear what he had to do next.

Artist laughed. "Okay. Step on the path and start walking."

Aspire looked forward at the fog-covered path. All of a sudden he felt anxious about walking through it again. He didn't want to repeat what had happened the day before. Not to mention, he didn't have Confident by his side to help him. He felt alone.

"I…I don't know."

"It's all right. Listen to me, and you'll be fine."

"Okay." Aspire took a breath and started walking on the path through the fog but then he paused.

"It's all right." Artist's voice was soothing, and it nudged Aspire forward.

Aspire started walking tentatively; he stared straight ahead to the ground before him. For some reason, it seemed even foggier this time. But strangely enough, Aspire felt fine. Artist's presence, even if it was merely a voice, gave him assurance. He was able to look past the anxiety of his present situation and press forward. Artist was helping him. He was going to make it.

"There is a rock on your right, and watch out. You're stepping off the path a little."

Aspire felt peace at the sound of Artist's voice. Yes, he was going to be able to do this. He carefully avoided the rock and corrected his direction on the path. It felt good. He pressed on feeling strong. He continued to keep his eyes on the ground before him determined not to walk off the path again. But as he walked, his mind began to wander.

He started to think about his home, his family and friends there. He began to see them in a new light as he saw their significance for the first time. He thought about what their dreams were. What they might deeply desire. Aspire had assumed that they were happy with jobs such as gardening, fence and furniture building, repairing homes, and the like. That's all they seemed to want to do. But maybe they wanted more too.

Aspire began to think about Confident and his old hometown. He wondered why it was only himself and Confident that seemed to be taking on the Adventure Trails to get to Destiny Falls. He thought that it should be everyone!

Aspire thought about his family again. He wanted them to meet Artist. He wanted his friends to meet Artist. Actually, he wanted everyone to meet Artist. Then, maybe they could all work together to bring the island back to what Artist intended it to be, the perfect artwork.

Aspire continued walking and staring at the ground as he went, but he was getting tired of all this thinking, so he had to give his mind a break. He asked Artist a question.

"Artist, have you known of me my whole life?"

"Of course, this island is older than you, Aspire."

Aspire could hear Artist smile, almost playfully.

"Oh." Aspire laughed at himself. "Were you always rooting for me even before I started my journey?"

"It was always in you, Aspire. I've always been rooting for you."

Aspire thought about the scope of that statement. He liked it a lot.

"Aspire, move a little to the right."

"Oh." Aspire corrected his direction.

"Careful to not go too far to the other side, Aspire."

Aspire adjusted his direction looking at what he could see of each side of the path and tried his best to stay in the middle. He saw a dry plant in the way and avoided it. Artist didn't tell him, and this made Aspire curious.

"Hey, you didn't tell me about that plant." Aspire waited for Artist's response.

"You saw it and avoided it just fine on your own," Artist spoke with a playful smile again.

"Oh." Aspire laughed but realized at that moment that he also had some power of his own to get through the fog. But he knew he needed Artist's help anyway.

Aspire continued to strive through the mist on the path. This wasn't so bad to him, and he found himself getting used to it. He had another question for Artist now.

"So did you name it? This island?"

"Yes, I have a name for it. Potentialand."

Aspire thought about it. He liked it, but he had another question.

"Were you sad when I got hurt during the journey?"

Aspire was curious. It had not been a comfortable journey whatsoever for him, and he wanted to know if Artist had seen it.

There was a moment of silence.

"Aspire, I don't want you to be in pain or in trouble. I didn't want the island to treat you the way it did. But think about this. Think about who you are versus when you first started. Do you remember?"

Aspire thought. He thought about who he was when he first started the journey, when he left Mundane. He thought about what he had learned and who he was now. There was a difference, and it actually seemed quite obvious to him now. He felt braver, stronger, and, quite frankly, more interesting. He had a story to tell.

He imagined telling his story to his family and friends and even creatures he didn't know. It would be a good one. Aspire kept walking for quite some time, eyes still to the ground, but he could feel something burning in his soul. He wanted to tell the world of his experience.

He felt strong and beautiful. It didn't matter that he didn't have his horn yet. He even forgot about what used to always bother him about himself. He felt almost whole and complete. He wondered if this was how a Majestic would feel. On top of the world, like he could fly, even in the fog.

Aspire did a little skip, but then remembered his actual limitations, and decided to keep his eyes on the path again. What an experience this was turning out to be for him. As he pressed on, he began to slip into his dream world again.

He imagined himself as a unicorn with the Majestics, leading in the front of the group. He imagined himself showing up before his family and friends. In his magnificence, they would ooh and ahh, but then he would tell them that they could be great too, maybe not as great but great just the same. Well, they could be just as great, he thought. It would be all right. He and Artist already had a special enough relationship for him not to worry about anything.

Suddenly, Aspire felt something brush against his foot. He looked down to see a plant in his way. Then he realized he was off the path. Worry flooded over him. It was happening again. He didn't want to be lost again. His heart started racing as he realized that Artist hadn't spoken to him in a while. He started calling for Artist.

"Uhh, Artist? Artist!" Aspire waited a moment before he called for Artist again. "Artist! Artist! Oh no, did you leave me? Oh no, oh no, oh no."

Aspire paced back and forth, and he felt a knot in his throat. He had no idea what to do. He tried to look for the path. He began to feel overwhelmed and confused, then his eyes flooded with tears. He remembered that Artist had told him to listen, so he tried that again.

He heard nothing, so he sat down. This time, he breathed slowly and tried to listen again.

"Aspire." It was a quiet whisper, almost inaudible.

Aspire perked up his ears trying his very hardest to hear.

"Aspire. You can hear me." The voice cut through the silence and warmed Aspire's heart.

"Artist!" Aspire felt sudden relief. "Artist, I got off the path somewhere. I'm sorry for not listening."

"I'm still here, Aspire. It's all right, just listen."

"Okay, what do I do?" Aspire wanted to get back on track as soon as possible.

"Stand up and keep walking forward."

"But where is the path?"

"You don't need the path, just listen, Aspire."

Artist spoke kindly, but Aspire wanted to have the path in sight.

"Okay. I hope you know what you are doing." Aspire stood up and tried to take a step forward. It was small. He stopped. "How will I know if I am going the right way or not?"

"I'll tell you." Artist's words comforted Aspire, and he decided to press forward as best as he could.

"Okay, I'm going straight. I'm still going straight… I think?" Aspire felt unsure as he walked forward slowly.

Artist affirmed Aspire, "Keep going."

"Okay." Aspire was still unsure, but he kept walking forward.

This was a tad frustrating for him. At least on the path, he knew a little of where he was going. The path helped him see better, but now, he felt he was walking forward blindly.

He only had direction and guidance if he listened to Artist, and he had failed at that a bit ago. He didn't know if he could trust this process. Most of all, he didn't know if he could trust himself anymore. He didn't know if he could listen well enough. Suddenly, Aspire heard a buzz. Then something spoke to him.

"Go left. Go left. That's the way to go."

Aspire stopped. That didn't sound like Artist. But what if it was, he wondered. He began to question his direction. He had already failed at listening. He didn't want to fail again. But he felt confused, and he started to get nervous.

He tried his best to remember what Artist had said before. Artist said stand up and walk forward. Aspire realized that going left didn't fit, and he was sure that Artist didn't tell him that because he remembered the buzz that came before the whisper. He remembered the sound from Liar's Loop. It had to be a gnat, and it was not going to get the best of him.

He continued walking forward disobeying the orders of what had recently spoken to him. But he was sure that it wasn't Artist, so he pressed forward. But suddenly, he began to worry. He feared that he may have made the wrong decision.

"Uhh, Artist? I'm going straight, right? Artist?"

Aspire tried to listen intently. He didn't hear anything. He started to worry again. He stopped and let the silence take over.

"Keep going forward, Aspire."

"Okay, yeah." Aspire felt relief and pressed on.

Aspire kept walking forward for some time. Artist wasn't telling him to do anything else except walk forward as far as he knew. But he began to wonder if he was accidentally tuning Artist out again. He worried that maybe Artist had given him new guidance but he didn't hear.

Nonetheless, he pressed forward, hoping that he was doing the right thing. He kept his eyes stuck to the ground before him, but there was not much to see. Occasionally, he would pass by a plant here and there, but it was mostly short grass ahead as far as he could see, which was only a couple of feet.

He tried his very best to walk straight ahead. But he would think that he was doing a good job, then he would almost immediately begin to psych himself out. He worried about the chance that he was leaning too far to one side or that he was straying. He didn't really know. The best he could do was keep walking forward to the best of his ability. So he did.

Aspire felt hungry and would munch on a plant that would show up here and there. It was quite nice to him to see so much green, and it brought him comfort, not to mention refreshment. After some time, he began to wonder if he was still going in the right direction.

"Uhh, Artist? Am I still going the right way?" Aspire paused and listened.

"You're doing great, Aspire. Keep going."

Relief fell over Aspire. "Yay, thanks!"

He pressed on with greater confidence, but the day was growing later. The bit of light that made it through the clouds above was dimming low, and Aspire could tell that night was arriving. He wondered how much longer he would be doing this as this challenge was tolerable but definitely not his favorite thing to do.

He continued walking forward nonetheless. He had no choice, and he wanted his horn. He also wanted Artist to tell him the secret as promised. Aspire began to wonder what exactly Artist would say to him. It gave him some excitement and helped him press through.

"Keep moving forward but move slightly to the right, Aspire." It was Artist, Aspire felt sure.

"Okay." Aspire took a slight turn to the right and kept going but quickly stopped. He needed affirmation. "Like this?"

"Exactly!"

So Aspire kept walking forward but much slower. He found he had to look closer to the ground as it was getting darker and therefore harder to see. But he didn't let it bother him and kept going. He reminded himself of what Artist had promised him and let that urge him forward.

He also tried to block out thoughts that weren't helpful to him. He even kept from daydreaming so he could focus and move forward correctly. He didn't want to overthink or get anxious. He didn't want to make himself question Artist's guidance. Artist was still there even if it didn't always feel like it.

"Aspire, you can rest and get some sleep now. We'll pick it up tomorrow. You did great today."

Artist's voice was nothing but soothing and comforting. Yet Aspire wanted out of the fog, so he felt uneasy and frustrated at the word *tomorrow*.

"Okay. But when am I going to get out of this fog?" Aspire was feeling a bit upset about having to stop.

"You've made much progress. Don't worry." The sound of a smile came through Artist's voice. "Just a bit ahead is a soft patch of grass for you."

Aspire looked forward and saw a welcoming patch of soft grass. He came up to it and laid down. He still didn't want to stop to rest but began to feel quite tired.

Aspire yawned. "How long until I get there, Artist?"

"Not much longer at all. Just rest for now. You'll be there in no time."

Artist was clear. Aspire had to wait for tomorrow again.

Aspire gave up and decided to rest as Artist kindly told him. He laid his head down as it felt very good to give his body a break from the day. He hadn't paid much attention until now to the ache in his body from the crouching to see in the fog. He decided to relax his mind as well, and before he knew it, he was fast asleep.

14

Aspire awoke but had to lie still for a moment; he was still feeling tired from the previous day, and he didn't want to get up. When he finally felt ready, he opened his eyes fully. It was hard to keep them open as they felt dry and tired, like they needed more sleep. Just the same, he looked around him to remember where he was.

It was easily recognizable, the fog and the dark. Memories from the day before came flooding back into his mind. He remembered some of the conversations that he had with Artist. He liked Artist quite a bit, though he still felt that he didn't know much about Artist as Aspire still didn't know what Artist looked like.

Then Aspire remembered the main reason why he was with Artist. He was going to get his horn. Maybe today would be the day! He felt ready, so very ready.

Aspire lifted his head to try and get up but felt an immediate ache in his head and neck when he did so. He laid his head back down. He tried to remember what exactly he did the day before. He had only tried to follow Artist's direction.

He did remember, however, that he may have been a little too tense in the process of listening. He had wanted to follow Artist's directions as best as he could, so he probably strained his eyes and held his body too tightly in order to see well and walk straight. Now, he was feeling it.

He decided there was nothing he could do, and he would just have to push through it. To forget the discomfort, he reminded himself of his goal. He knew that he was so much closer. He was certainly going to get his horn even if it took every last bit of him.

197

So Aspire pulled himself up. But it took a lot of effort, and he winced as he felt a big ache in his head. The muscles in his neck didn't feel strong enough to hold his head up well either. He decided that he wasn't going to let this take him out. He sat up straight looking ahead. He made himself feel ready for Artist's next guidance so that he could get to Destiny Falls and get his horn!

"Artist?" He waited in silence and took the opportunity to rest his eyes.

"Good morning, Aspire." Artist's voice was warm and cheery, and it gave Aspire so much hope. "How are you feeling?"

Aspire tried to stand up to show Artist he felt good and ready. But, in his effort, he stumbled and had to sit back down before he fell completely over.

"Uh. All right, I guess." Aspire closed his eyes to try and restart. "I did something to my head and neck yesterday, I think. Everything kind of hurts."

Artist's tone carried a smile. "It's all right. Aspire. You'll get used to it."

Aspire didn't know if he liked Artist's response, but he figured it was true. He would have to get used to this discomfort to keep pushing through to the end of the journey.

"Yeah, okay."

"Are you ready, Aspire?" Artist seemed to have a tone of excitement.

"Um, yes." Aspire got up, this time slowly and carefully to keep his balance and not hurt his head anymore in the process. When he finally found his bearings as much as he could, he took a deep breath and prepared himself. "Okay, where do I turn now?"

Artist still kept a tone of excitement. "You're in the right place. Just keep moving forward, Aspire."

"Okay."

Aspire took a step forward. It was small, but he responded to that one with another slow step that was bigger this time. He didn't want to cause his head or neck any more discomfort by walking too fast. However, he tested his boundaries until he found a good enough pace for himself and pressed forward.

As he became more accustomed to his aches and exhaustion, he began to look at his surroundings and discovered something new. He hadn't noticed it at first, but he could now see farther in front of his feet than the day before. The fog looked thinner today. This was a sudden comfort to Aspire. He felt that this meant progress and that gave him more energy.

So he pressed on, carefully paying attention to Artist's voice. This time, however, he made sure to loosen up so as not to add any more tension to his head and neck.

As he traveled, he would stoop slowly to get bites from the bright green plants that were appearing quite often, as he was very hungry and wanted more energy. Plus, the bright, fresh greens were very tempting and surprisingly very tasty.

When he finally felt more comfortable in his body and environment, he began to think. He liked that Artist was so kind as to help him and to stay with him as he ventured through the fog to get to the falls. He also liked how Artist seemed to want Aspire to get his horn just as much as he did.

Then he recalled that Artist promised to tell him something when he made it to the falls. Aspire felt sudden excitement about it. He wondered what it would be. His mind kept busy with ideas. Then a bothering question floated to the surface of his mind, and he needed assurance.

"Artist, do you really think that I am going to make it? That I am going to get my horn?"

"I believe in you, Aspire."

"Okay." Aspire pressed forward. He caught himself leaning to one side as his head felt heavy, and suddenly he couldn't hold his head up right. "I'm going straight, right? I'm going in the right direction…right?"

Aspire tried to listen but heard no reply. He felt anxiety grow and stopped. But in that moment, he decided to remind himself of what he knew. He had gotten this far with the help of Artist, and he knew that he was making progress. He was listening well and following Artist's guidance to his best ability.

If Artist didn't have any words of direction at this point, Aspire decided that he must be doing well. So he kept moving forward. He didn't psych himself out or give himself another choice.

"Okay then." Aspire pressed on. He tried not to worry if what he was doing was right.

"You're doing great, Aspire."

This gave Aspire the assurance he needed. He was doing the right thing, so he continued on even though his head still felt heavy and achy, and his neck at times couldn't take it. He lowered his head and continued to push forward.

As he walked, he couldn't help but imagine reaching the falls. He thought about being a unicorn. Oddly enough, this time around, he felt different about it. He felt that he could be significant; after all, he was going to be a unicorn. However, he didn't feel like he was going to be too special anymore, but in a good way.

He remembered that Artist wanted something big for everybody. Artist wanted everyone to get their dreams, for everybody to be something more. Aspire found himself welcoming that idea, something he had never done before.

Aspire began to embrace what Artist believed. He thought, yes, everyone should have the chance to get their dreams. Everyone was important, and everyone could be significant. It would be all right too. It would be okay if everyone was equally great.

Aspire began to think about Destiny Falls again. Now that he felt he was almost there, it was becoming more of an actual reality to him. He felt so close to being a real unicorn. The thought seemed so pleasant to him. However, on the other hand, when he began to imagine himself colliding with his dream, it seemed to bounce away, out of his grip.

Afterward, he couldn't picture his dream becoming a reality for him. He felt concerned and worrisome questions flooded into his brain. He knew he was on the threshold of this opportunity. But what if there was a chance he couldn't make it?

What if he took a wrong turn that he couldn't fix? What if he lost Artist's voice? He didn't like the feeling that was creeping upon him, not at all. However, he tried to remind himself again and again that Artist believed in him. Aspire tried to believe in himself as Artist did. He could do it. He would make it.

Aspire thought again over that fact that Artist was going to tell him something after he got his horn. That gave him more hope that he *would* get his horn. He wondered what Artist's words would be again. Artist seemed to sound excited about it. Aspire's curiosity was taking over him now, and he had some questions to ask.

"Artist?"

"Yes, Aspire?"

"Have you told anyone else what you're going to tell me?" Aspire waited in anticipation for the response.

Artist laughed a little. "And why are you worried about that, Aspire?"

"Oh, um, I don't know." Aspire didn't know at all how to respond to this question for a second. "Maybe, I just want it to be for me?"

"Don't worry, Aspire. I've got something just for you." Artist smiled through the words.

Aspire felt happy to hear that and continued traveling with renewed vigor.

Occasionally, Aspire would look up and notice silhouettes of what looked like trees to him. He was glad to see something new other than thick clouds even if the trees looked intimidating. The fog didn't help their appearance either. Aspire looked down again trying to rest his neck. He began to think about the last time he saw intimidating trees. It was in the forest with Confident.

At that moment, he remembered losing Confident all over again and all that they had been through together. Again, Aspire missed Confident. Aspire began to worry and wonder if Confident was all right, if he was lost, and if Artist would help him out too. He had to know.

"Artist? Do you know Confident?" Aspire realized how silly the question was. Of course Artist knew who Confident was, he thought.

"Yes, Aspire." Artist sounded happy to have Confident come up in the conversation. "Don't worry. I know where he is. I also have something special for him too."

"Oh, good." Aspire felt relieved. But then he had another question. "I'll get to see him again, right?"

"Of course, Aspire. You both have a good friendship. It's important."

Aspire smiled at this. It was true. He began to realize that Confident had become his very best friend over the journey. He didn't ever want Confident to leave his life. He and Confident also had to celebrate getting their dreams together; it had to happen.

Aspire pressed on feeling more encouraged and strengthened to keep going. He and Confident were both going to make it. He continued to push through the fog and tried his best to stay focused. He tried to walk as straight as possible. He still had no other orders from Artist, and he didn't want to mess this up.

But in the process, he began to wonder why it was taking so long. He had already traveled through the fog all day yesterday. This was taking longer than he thought or even wanted. As he continued walking forward, he realized he had another question for Artist.

"Artist, what did you feel when you created this island? Potentialand, right?"

"Yes, Potantialand," Artist began to answer fondly. "I felt excited. I felt excited to create something delightful that would be its own expression, its own thing. It would be independent and become what it wanted to be."

"That's cool." Aspire thought it over and hesitated to ask the next question but did anyway. "Did you think you would meet a creature like me? When you created this place?"

"I hoped to meet a creature like you, Aspire."

This made Aspire feel warm inside and even blush a little. He felt happy that Artist seemed to like him too. Even though he felt tired and achy and he still didn't know where he was or how close he was to the falls, even with the touch of doubt that would sneak up inside him every once in a while, he was strangely glad to be in this moment with Artist.

He realized that somehow, in this moment, he felt important and complete like he was all he needed to be, just in a new way. He felt peaceful and content and was somehow enjoying this weird experience with Artist through the fog. It was kind of an adventure in and of itself, and suddenly, it wasn't all that bad to Aspire.

So he pressed forward and kept going. He wouldn't let himself stop now. But as he continued walking, Aspire would sometimes have to pull himself out of a daze. He was still feeling tired and still couldn't see well through the fog. He would have to wake himself up by squeezing his eyes closed and quickly shaking his head.

In the process, he realized his neck and head were becoming less sensitive and were feeling better. He felt glad to be making this progress and felt strong for moving past his discomfort and exhaustion.

As the day progressed, Aspire managed to walk a while and even notice the fog clear up more. The silence of his surroundings was dissipating as well. At one point, Aspire thought he had heard birds.

However, he still had no idea where he was or how close Destiny Falls was to him. As the world around him grew a little louder with many undistinguishable sounds, he continued on. Until, rather abruptly, Artist caught Aspire's attention.

"Aspire, you can stop and rest now."

Aspire slowed but didn't stop. "But I'm not that tired. I can keep going!"

Aspire so desperately wanted to get to the falls now. He felt that he was so close, especially with the growing sounds around him. He was very willing to push through any exhaustion and ache to get to where he wanted to be.

"I know, Aspire. But it will be good for you." Artist's tone was understanding but firm and coaxing.

Aspire stopped, sat down, and let out a heavy breath. He didn't want to stop. He really wanted to keep going. He had to get to the falls as soon as possible, and resting wouldn't do that for him. It took everything in him to try to follow Artist's request.

"Go ahead, lie down." Artist sounded kind, but Aspire didn't want to listen.

Aspire lowered from a sitting position in slow motion and only partly laid down with a huff of rebellion. He didn't want to rest. He didn't want to rest at all. However, he did notice how tired he was, but he still didn't want this to be a time of rest. He had a destination to reach! He didn't want to wait any longer for it either.

He spent a couple of minutes in this rebellious state staring forward into the fog. He wished to push through it; he wished to keep going. What he didn't notice was that his eyes were getting heavier and heavier, and his head was sinking lower and lower. Eventually, he had to face the inevitable as he laid his heavy head down. Suddenly, against his will, he fell sound asleep.

Aspire slept and slept. He slept for hours. It could have been a whole day or a whole week, he would never know. But more importantly, it was peaceful and healing, and he needed it. The long journey had taken a toll on him, and his body was resting and recouping, greedily stealing all the sleep it could for some time.

Until…

A warm, gentle breeze blew over Aspire's face. It was fresh like mint hot chocolate. It pulled Aspire out of his deep sleep, and he slowly opened his eyes to a bright light.

Unhindered light was something that he hadn't been awake to in a while. His eyes had not adjusted, so he closed them quickly, choosing to sleep longer. But something pulled him back. When he came to, he began to wonder where he was.

He tried to open his eyes once again. He could only squint them, but he attempted to look at his surroundings. As his eyes adjusted, he could see green plants and trees everywhere around him. Suddenly, the whole world became alive.

As his eyes focused, he discovered banana, grapefruit, and passion fruit trees. Long vines draped everywhere in every direction. Lush foliage spread over the scene like frosting on a cake, and everything was glittering and green. The sun was high and looked as if it had just chosen its desired height for the day. He began to wonder where he could ever be.

At this point, Aspire was wide-eyed at the scene confused but also increasingly dazzled. Then almost immediately, an ongoing noise to his left caught his attention, so he turned to face it. Then he saw, to his surprise, a couple of feet away from him, there stood a shining, glittering pool of fresh, clear water. The water was unmoving at the edge of the pool where he was.

But as his eyes moved farther up the pool, he saw that the noise came from water gushing heavily down over a steep, rocky incline covered in moss and vines. The water fell directly into the pool leaving foamy ripples where it landed. All around the glassy water, vibrant trees bearing colorful fruit and dripping with thick emerald vines cascaded like a crown. It was quite regal and beautiful to Aspire.

Aspire also couldn't believe his eyes. He had to ask himself if this was real. He sat in shock at the scene. He blinked. Nothing changed. He blinked his eyes again and shook his head too. Still, nothing changed. Then it hit him. His heart began to beat, and hope flooded his head drowning out all sound. Was he where he thought he was? Could this be Destiny Falls?

Aspire's heart started beating faster. He quickly stood up to get a better view of his surroundings. He looked to see if there was a sign or anything to tell him if this was Destiny Falls or not. He spun around in a circle until he found it. Just before the falls, off to the side, stood a glorious wooden sign.

Aspire ran over to it. In aqua blue with big curly letters read the words "Destiny Falls" as if it was magic. He couldn't even breathe. He couldn't even think. He only stood before the sign in shock with his mouth gaping open. He had made it to the falls. He actually made it to the falls!

He turned away from the sign and looked toward the waterfall with exuberant joy. He was immediately mesmerized by the sights and sounds. It was the most remarkable thing he had ever seen. He walked closer and sat down by the water. Because of the pristine clarity of the water, he could see through to a floor of beautifully colored rocks. Many glittered as the sun shone over them.

It was a magnificent sight.

After Aspire sat a while, mesmerized by the glittering pool floor, he began to look at the surface of the water. He noted how still it was where he sat. He could clearly see the reflection of the sky and trees above.

But then, something sparkled differently in the reflection. It caught his attention. He looked to see what it was. He saw how it moved from a sharp end and swirled and twisted down to something familiar. He looked closer and surprised himself. It was his own head!

In a moment of sudden realization, Aspire stared at himself with his mouth gaping open even wider than before as he processed precisely what he was seeing. He realized, in that very moment, that the swirling, glittering thing was, in fact, a horn! A unicorn horn, and that horn was on his own head!

He closed his eyes tight and opened them again. It was still there. He moved his head around and watched how it moved and how the sun caught it letting it gleam and sparkle before him in the reflection of the pool. He sat in utter shock and wonder and let the idea sink in. He was a unicorn. *He* was a unicorn!

A unicorn! He couldn't contain it. He stood up and stepped away from the pool trying to fully understand what he had seen. He wondered if he was dreaming and poked himself. He took a deep breath to prepare for what he was going to see.

He leaned back over the pool looking at himself in the glassy water, and the glint of his horn drew in all the viewing ability of his eyes. He stared at it a long time. An opal-like blend of gold, pearly white, sea blue, and emerald colors jutted from his own head forming and twisting to a glittery point.

He tried to understand the truth, but it was becoming too much for him. He sat down by the edge of the water with his head drooping over the pool as tears began to flood his eyes. He couldn't help it, and just as soon as the tears charged in, the dam broke under the pressure.

It has been said that the little crystal pool raised an inch that day after Aspire became a wet, blubbering mess of joyful, grateful tears. They dripped from his face into the water muddling up his reflection. They were the best tears Aspire had ever cried. They were dream-come-true tears.

Aspire tried to hold his tears back so he could see his reflection in the pool again, but it was no use. He was completely overwhelmed with joy. So much so that he might've looked quite silly crying over his reflection like he was, but that thought never bothered him. He was utterly and wholly overjoyed at who he had become.

After moments of expressing his joy through tears, Aspire calmed down and sat up. All of a sudden, in a burst of excited energy, he immediately jumped up. He started dancing, kicking his legs, and swinging his horn all while singing and exclaiming his joy at the top of his lungs. He couldn't contain any of his emotions. He didn't even notice how dizzy he felt after the many spins and jumps he was pulling off.

Then, just as suddenly, another wave of the reality of the situation came upon him, and he moved back to the pool to look at his reflection. More sobs came, even louder than before, as he plopped down by the water in complete euphoria. This was it. The exact moment Aspire never knew he was waiting for, the realization that he was what he once dreamed about.

After more tears poured out, Aspire stared at his reflection. Another thought came across his mind as he remembered what Artist said about all the folks he left in Mundane and even the animals in nearby towns. They had just as much potential as him! They had no idea of their own beautiful horns hiding under the surface of their doubts! Or whatever they dreamed of becoming!

Aspire sat for a moment in silence in awe of who he had become and the potential he knew was before him. He was almost in a trance as he began to figure out how he could encourage others to reach for their dreams too. He had to do something about this.

Meanwhile, Artist was calling but had to repeat Aspire's name a couple times to get his attention.

"Aspire. Aspire." Artist didn't seem to mind and laughed as if to enjoy the moment with Aspire. "Aspire."

It was around the third time that Artist repeated Aspire's name when Aspire finally responded out of his stupor.

"Artist!"

Aspire looked around. With the fog gone, he wondered if he could actually see Artist.

"Artist, I don't know what to say…thank you for helping me get here!" Aspire continued to look around as he said this but could not find Artist anywhere.

Artist laughed again. "You're welcome, Aspire."

There was a moment of silence, and Aspire began to look confused and frustrated.

"Aspire, from where you are, you won't be able to see me very well. But look up at the sky."

Aspire looked up to the sky to see a mass of clouds gather and swirl like a bowl of whipped cream above him. Then, as soon as the swirl in the clouds started, Aspire felt a warm wind begin to encompass him like a hug. He found himself caught in a swirl of wind and with it came the scent of fresh mint and warm vanilla.

The wind was so strong and thick that Aspire thought he could touch it. He could feel his senses lifting higher than he ever imagined they would, and, at that moment, he believed he couldn't be any happier and more at peace as the wind enveloped him.

Then, as soon as it all started, everything stopped, but the scent still lingered. Sad that it had ended, Aspire looked to the sky with eyes begging for more.

"That was just for you, Aspire." Artist smiled, and this time Aspire could feel and smell the warmth of it like sun-kissed citrus. "It's just so you know I'm really here."

Aspire smiled. "Can you do that again?"

Artist laughed. "That's all you need, Aspire."

It was a beautiful moment that Aspire never wanted to forget. Then suddenly, Aspire's head filled with questions.

"So when you told me to rest, was I already at Destiny Falls?"

Artist laughed again. "You were, and I wanted to keep you from walking too far!"

Aspire laughed at the thought.

"Also, I didn't even have to touch the water. Right? But I have my horn!" Aspire did a little dance exhibiting his horn, letting it glint in the sunlight. "What happened?"

"*I* gave it to you, Aspire."

"Oh!" Aspire welcomed that knowledge. "Did you give it to me when I was sleeping then?"

"No, actually. I gave it to you before."

"Wait, what?"

Aspire tried to think back. He thought hard. So much had happened that everything behind him was a distant, blurred memory. Then it came to him. He remembered when he woke up with the pain in his head and neck.

"Wait, was that why my head felt so heavy and achy?"

"Yes! I told you that you would get used to it. I couldn't wait to give it to you, Aspire, so I gave it to you as soon as you followed me into the fog."

"Wow..."

Aspire sat in awe at the kindness of Artist. He decided right there that this was the best day of his life, ever, and Artist was the best, ever.

"Now, Aspire, I need to tell you something."

"Yes?" Aspire remembered Artist's promise to tell him something. He sat up straight ready to hear what Artist had to say.

"Aspire, I want to first begin by telling you that I have a new name for you. But only I will use it if that is what you want."

"Okay!" Aspire was beyond curious about what Artist would name him.

"I want to call you Inspire. For this reason, I told you that I want something more for every creature of Potentialand. I want every creature to have dreams and to reach them like you, Aspire. But you see, very few of them allow themselves to dream, and if they do, some don't think their dreams are attainable. Others don't feel capable enough to reach their dreams. Or, sadly, some get distracted. You have a strong mind, Aspire, and I want you to help them. I want you to inspire them. I want you to show them what they can be if only they would just reach for it."

Aspire sat for a moment taking in the weight of Artist's words. This was a big deal. He knew it. But he didn't know if he could do it. He felt honored, though, that Artist would ask him to take on such a role. Aspire knew that is exactly why he should do it.

He rose to the challenge and, with a strong voice, said, "Okay, Artist. I'll do it."

"I knew that you would, Inspire." Artist's words carried a big smile and the sound of adventure.

Aspire smiled too, especially at the sound of his new name. He liked it. He liked it a lot. He felt that it gave him strength and dignity.

"Now I have something else for you, Inspire." There was a thread of fun and play in Artist's voice.

Immediately, Aspire felt a tap on his leg. In a moment of sudden surprise, he turned and looked to see what it was, and a warm, smiling, familiar face greeted him. It was Confident!

"Confident!" Aspire immediately tackled Confident in his excitement, and the two rolled over laughing. "I missed you so much!"

"I missed you too!" Confident laughed at Aspire.

They both laid down side by side and looked up at the sky. Aspire was in complete contentment. He and Confident made it, and all was well.

Aspire turned to Confident. "How could I have ever lost you, Confident? That can't happen again!"

"I honestly don't know what happened. But I know it happened when the trail ended."

"The trail ended?" This was news to Aspire. "You mean it didn't go all the way to the falls?"

"Nope."

"Oh." This brought a whole new light to the situation for Aspire.

Those moments when he thought he had failed and stepped off the trail were only the moments when he had reached the end of Adventure Trails. The moment right before the next and final steps would lead him to magic.

"Wow."

"Yeah, I didn't know what to do. Artist helped me though."

"Yeah, me too!"

"We had some good talks."

"Yeah, we did too."

There was a moment of silence as Aspire and Confident stared up at the sky. Aspire embraced, with pure ecstasy, the fact that he and Confident had finished the journey and were together again. This time, they had accomplished their goals. They were living out the dream.

"I see you got your horn. It looks great." Confident looked over at Aspire and smiled.

"Yes. Artist gave it to me!" Aspire smiled back. "What about you, what happened to you?"

"Artist made me a king. He said I was ready. He even sent me some creatures for my tribe. They're young and wild, but I like them a lot. I gave them a free day, and we'll meet up again tomorrow for breakfast. I've got some things planned."

They both watched clouds float by above basking in the glory until Confident finally broke the silence.

"Aspire, you know what I want to do?"

"What?"

"I want to swim in that pool." Confident sat up with a glint in his eye and pointed over to the falls and the cool, fresh, glittering pool.

Aspire sat up with him and shared the glint. "Yeah, me too."

They smiled mischievously at each other. Confident jumped up, and Aspire followed. They both ran without restraint until they reached the pool. They didn't even take time to pause before they both splashed into the water.

For the rest of the day, they played in the water, swung from the vines, danced undignified, and enjoyed the fruit of the trees. They each talked about their time with Artist through the fog until the sunset. Then, Confident tested his newly found "kingly" ingenuity. He made both him and Aspire banana leaf hammocks to sleep in next to the sound of the falls for the night.

When Confident finished, both Aspire and he rocked in them being lulled to sleep by the sound of the water and birds in the trees as dusk turned into dark.

"Good night, Aspire the Unicorn."

"Good night, King Confident."

Aspire had never felt happier hearing and saying those words as he and Confident fell fast asleep in fulfilled and satisfied exhaustion.

15

*A*spire woke up to the sound of birds singing. He opened his eyes to the daylight and looked around lazily lying in his hammock. He could not have felt more relaxed as the sun shone through the banana tree canopy overhead.

Nearby, the waterfall poured down, awake and lively, into the pool of sparkling rocks. The whole scene was vivid and colorful. It felt like a dream, and he couldn't believe he was there. He couldn't help but wonder if he actually was dreaming.

He closed his eyes, laid his head back, and tried to not wake himself up from the dream. But then he so badly wanted it all to be real that he pinched himself then squirmed and wiggled. However, to his surprise, the hammock fell apart near his head in the process, and he came crashing to the ground.

He landed with his back end up, his body scrunched now on the broken hammock still clinging to the other tree. He let out a noise out of shock, not pain, as he fell, and it woke Confident. Confident sleepily peered out of his hammock slung around two nearby trees.

"Are you okay?" Confident yawned, his concern disappeared when Aspire smiled sheepishly.

"Yeah." Aspire laughed off the surprise and got up. "I don't know what happened. I was just trying to make sure that this wasn't a dream."

"Oh." Confident squinted his eyes and took a better look at Aspire and the mess he created. "It looks like your horn ripped through the hammock." Confident was laughing now. "You might want to get that piece leaf off your horn." Confident continued to laugh.

Aspire looked up discovering that he couldn't actually see his horn from that perspective. But he did see what looked like a bit of leaf floating above him, moving when his head moved. He laughed an embarrassed laugh and tried to pull the leaf off his horn. He realized at that moment that he still had to get used to this new addition to his head.

When Aspire was finally able to pull the piece of leaf off, he and Confident, who was still relaxing in his hammock, spent quite a while in silence. Aspire embraced the sounds and visuals of the space getting lost in the beauty of this new world. It was everything and more than what he had ever pictured. Confident finally broke the silence as he switched positions in his hammock staring up at the green canopy above him.

"Aspire, we made it. We made it!" Confident stared wide-eyed up at the canopy.

"We made it," Aspire repeated, looking from Confident to the waterfall again. He was still lost in the beauty of the scene.

Confident turned and looked at Aspire. "I just wanted to tell you that. Just to make it official." He smiled. "So we can talk about it later. It's our story. We actually made it, Aspire."

Aspire looked back at Confident realizing the significance of this moment. They had made it. Tears welled up in his eyes again. This was better than he could have ever imagined. At this moment, it was so good he almost felt that he didn't deserve any of it.

"Hey there, no time for tears, well, unless they are happy." Confident smiled and lay back in his hammock still saying under his breath, "We made it. We made it!"

After some silence, Confident turned to Aspire and asked a question.

"Aspire, did you talk to Artist after it all happened?" Confident looked curious.

"Actually, yeah." Aspire fell into a trance in the pool of sparkling stones as he thought about the last conversation he had with Artist. He suddenly remembered it didn't formally end as Confident interrupted the moment. Aspire looked at Confident. "I was actually just talking to Artist before you showed up." Aspire started to wonder where Artist went after that.

"Oh." Confident was quiet again. He looked as if he was trying to find words to say something. "Aspire...Artist gave me a new name."

"Wait, really? Me too!" Aspire felt excitement remembering his new name. He was equally excited that Confident was able to share the riveting experience with him. "What did Artist call you?"

Confident laid back in his hammock. "Artist called me Courage. Artist said that I am a leader and that I'm brave." Confident paused. "Artist said that so many creatures are afraid or timid. I'm supposed to take them under my wing and help them. I'm supposed to help them reach for more."

"Wow, that's so cool!" Aspire paused a moment too. "Artist called me Inspire. Artist said that I'm supposed to show everyone what they can be. I'm supposed to help them dream and believe. Help them know that they can be more."

Confident sat up and turned urgently toward Aspire. "Aspire, you know what that means?"

"No." Aspire felt surprised by Confident's urgency.

"It means"—Confident hopped out of his hammock and sat by Aspire looking directly into Aspire's eyes; Aspire could see passion burn in them—"this place isn't just for us. We have to help other creatures get here too."

Confident turned toward the beauty of the scene. "This place is for every creature to reach too." He looked back as Aspire with watery eyes. "We have to let every creature know it's possible. They need to know that they can make it too."

Aspire sat there staring at Confident, who now seemed to be overtaken with strong passion for this purpose. Aspire had nothing to say. He knew in his heart that it was true, and that is exactly what Artist wanted them to do. He and Confident each had an important role. They needed to bring everyone they could into the shore of Destiny Falls.

"Yes, Confident." Aspire started to catch fire with Confident's passion. "Let's go."

Confident smiled big after he saw that he had caught Aspire on fire as well. Confident nodded, looked around him, and then turned straight ahead. Aspire could see determination grow and grow in Confident as he stood up tall with purpose.

Then, before Aspire could get ready, Confident started to run. He ran out of the trees, away from the waterfall and pool, and kept running to the open, grassy field before just outside the Destiny Falls oasis. Aspire was not ready to run, but he didn't want to lose Confident again.

"Confident, wait!" Confident clearly didn't hear him, which frustrated Aspire. "Confident, wait up! Wait for me! Confident!"

Confident heard this time and stopped, turning around to look at Aspire. Even though he was far, Aspire could see that Confident was antsy and was giving a stare that said exactly what he yelled next, "Well, hurry up now! I can't wait any more to do this! Plus, I have to tell my tribe what I am doing!"

Aspire remembered Confident has a tribe to take care of now! Aspire picked up his pace and sprinted to meet up with Confident. As soon as Aspire reached Confident, Confident started running again giving Aspire no chance to breathe or to prepare for the pace, but he kept running.

Confident ran fast too, and Aspire, to not push himself too hard and to not lose Confident again, breathlessly requested they slow down. Confident agreed, and the two ran a quick but steady pace away from the falls; for now, they had a mission to complete.

"Confident, where are we going?" Aspire tried to sound like he wasn't breathing so heavy, but there was no use in trying; Confident was fast.

"First, I am going to tell my tribe at the meeting spot that they can have another day off or they can join us. Then, I know that we can go to Ever After, to the mountains you were talking about, and get everyone's attention. There are a couple sparrows and a falcon in my tribe, and I am going to send them to the towns to invite creatures to the mountains so that we can talk to them." He looked at Aspire with a smile. "So that we can inspire them and give them courage."

Aspire smiled back. He liked the plan. He was also in awe at the kingly leadership Confident was giving at that moment. Aspire remembered that he knew from the beginning that Confident would be great. Immediately, he found himself so proud of the fact that he and Confident were living the life they now had. It was too good to be true, better than Perfect's life, Aspire thought.

Aspire and Confident ran straight ahead for a while, slowing their pace only a tad. They also took a moment to pause for food and pressed on again until they reached the orchard. They stepped in and slowed down as a sweet wave of the familiar peach scent reached their noses.

"Confident, why did it seem like we got here so much faster from the falls, but it took so much longer to get to the falls?" Aspire was very curious and confused about the reason.

Aspire wasn't surprised that Confident, after a moment's thought, seemed to know the answer almost right away. "We followed the path the first time." He pointed into the orchard to the path. "It goes around the long way. Plus, the fog slowed us down a lot."

"Oh, yes." Aspire thought for a moment. "Wait, you mean if we had just cut through here and ran that way, we would have made it to Destiny Falls sooner?" Aspire pointed in the direction they came from with a bit of frustration in his voice.

"Well, yeah," Confident stated calmly. "But it was worth it. At least to me."

Aspire thought. He thought about the frustrating experience in the fog. He didn't like that. But then he remembered the bluff that had invigorated him and Confident. He also recalled his experience and conversations with Artist. Then he had to agree with Confident.

"Yeah, it was worth it."

Aspire followed Confident as he ventured through the orchard to the tribe's meeting spot.

"Have you met them yet, Confident?" Aspire was curious about this group.

"No, just the sparrow and falcon. They had been looking for a king for their tribe, and Artist sent them to me. We agreed to meet at a clearing in the orchard straight down from the falls. Ah, and there they are."

Confident nodded toward a group of creatures gathered in a clearing laughing and talking. There were about twenty or so. They seemed to be full of energy and excitement. As Aspire and Confident reached the group, Confident greeted the tribe with enthusiasm and boldness. He looked so ready for this.

"Hello, all!" Confident walked in the clearing and sat before the creatures. Aspire watched as the two sparrows and falcon that Confident mentioned flew down and sat next to him. "I'm Confident. I've been chosen to be the king of your tribe."

The sparrows and falcon began the cheers, and all the creatures surrounded Confident. They lifted him up in the air in their excitement. Everyone was showing energy and enthusiasm, except Confident.

"Okay, everyone. You can put me down now. Okay, put me down now!"

This caught everyone's attention, and they obeyed, putting him down almost immediately. Confident, appearing slightly embarrassed from the experience, cleared his throat. But then he began to talk to the creatures about his readiness and excitement to be their king. The animals seemed to be happy about it too. Then, Confident went on to explain the mission he was ready to begin.

In his passionate expression, he told them about his interactions with Artist and what Artist told him to do. He explained how he was going to do it. He made his request known to the sparrows and falcon to send out the critical message and finished with a question for the rest of the tribe.

"Would anyone like to come with me?"

There was a moment of silence. Then, a bullfrog, a fawn, two cats, a wolf, a donkey, and a groundhog lifted their arms. Aspire lifted his hoof. Confident was inspiring him too!

Suddenly, a little mouse shouted out and pointed to Aspire. "Who's that?"

Confident looked back at Aspire who sat behind him.

"Oh!" Confident looked at his tribe. "This is my good friend, Aspire. He will be leading the mission with me."

The animals cheered for Aspire. He felt his face get hot. He was not used to that kind of response. Confident began to call the creatures who wanted to help up front to figure out a plan. But suddenly, at that moment, Aspire turned and saw a gathering of unicorns walking through the orchard together carrying some fruit in baskets. There seemed to be about seven of them.

They must be the Majestics! Aspire had to go and meet them.

He turned to Confident and whispered, "I'll be right back."

Aspire turned around to see where the Majestics were heading and ran after them. They were taking a path that Aspire found familiar. It was the Adventure Trails' main path. He ran over to it and watched as the group of Majestics turned off to a smaller path. As he got closer, he felt quite jittery and nervous.

When he got closer to the Majestics, he realized that he didn't know how he was going to start talking to them. He didn't want to scare them by shouting too loud from behind. But he didn't know how he was going to avoid that. He thought about it. He decided he was going to have to try to speak loudly. He came up slowly behind them and cleared his throat.

At the sound, quite a few of the unicorns in the back of the group stopped and turned quickly. It caught the attention of the other unicorns, and suddenly they all stopped. Now, they were all staring straight at Aspire.

Aspire had no idea what to do or say. He caught himself pulling back, almost to a sit, as he felt instantly intimidated by the group of Majestics. Then he decided that there was no time for that, so he stood up straight and cleared his throat again.

"Hi! Uh, I'm Aspire!" He smiled and held out his hoof, and no one shook it. The unicorns just stared. "Um, I'm new." Aspire laughed nervously and placed his hoof down.

One of the unicorns finally pushed through the group and spoke. "Hi, Aspire. You're real, right?" He gave a nod toward Aspire's horn.

Aspire nodded and showed them a better view of his horn. "It's real, all right!"

One of the unicorns whispered to another, "He's not from around here. He probably went to the falls."

"Oh." The first unicorn was still observing Aspire's horn. Then he looked Aspire in the eyes and held out his hoof. "I'm Dignity." He and Aspire shook. "How long have you been here?"

"Oh, uh…" Aspire thought. "Two days…I think." He looked at Dignity, waiting for a response.

"Ah, we got ourselves a newbie!" Dignity turned and looked at the other unicorns.

They all chimed in with slightly interested "aahs," shaking their heads in agreement as they stared at Aspire.

Aspire never felt so inspected before. He felt like a specimen under a microscope. He nodded along with the other unicorns. He didn't know what to do.

"Come on, we'll show you around Ever After." Dignity nodded to the direction he and the other unicorns were headed.

"Oh, sure!" Aspire instantly remembered that he and Confident were supposed to be on a mission. "Oh, but I was planning on going to the Ever After Mountains with my friend."

Dignity shrugged his shoulders. "Okay. But you'll have to go through Ever After to do that anyway. When are you meeting up with your friend? You can come with us since you'll be walking in that direction anyway. Or you could meet up with us later."

"Okay. Uhh."

Aspire looked back to where Confident was speaking with his tribe. Confident was laughing with a turtle and a flamingo. Aspire didn't know what to do for a second. He really did want to go with the unicorns. He had dreamed of being a part of the Majestics for so long. He didn't want to hold off on it anymore.

However, he and Confident had a vital mission to complete. He also didn't want to miss out on anything that Confident and his tribe were planning. However, they were all walking that direction. Plus, Confident might be spending time with his tribe a while longer. Aspire should give him space.

He could go with the Majestics so they could show him around Ever After. Then, Confident could meet up with him there. Afterward, they could go to the Ever After Mountains and complete their mission. Aspire liked that idea and chose to follow through with it.

"Is that your friend?"

Aspire turned to face Dignity to see him nodding off to where Confident was standing.

"Uh, yeah. Yes." He looked back at Confident and then back to Dignity. "Just give me one second. I'll just tell him to meet up with me at Ever After."

Dignity nodded. Aspire ran back to Confident and his tribe. When Aspire made it to Confident, he told Confident his plan.

"Hey! So I'm going to leave with the Majestics now, and they're going to show me Ever After. It's on the way to the mountains anyway. We can just meet up there or at the mountains?"

Confident looked over to the Majestics and looked back to Aspire.

"I guess." He paused. "I do have some things to finish up here. I'll meet you in Ever After then."

"Okay, cool!" Aspire smiled and turned to walk back to the unicorns.

"But don't forget our mission!" Confident shouted out.

"I won't!" Aspire shouted back and then ran to meet up with the unicorns.

As Aspire almost reached the unicorns, they started walking, and Aspire followed behind. Dignity led the way, chatting with another unicorn. The other unicorns were talking amongst each other as well. Aspire felt like an odd one out, but he didn't mind too much. He was walking with the Majestics, as a unicorn himself.

They led him out of the orchard and down the path into a field full of hills. Not too long after, they rounded a small corner, and there it was. The glorious sight. Sitting off a small distance before them, under the happy light of the sun, were numerous homes and buildings clustered together. As they came closer, Aspire saw a grand blue-and-white sign with swirling details that read in big cursive letters, "Town of Ever After."

As they walked, Aspire began to observe the homes and buildings. They were all white, with red tile roofs, and blue-trimmed windows and shutters. There seemed to be a few buildings scattered around made of white or light pink-colored brick with blue roofs as well.

The closer they got, the more Aspire could see very detailed architecture and decor. Immense amounts of flowers and greenery decorated the homes and buildings as well, and there were strings of beautiful lights strung overhead everywhere.

Aspire's eyes sparkled along. He was in awe of the sight. When they arrived at the threshold of the town, Dignity looked back to speak to Aspire.

"Here's Ever After. Welcome." He turned back and began to lead the group through the town, nodding and smiling to other unicorns as he passed through.

As he followed, Aspire gaped at the quaint beauty of the town. He loved the place. He loved the flowers and wreaths decorating almost every home. He loved the tranquility of the place and the cobblestone walkway made of white rock.

Truly, he loved it all. He tried smiling at a few unicorns as he passed through but found it odd that he was gathering strange and confused stares instead. He tried to remind himself that it was because he was new. They would eventually like him, at least he hoped.

Dignity led them to an opening in the town where a beautifully ornate fountain stood in the middle. The centerpiece had a golden sunflower jutting up from the center of the fountain. The place contained lush shrubbery and all kinds of unique flowers.

Inviting seats and tables with blue umbrellas sprinkled the area as well, and little shops surrounded the opening. This was where Dignity decided to sit down. A couple of unicorns stayed, but the rest left. Dignity caught Aspire's attention.

"This is the main square. We call it Sunflower Square. We meet here a lot to hang out or talk about town stuff. This is where most of the shopping happens. Most of these streets have homes on them.

This one"—Dignity pointed to the right down a street—"has our town movie theater, and next to it is the grocery store." He turned to look back at Aspire. "That's really all you need to know. You can figure the rest out. I can find someone for you to stay with if you want until I know of a house that is available for you."

"Oh." Aspire felt surprised at the brevity of the tour. He was also surprised that even though the space seemed so welcoming and happy, the unicorns weren't quite so.

"Yeah, so do you have any questions?" Dignity looked at Aspire.

"Um, no, I guess." Aspire thought. "Well…"

Dignity waited.

"Do you have any town events, like parties?"

Dignity took some time to think. "There was one day a lot of us decided to watch a movie together. But we kind of all do our own thing. There is one party that we have once a year to celebrate being Majestics. We have it here in the square. It's clearly exclusive. That's fun."

"Oh." Aspire found Dignity's words unsettling. It didn't quite sit right with him.

"Yeah. We mostly just hang out in our homes. They're really nice. We go to the beach a lot." Dignity pointed north. "We enjoy the sun over there. It's too hot over here sometimes."

"Okay." That was a slight improvement for Aspire. Then Aspire, remembering his mission from Artist, had another question. "So do you get a lot of new creatures over here?"

Dignity thought. "Not really. No. It's been a while since we had someone like you. Actually, I can't remember the last time."

Aspire wasn't surprised, especially after all the reactions he was getting from the other Majestics. "Do you ever…invite other creatures over here?"

Dignity laughed. "No. There are certain likes of creatures we don't want around here. We like to keep our town pure. You seem fine so far, but they'll want to make sure you fit. You know, if that horn is actually real." Dignity pointed to Aspire's horn.

"Oh." Aspire didn't know what to think. He was shocked. He had a sinking feeling that this probably wasn't exactly in line with what Artist had wanted him to do.

"So what are you going to the mountains for?"

Aspire didn't know what to say. He felt that Dignity was probably not going to like his answer. Just then, a noise interrupted them. Aspire looked over to see Confident leading his tribe of fun-loving creatures. They were vibrant and energetic, very opposite of every unicorn Aspire came across in this town. Just then Confident spotted Aspire and walked over to him.

"There you are! Are you ready?" Confident smiled, and Aspire could see Confident's eyes were still burning bright.

"Y…Yeah." Aspire looked at Dignity, trying to figure out what to say.

"What are you doing?" Dignity tilted his head, looked at Aspire, and then at Confident confused.

"We're going to the Ever After Mountains!" a donkey shouted from the back.

"Yes." Confident laughed. "We've invited any creature to meet us on the other side. We want to inspire them and give them the courage to take the journey to make it to the falls."

Aspire looked at Dignity to see his response.

"Ah, interesting." Dignity looked like he was thinking about what to say next. He didn't look very approving. "You don't think they'll do it, will they?"

"The hope is that they do!" Confident smiled.

"Hm." Dignity sounded disapproving this time. "Well, if they aren't a unicorn, they're not allowed to stay here, so you know. It's the rules."

Aspire watched as Confident's smile disappeared. "All right. Well, we'll get going then. We won't be there long."

"That would great." Dignity looked over the other creatures; he didn't look like he enjoyed their presence there.

Aspire's heart sunk low. This was not how he wanted Ever After to turn out. This was not what he dreamed about whatsoever. He stood for a moment feeling quite upset, trying to process what had happened, what Dignity had said. Aspire began to realize that if he lived with the Majestics, he would have to live far from Confident, his best friend, and his fun-loving tribe.

Aspire looked at the creatures who had agreed to join Confident on the mission. They were full of life, and they were so sweet. Aspire liked them. He thought about the parties that they would have. The memories that they would make. Aspire didn't foresee that here in Ever After. Plus, it would probably take him a long time to feel accepted, considering the fact that new town members were rare. They clearly didn't trust that his horn was real as well.

Aspire understood that Dignity had tried to not-so-subtly point out that other creatures weren't wanted there. He thought about Artist, their conversations, and what Artist asked of him.

"Well, we're going to the mountains now, Aspire." Confident looked at him with the unspoken question in his eyes.

Aspire couldn't respond quite yet because he felt torn and upset. He didn't know what decision to make. Then, Confident started to lead his tribe to the mountains, and Aspire couldn't handle his emotions. He felt frustrated with the whole scene. He wanted so badly to live in Ever After. However, he and Confident had become good friends. He just couldn't ditch Confident or their mission.

He turned to Dignity, and with every ounce of strength in him, he made his decision. "I...I can't live here." Aspire felt strength rise up in him. "Artist gave me a mission, so I'm going with my friend."

With that, he turned and ran off to catch up with Confident, leaving Dignity and Ever After behind.

Confident smiled at Aspire when he caught up with the group. "I'm glad you chose the mission."

"Are you kidding? I'm not turning my back on Artist. Or you." Aspire looked down as he walked. He was glad about his decision, but he felt hurt by how things ended with Dignity and Ever After. It wasn't how he thought it would be. He felt a knot in his throat and held back tears.

"I'm sorry. Ever After sucks." Confident looked apologetically at Aspire.

"It's okay." Aspire smiled. There was no time for tears. He looked straight ahead. "Let's go do this thing!"

Aspire, Confident, and the tribe charged for the mountains. They had a mission, and nothing was going to stop them now. When they made it to their destination and reached the overlook spot, they stood over to discover quite a small cluster of creatures.

Aspire and Confident looked at each other. This was not expected.

Confident breathed out a heavy, disappointed sigh. He obviously wanted more creatures to come than that. Aspire shared the same feeling; his family wasn't even there. Just the same, Aspire and Confident did what they had set out to do.

Aspire and Confident shared their story with the creatures below. They did their best to give inspiration. They tried their best to send courage. Nonetheless, to their dismay, the animals seemed impressed, but very few showed interest in the journey.

Aspire began to think back to when he first started his journey. He remembered the sad truth: few creatures made the journey, let alone even tried. After Confident finished giving instructions to the few who showed interest in taking the journey, Aspire and Confident looked at each other. They gave each other concerned looks.

They had done all that they could. But now, those creatures had to decide whether or not to go on their own. Aspire and Confident thanked the creatures for their time and let them go off to their other plans. Then, Aspire and Confident left with the tribe following close behind.

"That was amazing! You did great!" Many of the tribe members expressed their newfound inspiration and courage. They seemed very excited about the future.

"Yeah, but I don't know if anyone else caught on." Confident sounded beaten down.

Aspire didn't know what to say. The whole chain of events after meeting the Majestics had confused and upset him. He didn't think that any of this would ever happen.

Aspire and Confident tried their best to quickly pass through Ever After, avoiding eye contact with the Majestics. Aspire couldn't handle the judgmental stares of the Majestics after choosing not to live there and failing his mission. He felt tears well up in his eyes again. When they made it back in the orchard, they walked to the clearing where the rest of tribe was.

The tribe greeted each other happily, but Aspire and Confident sat down on the outskirts feeling entirely defeated. This was not how Aspire wanted the day to end. Confident seemed to express the same feeling as he looked off in the distance frowning. Aspire figured that Confident felt just as confused and frustrated as he did after the strange turn of events.

Together they watched as the sky began to change color through the trees. The creatures that took part in the mission with Aspire and Confident shared their newfound inspiration and courage with the rest of the tribe. Now, everyone was feeling ignited and uplifted, cheering and shouting. There was so much energy in the air. Aspire observed it, and a realization struck him.

"Confident, look." Aspire pointed to Confident's tribe. "Look at what happened."

Confident observed it. His head perked up from the energy in the air then quickly sunk. "But what if no one else listened?" He sounded upset.

"Then…we'll do it again. And again…and again." Aspire felt his spirits lift. "We owe that to Artist."

Aspire began to think more about what happened earlier. "And, Confident, who knows, maybe in time, because of our story, we will see new creatures at the falls. Even if it is only a few, even only one, we at least did something."

Aspire felt excitement grow at another realization. "Confident, we did inspire! We did give courage! Look at your tribe!"

Confident began to soften to the idea with a small smile as he watched his tribe celebrate together. Aspire could see passion growing back in his eyes like a low flame that only needed a little extra oxygen. Confident started to nod, and then in a burst of inspiration, he stood up tall.

"Yes. Yes! And I think we should consistently go to the mountains. Let's make it a regular thing!" Confident turned to the tribe and made a decree.

"Hey, everyone! How about we make this a regular thing! Let's go every week to the Ever After Mountains and share our stories!"

Confident's tribe cheered in response. It was settled. They were not giving up on this mission from Artist no matter how long it took. Then in a rightful response to completing their first mission, they partied the rest of the night.

In the midst of it all, Aspire and Confident shared a smile. They never knew of the impact of their decision that day, and little did they know of the beautiful change they would ignite in so many creature's lives, for the better from henceforth.

For that day, Aspire and Confident became far more significant than they could have ever imagined. The most magnificent unicorn and king to exist, because they made it known that it was simply a gift given to them. They wanted everyone and anyone to know that they too can reach their goals and dreams, and it would not be because of their effort but because of the help of the owner of their island. They could receive their gift only if they so decided to take the journey, to accept it, and not give up on it when it got hard.

It remained established: Aspire and Confident were no longer their old selves—they were Inspire and Courage. Fully themselves and entirely who they were meant to be all along, discoverers of their pure, raw identity. They became an inspiration and strength for all creatures who chose to dream and dare to believe that they could find themselves too. From that day on, Aspire and Confident watched as the tribe grew until it was so big it became a city itself. A city of the inspired and courageous where the Stars shone brightly every night.

Note to the Reader

*Y*ou may have finished this book with questions. If so, and if they bother or frustrate you, I apologize. I still have questions too. I don't know if any or all of them will ever have answers. However, all I want to tell you is, it's possible.

Though the journey is hard and rough. Though heartbreak and disappointment knock at your door. Though things don't seem to pan out the way you imagined, you can and will reach your dreams.

Just keep going. Don't give up. I'm not the only one believing in you either. You are not too young; you are not too old. You are not too this or too that. You are worthy of your dreams should you choose to believe in them and take steps toward them.

It may hurt, it may be scary, but you have got this. I wish and pray the best for you. So here's to you and your dreams coming true. May you make it to your own Destiny Falls and encounter the Artist along the way.

About the Author

*T*hough a daydreamer from birth, Angela Engnell never dreamed of becoming an author until *Destiny Falls* came to life from an attempt to write an amphigory (nonsensical writing). What started as insignificant became something brimming with deep and intricate meaning to her. She has realized that life journeys and experiences most often end up that way too. Hers being no exception. Though she is still on her journey and has more destinations to reach and things to accomplish, she is grateful for how far she has come. As a lover of music and all things creative and whimsical, she sees that life always offers more of a blank canvas to paint what she has learned and experienced with her words and melodies and desires to offer hope and inspiration to others and along the way. Born in Metro Detroit, Michigan, Angela now has her roots in Los Angeles and hopes that her time there will continue to draw up more stories to come.

Melissa Van Der Veen is an illustrator who grew up living in her imagination, creating worlds and creatures to befriend. She has a deep love of anything that involves magic, adventure, nature, and a tiny bit of mayhem. So when her friend, Angela, told her about an epic, magical adventure about a small pony with big dreams, she was thrilled to be a part of the journey! No dream is too big, and there is magic in the world if you take the time to seek it. Melissa currently lives in Seattle, Washington, with her pup and her sweetheart, Austin, and when she is not covered in paint, she's covered in mud exploring with her horse friends.

CPSIA information can be obtained
at www.ICGtesting.com
Printed in the USA
BVHW090607161121
621700BV00016B/535